OUT OF THE BLUE

By
Nick Smith

Published by Proper Job Media 2013

Cover Design by Spiffing Covers.

ISBN
Paperback - 978-0-957636-62-0
ePub - 978-0-957636-61-3
mobi - 978-0-957636-60-6

For John Page

"There's some art to faulting the liar. Of course there is. But the real art lies in recognizing the truth, which is a great deal harder."

George Smiley – The Secret Pilgrim

Prologue

17 November 2008

The killing has become less of an enjoyment as I have grown older.

I am evil.

I do not feel evil. I do not feel anything. I have been told that I am evil and, even from this distance, from my long-dead accuser; I can see that it must be true.

Was I born evil, or did evil grow within me?

Believe me; the latter.

The loss of the youthful enjoyment of killing darkens my mood. Many may diagnose depression; it certainly depresses me.

At 0400 each morning I wake up living in my joyous past. Sometimes it is 0358. Once 0359. My mood turns soot black as I realize I have only been dreaming. My dreams are the undreamed nightmares of my slumbering victims.

Disturbed sleep is a symptom of depression you know; a classic symptom.

I cherish my past. If only the joy would return. The assassination business is a growth industry. I am a market leader; I name my price. I should celebrate.

Instead I am a corpse walking around.

Take now for instance. Yes? Right now.

Pay attention. Turn away if you do not want to look at me! Or, look at me in disgust if you must. Can you prevent me from doing what we have to do?

You are still here?

Of course you are. Look. Look here. Look down. "The keyboard?" you ask. Yes, the keyboard. Just the strike of one key starts the whole perfect murderous business.

I'm not writing this for me. Why should I? I know what is going to happen. Death.

Ah-yah.

Sorry, I yawned. Same old work. I'm just like the man who takes your money at the toll booth, or the woman at the supermarket check-out, or the check-in clerk at the hotel. We're all the same. We carry out the same tasks, day in, day out. Such is the repetitive life in the service industries.

Back to the keyboard. Look down. Fourth row down. Look down will you! The killer key is on the right-hand side. The starboard side; that itch Stone would say. The letter "L" orders the kill. "L" Lima. "L" Lukasz.

That is the key to the killing. Strike it – death. Yet again.

How rude of me. Would you like to do this one? You could lightly tap it or slam it with the vigour I used to have and that same vitriolic cheer? The choice is yours. I won't criticize your technique.

Pull up a chair; you'll need it. The first job can affect you.

Now you know what has to happen you're my accomplice. Are you so reluctant to do the deed?

I shall have to do it.

Tap.

There. Done.

They are dying now, my friend. Can you hear them?

Turn away. Go and make some tea. I read somewhere that it is an effective cure for shock. As it brews, remember this; I know who you are. You are my accomplice.

They will come for you. Not me.

1

13 February 2003
Amsterdam, the Netherlands

“Diamonds, Jay, diamonds.” The Governor swirled two blocks of ice around a tumbler. He watched the tiny waves lap at the edge of the glass.

The Governor waited for a reply. Lamb said nothing.

“Why would I want to join your cash scheme? Diamonds make so much more sense?” the Governor asked unnerved by Lamb’s silence.

Lamb shrugged. “You’re the Governor, Bill. I can’t teach you anything,” Lamb said sipping from a glass of mineral water.

“Stop messing with me Jay,” the Governor said slamming the tumbler onto the table in front of him. “I didn’t come here to be jerked around. What’s the deal?”

Lamb stood and walked to the starboard side of his hotel room, shifting a curtain to look at the canal below.

“Diamonds, “Notoriously untraceable”,” Lamb said releasing the curtain and turning back towards the Governor. “Except for one hefty weakness, that would be absolutely true.”

“Spare me the riddles Jay. I’m too old for it,” the Governor hissed. “What hefty weakness?”

"The guy who sold you the diamonds," Lamb explained walking confidently towards the Governor. "He knows who you are."

"So?"

"So how discrete do you suppose he's going to be under pressure, Governor? Scratch that. How loyal do you suppose he will be staring down the barrel of a gun?"

"Jay, we're in Amsterdam," the Governor laughed. "Not Tallahassee. They don't care who I am."

"Don't your political enemies hold passports? You're up for re-election. Diamonds might be a girl's best friend but they're not yours."

The Governor stood, towering over Lamb. "That's a garbage line Jay and you know it."

"It's not garbage. It's true," Lamb said, staring up insolently into the Governor's face.

"Go on. Give me your pitch," the Governor conceded.

"Another drink?" Lamb asked gesturing towards the Governor's glass.

The Governor nodded, "Double."

Lamb walked slowly to the vodka and ice next to the television. He was in no hurry.

As Lamb returned to his guest he prepared to explain. "Governor, I have an associate with old college friends in the secret services," he lied. "Clearly you have connections too, your brother being…"

"We both know who my brother is Jay," the Governor said downing the vodka in one go.

"My associate has undertaken some research on the people you have been trading sparklers with. His report is ugly reading."

"Report?"

Lamb walked to the open left louvre door of the wardrobe and punched a code into the room safe. He extracted a buff-coloured folder. "Here," Lamb said passing it to the Governor. "Gratis."

"What does it say?" the Governor asked warily passing it back to Lamb unopened.

"It says that Willy and the gang that you've been so naively dealing with are all in the employ of your political rivals."

"What?"

"I think you heard me Governor," Lamb said quietly passing the file back to him. "Take a read."

The Governor opened the file and started to read. Lamb and Mills had worked long into the night to make credible the lies it contained.

"Enough," the Governor said, throwing the file back at Lamb.

Yes Governor, enough, Lamb thought.

"Are you going to wait for this to explode? All over your election campaign?"

"My brother…"

"We both know who your brother is Governor, as you reminded me. Do you really think the White House is interested in covering up your activities?"

"No," he replied resignedly.

"No," Lamb retorted, gaining in confidence. "Give me the diamonds."

"What?"

"Give me the diamonds."

"Why would I do that?"

"Because I am going to make the diamonds, the dealers and your political death all just disappear."

"My money?"

"Governor, we both know it isn't your money. But, you will find that you have been credited with three hundred million dollars in an investment fund. A fund managed by me." Lamb stood and patted the Governor's shoulder. "Just carry on governing, Governor. You're doing a great job."

In the street below the hotel standing by the canal Alexander heard the control words – "Great Job." Slowly he turned away from the canal and climbed into the silver Mercedes waiting for him.

“Go,” he murmured to the driver. He did not look back at the three gunmen behind him. They would be dead by morning.

The Mercedes slipped quietly through the damp backstreets of the city. Two drunks watched the five men inside. Despite the drink they wisely looked away.

Why always a Mercedes? Alexander wondered. We might as well have ‘mercenaries’ in lights.

Towards the northern edge of the city the car approached the gates of an industrial estate. The youngest of the three assassins in the back of the car cleared his throat and shifted uncomfortably in his seat.

“Problem?” Alexander barked.

“No boss,” he replied.

Two black Audi A8s were parked either side of a street door, the only entrance from that side of the building. Alexander had scoped the building out earlier that day.

As the five assassins got out of the car he instructed two, including the nervous youngster to cover the back of the building.

“They come out, you shoot. Got it?” The two nodded.

“Say it back to me.”

“They come out I shoot,” they said quietly.

“Go. You two,” he said beckoning, “with me.”

Alexander controlled his breathing as he pressed the buzzer next to the door, as he had done so many countless times before. Nothing was said, but he heard the door lock released.

"All of them and quickly," Alexander said.

The three gunmen entered the building and followed the sound of a blaring television set along a narrow corridor.

"Brit boys! We are in here."

Willy sounded drunk. If his friends were too, the job would be easier.

Light was coming around a door ajar on the left side of the corridor. Alexander nudged it open. Jan was sprawled on a filthy rug, his arm around a tall blonde girl who seemed unhappy to be there. Two overweight and under-washed men sat at a small table playing cards surrounded by bottles of spirits.

Four targets, three gunmen.

Willy tried to stand, staggered with a hand outstretched towards Alexander. He never saw the pistol that shot him between the eyes. The blonde was not so lucky.

The two gunmen behind Alexander shot the card players before they were able to reach for their guns. Military precision.

In the Mercedes on the way back to Lamb's hotel, Alexander called The Honest Lawyer.

"Tell him it's done," Alexander instructed.

Lamb hung up.

"Relax Governor. Problem solved."

"Thank you," the Governor murmured quietly. "I guess I owe you."

Lamb smiled. "I guess you do."

The Governor stood to leave, "I…

"Just go, sir," Lamb said holding the door open for him.

In the street below Alexander waited in the Mercedes ready to drive the Governor to Schiphol Airport. The gunmen were in a bar celebrating the ease of the kill. Later when they were sufficiently stoned or intoxicated, the driver would kill them and dump their bodies in a canal. He too would then make his way to Schiphol and leave the country.

Lamb sat on the sofa and opened the soft black velvet pouch which contained the Governor's diamonds. What was the going rate of commission for corrupt land deals, property rights, prostitution, drugs and murder he wondered? If you pay the guy in charge of a billion dollar budget a hundred thousand a year of course he will help himself Lamb reasoned.

Lamb's cell phone rang. It was Alexander.

"The Governor caught his flight. You want me to come and pick you up?"

"One more job. Drive to Prinsengracht. Wait by the bagel store. A woman will walk towards you…"

"Is this your plan? If it is you can do it yourself."

"This is a Mills' plan. If you do not believe me, feel free to call Jack directly."

"I will. What does this woman look like?"

"Six feet tall, blonde, elegant. She should have nothing larger than a handbag with her."

"Then what?"

"Bring her to me, if you please. Or even if you don't."

"I don't like this," Alexander barked.

"For pleasure in this city may I recommend the Van Gogh Museum? For work, please do as I say."

Lamb switched off his cell phone. He scooped up the diamonds, dropped them back into their pouch and locked them in the safe next to the bogus file on their suppliers. He sat back down on the sofa and listened to the distant hum of the elevator winch. He felt satisfied. Firstly, he now had protection for his fraud at the highest level. Anyone found snooping around his scheme would find their life very unpleasant indeed. Secondly, he had just tucked away the final payments on 'AZUL' into his hotel safe. Good job.

"Did he suspect?" she asked.

"Of course not. Fear of exposure for a man in his position is bad enough. When your brother is President of the United States of America, there's really nowhere to hide."

Lamb watched her walk across the room to the safe.

"May I?"

"No," he laughed. "Sit."

She was not used to taking orders. But for four hundred million dollars some indignity could be tolerated. She perched provocatively on the bed.

"You know that doesn't work with me," Lamb said with his back to her. He unlocked the safe. "The transfer was made at 3p.m. Two hours late," he added. He sensed her stiffen.

"But you have the money."

Lamb punched in the access code.

"I have the money," he said opening the door. "So you shall have your diamonds." He withdrew the velvet bag, stepped slowly towards her and said, "Examine them. Next time, don't be late."

She hungrily opened the pouch, spreading the diamonds out over the bed, the glamour displaced by raw greed.

"Next time?" she asked.

"I assume that you would like a 'next time'. There is after all four hundred million dollars down there, a tidy profit."

She rearranged her body and the diamonds.

"That's better," Lamb said.

"I am sure we can do business again," she said, standing.

"That is all I needed to know," Lamb replied.

More protection. The Honest Lawyer.

2

27 November 2008. Thanksgiving Day
Tampa, Florida

"Good afternoon, Mr. Stone. I hope you bought the insurance."

A smiling policeman. Through bleary eyes I could just about read his badge. A very senior, smiling Hispanic policeman, sitting on a bed. A hospital bed. My hospital bed.

"How are you feeling?" he asked leaning towards me. I smelled stale Cuban coffee.

All limbs still attached; shins painful, neck in a brace, head sore.

"Never better," I replied.

"Brits," he huffed. "Your vehicle looked as if it was driven into a wall," he added standing. He was around two metres tall, early forties I guessed although his jet-black hair made him appear younger.

"Was my call recorded?" I asked shifting uncomfortably in my bed.

"Sure," the policeman replied languidly stretching out his toned arms then cracking his knuckles. "Our dispatcher was very distressed."

"I have had happier days myself," I said struggling to reach for a glass of water on the nightstand alongside my bed. The officer made no attempt to assist me.

"I am sorry that we failed to provide the protection you required," he lied.

Your paymaster wanted me dead. Try "sorry" on him, I thought sullenly while sipping tepid water from the glass.

The policeman walked to the door of my private room and closed it. He sat back down on the bed and leaned in so closely towards me that his nose was almost touching mine.

"You've been spending lot of time in Florida recently Mr. Stone."

"As you say," I replied.

"I do not enjoy your visits," he hissed. I could see a tiny surgical scar in his left eye. The rancid smell of stale coffee mixed with whatever solution was being drip fed into my right arm made me want to heave. I wasn't going to let him win. Suddenly he stood up. "During your call to my dispatcher you said that you would explain to my attending officers why you felt threatened."

"That's correct," I replied insolently, before sipping more water.

The policeman spun round and rammed his face into mine. "Let me cleanse your memory of today Mister Stone. I could not care less why you felt threatened. You, sir, are in the wrong place."

"If you kill me they will just send another," I said pushing forwards towards him, despite the pain wracking my body. "As I see it you've rather more to worry about than me. You failed; I survived." He said nothing. I dropped back against the pillows. "Don't worry officer. I will not be filing a complaint about your corruption."

“I am glad to hear that, sir. And you will not be asking us to commence an investigation into who did this to you either.” It was a statement, not a question.

“Then we understand each other.”

“Yes, sir, we do.”

I said nothing.

“While you were sleeping my officer received a call from a cellular telephone. The phone was stolen yesterday from a yacht crewing agency in Fort Lauderdale. The cell phone has been found. The caller remains at large.”

“What did the caller say?” I asked wearily.

“The caller said, “Tell Stone that this is only the beginning.” I’m sure that is a warning that you understand. Also, I had my office run a national check on you. Not too popular with the D.C. Coast Guard, are you?”

“No.”

“I made some calls earlier. I have made sure your unpopularity has spread to every United States government agency.”

“If you are expecting fear, officer, let me disappoint you. You know I have too much intelligence stored away from the United States to worry about your threats. Heed some good advice. Save yourself.”

I delivered those words with more strength than I knew I had in my aching body.

“I have spoken with your doctor,” the condemned

man said. "Nothing is broken, no concussion, and that neck brace is purely to prevent you bringing a malpractice lawsuit against the hospital. In fact you are free to leave."

"Great," I said with little enthusiasm.

"Isn't it just? In fact we got so excited that my office called your client in London."

Rachel? Now I was in trouble.

"We recommended that they arrange a flight home for you as soon as possible. You are leaving Florida for London from Tampa International Airport tonight. Isn't that wonderful news?"

"You are deporting me?" I asked.

"No sir. I am not deporting you," he sneered. "That would require paperwork and the creation of records. I have never met you. The dispatcher unfortunately deleted the recording of your call."

The man stood up and walked slowly towards the door. With one hand on the handle he stopped. Without turning back he said, "One final thing Mr. Stone."

"Yes?"

"Some sound advice. Do not attempt to enter the United States or our territories again. No business trips. No vacations. No checking on the mouse. Nothing. Understood?"

It hurt. But I laughed.

3

17 November 2008
Lloyd's, One Lime Street, City of London

I sprinted up the Lloyd's staircase, nodded at the two 'Waiters' guarding the revolving door, and jabbed my security pass at the barrier scanner. Why today? Henry Coles & Others, Syndicate 8001 if you prefer, were loyal clients but, right now, they were inconvenient.

As I bounded into 'The Room' I was aware of dozens of pairs of nervous eyes upon me. I am never a welcome appearance on the trading floor. I know that more than one of my clients refers to me as the "Prophet of Doom". I profit from doom.

I charged angrily past the rostrum with the famous Lutine Bell hanging beneath it. My friend Nigel Wright spotted me and started walking towards me. He is Lloyd's top gas tanker broker.

"Lukasz," he greeted me warmly.

"Not now Nige. Sorry."

He turned on his five hundred pound heels.

I arrived at Underwriting "Box" 23 only to find the H.R. Coles and Others Syndicate had moved yet again. I had been there only two weeks before. I did not have time for this. The six-seat rectangular desk was empty bar a slim, blonde late teenaged girl giggling whilst reading something on her BlackBerry.

"Where has the Henry Coles Syndicate moved to?" I asked her.

"Never heard of him," she replied reluctantly looking up. "How can I help?" she asked and then froze. "I know you. You're him."

"Who?"

"Him. You're that guy in 'Limelight' with the green tie." She reached across the Box and excavated a trade magazine from under a pile of renewal statistics. "You're him," she said jabbing a professionally manicured nail at my picture on the cover.

"Please. I just need to find Henry Coles."

"You do the disasters," she said.

"I do the disasters," I agreed smiling. "Henry Coles? Please? There's been a disaster and I'm in a hurry."

"Hang on." The girl picked up the receiver of a black slimline phone. "Lucy, it's Bling."

Bling?

"I've got that disaster guy from the magazine here..." She paused, looking me up and down. "Taller. Look, do you know where Henry... sorry," she said to me screwing her face up, "Henry who again?"

"Coles!" I boomed.

"Where Henry Coles is?" she said. "Box 123... thanks

hun.”

I sprinted towards the escalators and ran up to the first floor.

Henry had a broker with him. When he saw me I could tell from the way his eyes locked onto me that I was in trouble again.

“Robert, would you mind if we talked about this again later? It is a very interesting proposal and I wish to give it my full attention,” Henry said to the obese broker struggling to balance on the stool next to the Underwriting Box. “I have to speak with Mr. Stone urgently,” he whispered. The broker looked at me disapprovingly and moved away.

“Thank you so much Robert. Say half an hour?”

Half an hour? Please not that long.

As the broker reluctantly left us Henry greeted me, “Lukasz. Thank you for coming in. Please, sit down.” It was an instruction not an invitation. I sat on the low stool next to Henry. He was a tall man, well over two metres in height. He was straight backed with a presence that belied the brilliant military career he had enjoyed before he joined Lloyd’s. Although Henry had been a loyal client and a patient friend I often found him unintentionally intimidating.

“Christian tells me there are numerous problems with the Mills case,” Henry said looking around the Underwriting Room as Lloyd’s underwriters habitually do. “What are they?” he asked quietly.

I then noticed Christian Unstead-Matthews (“Chum”)

seated at the right hand of Coles.

He leaned forwards, both he and Henry facing me earnestly. I did not have time for any of this.

Tanya, the new Box assistant sat down opposite Henry. Normally we would all have greeted her.

"Hi Lukasz," she said.

"Your investigation has, thus far, taken forty-two days and remains incomplete," said Coles. "As you know, Lloyd's Rules – issued from eleven floors above our heads – allow just thirty-five days…"

"Unless a 673 has been submitted to Lloyd's by the investigator within four days of the approaching prescribed limitation period," interrupted Chum in his weak nasal voice.

"Thank you Christian," Henry said coolly. "I understand that no 673 has been filed. We understand from the broker that Mr. Mills is formulating a complaint. So, I will ask you again, Lukasz. What are the issues with the Mills case?"

"Your client is lying Henry. Mills knows exactly where his "stolen" yacht is…"

"There is nothing on the file to substantiate that," Chum interrupted leaning angrily across Henry trying to get to me.

I pressed forward in front of Henry to face up to Chum. I then slowly announced, "I have found the yacht."

Five short words that I would later regret.

"I knew you would," Tanya said cheerily, rummaging in her Louis Vuitton handbag.

Henry and Chum were silent.

"You always find them," she added lifting the latest model smartphone from her bag.

"What?" asked Chum in a whisper, his eyes bulging. I watched, fascinated by a pulsing vein in his left temple.

"I have found the yacht," I repeated loudly enough to be heard beyond the Box. Suddenly aware that Henry was sandwiched between Chum and me, I pulled back from Chum.

Can I please go now? I wondered.

"There is nothing on the file!" Chum fumed slamming his back against the Box.

"You've found her? Good. Very good," said Coles, straightening his already perfectly knotted tie while trying to suppress a smile. "Well done Lukasz. That is a relief. Isn't it a relief Christian?"

"May I please go now?" I asked.

I saw Henry about to agree until Chum intervened.

"You know nothing!" Christian shouted.

Silence fell around the Box. A broker at Box 127 laughed.

Mistakenly, I assumed Chum's outburst was due to his humiliation. In hindsight he was right, I knew nothing.

"I have credible information that the Mills' yacht has

been found and is under tow right now closely followed a coastguard cutter," I explained hurriedly.

"Excellent. Follow the procedures next time, please Mr. Stone," said Coles, attempting once more to conclude the fiery meeting.

I liked Coles and always regretted causing trouble for him.

"Credible information? Not Banksy again?" Chum sneered.

"Christian," I almost pleaded, "I am running out of time. Ask all the questions you want but, please, do it by phone."

"Why isn't this discovery on the file?" demanded Chum, thumping angrily at his computer keyboard. "I checked the electronic file before you arrived. There was nothing there. Let me check again." He delivered three more hefty strokes. "There! Still nothing," he declared pointing at the screen in front of him.

"Christian, we found her at two o'clock this morning. If I hadn't been called here I would be on the escort boat with the authorities, getting her arrested before Mills makes his yacht disappear again. Instead I am here answering bureaucratic questions from you!" I realized then I too was shouting.

"Meeting over," Henry ordered.

As I stood up to leave, I heard Henry say to Chum, "Christian, clearly procedures must be followed. I just hope Mills has not heard of Lukasz's discovery. Forty million euro isn't much, but I'd rather keep it than give it to that criminal."

Finally free to get on with my job, I ran back down the escalator across the ground floor and through the revolving doors back onto Lime Street. I sprinted over Leadenhall Street to my office on St. Mary Axe. I leaped down the stairwell to the underground car park, taking two or three stairs at a time.

"Flying visit," observed Jerry our one amiable security guard as he opened the garage doors.

"Wasted visit," I called back.

"Chum?" he asked, in mock salute as I threw the Mills file onto the back seat of my car.

"Spot on Jerry. You should do my job."

In the rear-view mirror I saw his mouth form the words, "No thanks," as I shut the door and jabbed the ignition button.

4

Surrey, England

I am standing in front of a row monitors watching my quarry again. I have watched him charge across the Lloyd's trading floor, barking orders and bounding up the glass-sided escalators. I watched him brush off Nigel Wright and saw his encounter with the swooning blonde. I have replayed that scene several times.

I am watching him now with Coles and that fool Unstead-Matthews. He is delivering what he believes to be his good news. That is the news that I have chosen to give you Stone. I delivered it into your hands. There is nothing 'good' about it, as you will discover in my own time.

He is running out of Lloyd's now, like a greyhound out of a trap. The dog never catches the hare, Stone.

So, Stone is dutifully following the trail I have laid down for him. I feel disappointed. This is, after all, a man who appears on the front covers of magazines. I had expected better. Slow down and think a little Stone. Englishmen walk; they never run. Of course I too in my early career was close to appearing on the front pages. It is surprising how flammable editorial offices can be.

During his hasty exit from the Room, Stone almost collided with the lapel camera. I cannot recall which charity pin Alexander said he had adapted this time. I have just frozen the frame where Stone's harried eyes are closest to the camera. They are sea green.

Something unusual is occurring. What is it? I realize that I am laughing, genuine, guttural laughter.

“Maybe you will bring me back to life, Mr. Stone?” I am saying to the monitor. “As I slowly kill you.”

5

River Hamble, Hampshire

By the time I had been released from Lloyd's to get on with my job, Banksy had the Mills' boat hauled. He was carrying the mast with a large mobile crane as I skidded into the yard car park. The mast was constructed from carbon fibre, a difficult but not impossible material to repair. Banksy was gingerly moving the rig towards some carefully erected cradles. Forty-five metres in length (or ten million euro if you prefer) there was no room for error.

As I grabbed my kit from the boot of my car I scanned the yard for any sign of the coastguard. Nothing. Too late. Thank you Chum.

The engine of the crane stopped. The long ebony coloured mast now lay safely in the cradles.

As Banksy climbed down from the cab of the crane he yelled, "I've been looking at the hull number. It's been changed. They've done a good job. Very professional. In fact it is so professional I'm worried they might have changed the hidden number too," he added jumping the last two steps. "They knew what they were doing that's for sure. Yogi at the Marine Police is calling the builders for the location of the hidden hull number. I'll call them later. They'll be more likely to tell me where it is located than him."

The diesel engine from a winch to our left further up the slipway fired into life. We stood and watched as the high-gloss black forty metre yacht, inched her way up the railway into Banksy's largest shed at a pace slower than a funeral cortege.

"Who paints a yacht that colour?" Banksy asked as we walked alongside the ascending yacht.

"I don't know Banksy, but whoever it was paid a lot of money for it." I held up a hand towards the gleaming hull. "Look at that. No distortion. No orange peel. Even without putting a meter on it I would say that gloss level is almost perfect."

"Those Italians know how to build a fine sail boat," Banksy shouted above the noise of the winch gear.

"Lovely lines, even out of the water," I admitted. "Shame that something so beautiful is involved in such a grimy business."

"It's a grimy business that keeps you in business, Lukasz," Banksy reminded me as the bow of the yacht entered the shed.

"Has the coastguard left?" I asked.

"The coastguard said they couldn't wait any longer for you. I tried to keep them here but there's only so much coffee and biscuits that men can take."

"Thanks for trying."

"Yogi said he'd come back later and plaster her with police notices. It's not as good as an arrest but it'll buy you some time to get your legal stuff underway."

Ping. My phone.

"Sorry Banksy, excuse me."

I walked back down the slipway. The alert was an e-mail from Chum:

"Subject: 'AZUL' – Disappeared off Puerto Rico." the body of the email read "No news on 40 crew. Flights booked for you as follows: 1900 LHR – MAD. 0800 MAD – SJU. 1300 SJU – EIS. You meet owner's representatives in Road Town, Tortola 1500 local tomorrow. Contacts to follow. Kind regards, Christian."

It could not be that 'AZUL' I thought, although I knew Henry insured her. 'AZUL' – cloudless sky – the largest yacht in the world. At two hundred metres she was two thirds the length of 'TITANIC'. She was known to be privately owned but beyond that nothing was certain. I had heard rumours that the Boss was from the Middle East. Or Russian. Or "totally American". No one knew. Besides, if it was that 'AZUL' Chum would conduct the investigation. His 'investigation' would be over within thirty-five hours, forget thirty-five days. All the forms completed. Everything neatly placed on the file.

I replied to Chum's e-mail:

"Received. On my way. Please send usual documents."

As I had no regard for Chum, kind or otherwise, I hit the send key. The 'usual documents' were copies of the underwriting files.

I returned to the shed just as the yacht came to rest and the twin doors started to close.

"Banksy, can I ask a favour?"

"Sure," he said, as he always did. He turned off the

railway winch. “What is it?”

“When you get the second hull number, text it to me?” As I headed towards my car I shouted back, “And bill me for the haul out, crane and storage, this time.”

Banksy laughed, “Get out of here.”

“It’s time you made some money out of this grimy business of mine.”

And so I got out of there. Looking back, I wish I hadn’t.

6

M25 Motorway

I was sitting in stationary traffic when I received an e-mail from Rachel.

"Hey, It's the 'AZUL' Lukasz. Go online. She's gone. It's all over the television. We insured the lot. Joe is locating our reinsurance."

Insurance really isn't my thing. I am just insurer's hired hand when things go wrong. Henry Coles would explain the little I needed to know as I needed to know it, but even I understood what this meant. 'AZUL' must have been insured for at least a billion dollars, probably more. The Syndicate could not retain that amount of risk so they would have insured themselves against a major loss, probably with other Lloyd's Syndicates. Henry Coles would never have allowed it any other way. I knew the Coles Syndicate never retained any more than two million dollars on any one risk without insuring themselves for the rest.

Ping. Rachel again.

"No reinsurance in place. Chaos here. X."

Impossible; Henry would never have left the Syndicate exposed to a potential billion dollar loss, it would bankrupt the Syndicate. I guessed with no reinsurance in place and the high publicity, the case would very quickly attract the attention of Lloyd's twelfth floor.

As the traffic started to move, I picked up a news report on the radio. 'AZUL' was headline news:

"It has been reported from the Headquarters of the United States Coast Guard in Washington D.C, that 'AZUL', the largest privately owned yacht in the world disappeared off the north coast of Puerto Rico in the Caribbean Sea early this morning. The last known location of the yacht was above the area known as 'The Puerto Rican Trench' due to its vast depth. The yacht, said by experts to be worth in excess of one hundred million pounds, is believed to have sunk rapidly, during the hours of darkness. A huge search and rescue operation is underway by the U.S. Navy and Coast Guard from bases in San Juan and Fajardo. A short time ago the authorities said that all hands are feared lost. The U.S. Coast Guard will hold a press conference shortly."

I recalled having met the captain of 'AZUL' once outside "Stars and Bars" beside Port Hercules in Monaco. I thought his name was Sharpe. I remembered hoards of excitable young deckhands jockeying for his attention. The yacht herself was too large for the port and was at anchor in the bay outside. The captain stood with a detached calm that set him apart more than his gold epilates. You can always tell a good captain by their eyes; calm confidence and authority.

I have no idea what my eyes said about me.

7

Surrey, England

Now you know what happened when we pressed the "L" button together. You could have tried to stop me, couldn't you?

I have just spoken with Alexander our most talented and conscientious colleague. I congratulated him on his work so far.

Why do you query, "So far?"

Of course there is more to come. So very much more.

8

Terminal 5, London Heathrow Airport

I parked my car in short stay. If the Syndicate was to pay out a thousand million dollars, my parking expense was irrelevant.

I grabbed my ever-ready, heavily battered, packed bag from the boot and headed through fast track.

I stopped counting my air miles after the first million. I've earned my wings for fast track, business class, and airline lounges.

In the lounge I looked for a spot where I could be alone to read my e-mails. I did not need privacy, but I needed to be away from the regulars. They are the men who have managed to get an upgrade. They would be on the phone to their friends bragging loudly, gulping down free alcohol. There would be at least three French or Spanish tourists laying out their expensive jackets and luggage for us to examine like heirlooms at a car boot sale. Then there would be the nouveau riche wives with their exhausted husbands, engaging the waiters by their first names in wearisome, dreary stories of the places they have been, and in which row they sat en route. Then a few kids on their way to... who cares? I didn't.

Then there would be me. I can just about put up with me.

I found a space in the library and started to read. Rachel – my ever trustworthy contact within the Syndicate office – had sent me my hotel and rental car arrangements. For other clients I make my own arrangements but Rachel is so good at it I let her get on with it. Chum had told her to instruct me not to speak to the media as if I'm a novice. There were questions from the trade press and twelve messages from the dailies. I ignored them all. Another message informed me that Coles had resigned. So soon? I reread the e-mail:

"It is with regret that Board of H.R. Coles & Others announces the immediate resignation of its active underwriter, Henry Coles. The Board wishes to express their thanks and appreciation to Mr. Coles for his invaluable contribution to the growth of the Syndicate and its past success. We wish Mr. Coles well in his future endeavours."

I placed my phone on the small table in front of me. I did not understand why but all I could think of was Chum's final words this morning, "You know nothing."

Ping. A new message from Rachel:

"Hey. Sorry about those poor people." I knew that she was sincere. "Please keep safe."

The "Please keep safe." part caught me off guard. Of all the places I had been sent around the world, my final destination of Tortola, British Virgin Islands, was amongst the safest.

I looked up from my phone and saw a vision of everything I hate in a business lounger drag her jewellery to the bar and, while overtly flirting with the young waiter, order a Baileys on the rocks.

Ping. A new e-mail from Chum. "Lukasz, we wrote the War Risk Insurance too. That means that if the yacht was destroyed by a bomb we still pay."

I imagined the fever at Lloyd's. I looked at my watch, six o' clock. One Lime Street would be moving to The Lamb, The Ship on Lime, the East India Arms or, for those with corporate credit cards, Corney and Barrow. There would only be one topic of conversation and speculation in all of them.

....

I knew that I was being watched. I sensed that the spy was behind me. Three or four chairs back I heard a newspaper being folded, followed by a woman say very softly, "Thank you." It was so soft that I could not identify her accent. I then heard chair legs move over the wooden floor and she was gone. I resisted the urge to look at her.

Why isn't Chum handling this, I wondered? He needs to be in London of course canvassing for Coles' job!

My flight was called. On my way to the gate I stopped regularly and took a detour to see if the lounge spy would reappear. She did not. I was disappointed; I grabbed a copy of the evening paper from a dented newspaper stand as I walked down the jet bridge, my shoes drumming on the bouncing floor. 'AZUL' was on the cover and filled the first five pages. To the right of the cover page was a photograph of the captain of 'AZUL', the man I had met in Monaco. I was right, it was Sharpe. On the third page a montage of most of the crew had been published.

As I felt the aircraft wheels retract beneath me I puzzled again on Rachel's words. "Please keep safe."

9

Surrey, England

"I hope he will not continue to be so predictable Alexander."

"I left him alone at Heathrow. We know where he's heading. We'll pick him up again when he arrives."

"My new friend finds our business unsettling."

Alexander says nothing. He does not approve of you joining our firm. It is essential that I unsettle him on occasions, it prevents complacency.

"I said, my new friend…"

"I heard you," Alexander interrupts. "If you will excuse me. I have work to do."

10

18 September 2008
Off Port Hercules, Principality of Monaco

Standing on the bridge of 'AZUL', surrounded by a dull red light and watching the close-range display of three radar screens, captain William Sharpe received his orders from Alexander with bewilderment.

"Say again," Sharpe asked over the yacht's encrypted satellite telephone.

"The Boss wants you and your entire crew to go ashore tonight," Alexander repeated.

"Alexander, I cannot leave the largest yacht in the world unmanned at anchor off Monaco! It's the yacht show. There are over sixty superyachts out here. There are tenders, rigid inflatable, jetboats you name it buzzing all over the bay. The radar screen looks like an ant race. I can't do it."

"In exactly one hour you will see a target appear from the west. The target will stop and start at one minute intervals between each movement towards you. At a distance of one mile off, view the target with binoculars. You will see two flashes from a handheld flashlight. The flashes are your final orders for you and your crew to go ashore. I will board 'AZUL' with the Boss and a riding crew. Understood?"

"Understood," Sharpe lied.

"Good. The Boss has urgent business aboard tonight. He wants his yacht to himself."

"Very good," said Sharpe although he sensed there was nothing good about it. He had no more reason to trust Alexander than Alexander had to trust him. They were both, after all, hired for the same reason – trained killers with an unblemished record in following orders.

"Out!" snapped Alexander as the line went dead.

Sharpe replaced the handset. All luxury yacht captains are accustomed to erratic decisions of owners. Some fight against them usually finding themselves instantly on the dock looking for a new position. Sharpe could, until very recently, have honestly said that the Boss of 'AZUL' had been reasonable as to the limitations of the ship (for a ship was what 'AZUL' assuredly was) and considerate to the crew almost to the point on being, well, boring. What had changed? Why was the world's most private yacht sitting at anchor outside Port Hercules, Monaco during, arguably, the most public yacht show in the superyacht calendar with three hundred underwater lights illuminating her like Times Square? She could not have been more conspicuous if she had berthed within Port Hercules (an impossibility of course at her size).

Sharpe stepped away from the radar screens and looked at the clock behind the mahogany chart table. Launch three tenders and go ashore in five trips? Ten minutes to the dock wall, two to drop off, and ten back; there was insufficient time. Damn Alexander.

Sharpe radioed the Chief Officer from his walkie-talkie. "Orders from the Boss Ben, we're all going ashore; me included. Launch three tenders and get the Viking Sportsfisher out too. We have about forty-five minutes. Get the boats to the starboard garage door as quickly as possible." Sharpe then added, "Out," to indicate the matter was not open for discussion.

The captain then radioed the Chief Stewardess. “Kathryn, we have all been ordered ashore within the hour. Prepare all crew please. Out.”

Sharpe imagined the excitement below his feet as news spread of the run ashore. He wished he could share in it.

A buzzer sounded and a red light flashed to the right of the bridge indicating that the starboard quarter garage door was opening towards the end of the ship. He switched the CCTV monitor to station ‘GAR02’ and watched his crew expertly manoeuvre the tenders one by one into the slings of the crane. Although the image was grainy, he could see the delight on their faces. Apart for runs ashore for supplies most of Sharpe’s crew had not been ashore for nearly three weeks. Each night they could see the enticing lights of Monte Carlo, but not for them. So near, yet so far. The crew of charter yachts had it far worse; Sharpe would lecture in the crew mess, trapped aboard serving the every need, however bizarre, of the charterer; working twenty hours a day for weeks, sometimes months on end. Our Boss just wanted privacy; until now.

Sharpe saw the last of the three tenders enter the water. An amber indicator light lit up indicating that the crane for the Viking Sportsfisher was drawing power. When it turned green the crane would be in operation.

Sharpe knew his ship. He knew that almost thirty kilometres of wiring had gone into her construction and the quality of the build was astonishing. Sharpe and his crew had accessed every area of the ship, however small, to maintain her. Some of the spaces were so small and remote that no Boss, however fascinated by his toy, would ever access.

The story was the same wherever Sharpe went; a fastidious attention to detail. Every sole plate in the engine room crafted from aluminium diamond plate matched its neighbour to the millimetre. The marble in every head (bathroom to the Boss) had been crafted from an individual piece of marble without interrupting the intrinsic pattern, even in the crew quarters. This was without precedent. The gap around every single door and hatch in every compartment was uniform all the way around. Sharpe marvelled at the workmanship. He was used to destroyers aboard which there were no aesthetics; function over form.

Sharpe was expected to leave all of this beauty in the hands of a barely refined thug like Alexander?

Sharpe's radio crackled. "Half of the crew is ready to disembark captain," the Chief Stewardess informed him.

"Send them to the starboard garage and send ashore," Sharpe replied without enthusiasm. He watched as the first group boarded the tenders. He saw hands slip and slide all over his crew. Most of it was if not innocent, consensual. He saw, not for the first time, the Chief Engineer close to that stew from Florida. He was smiling too much pushing her towards the tender. She made an obvious effort to get away. Sharpe toggled the zoom control and saw the fear in her eyes. Sharpe grabbed the public announcement microphone and jabbed at 'PA:GAR02' on the left-hand side of the CCTV screen.

"Chief Engineer to the bridge. Out," he commanded.

Sharpe watched the relief in the stewardess's face match in equal measure the dismay in that of the Chief Engineer. He disappeared from shot as she climbed aboard the second tender.

As he waited for the Chief Engineer to reluctantly attend on the bridge, Sharpe looked again at the clock above the chart table. Alexander would never be late. He guessed that the Boss would have boarded Alexander's boat at Beaulieu to the west. Sharpe watched the near-range radar screen. Precisely on time a target appeared on the left side of the screen. 'AZUL' was sitting at anchor with her bow facing south-west.

"Here we go," Sharpe said to himself.

The Chief Engineer entered the bridge.

"Captain?"

"Just a minute Justin," Sharpe said fixed upon the target which appeared to be heading directly for 'AZUL'. Sharpe pressed a button alongside the screen marked 'ARPA'. Instantaneously the screen was overlaid with what to the untrained eye would look like a laser show of straight lines. Sharpe followed the line from the target to 'AZUL' and saw it heading for his ship exactly amidships. "Nothing if not accurate," Sharpe murmured punching the ARPA button again causing the laser lines to disappear. Recognizing the target as Alexander, Sharpe watched the image intently.

"Captain?" the Chief Engineer asked again.

"Not now," Sharpe said slowly. The target stopped moving. Sharpe noted the time on his watch. Exactly one minute later the target moved towards him again. Sharpe turned to the Chief Engineer. "Sorry Justin. I thought we had a problem. We don't. Join the others, go ashore."

Sharpe raised a pair of binoculars in the direction of the

target. Two flashes.

Sharpe radioed the Chief Stewardess. “All ready to go ashore?” he asked.

“Just a little,” she replied laughing. Sharpe could hear singing in the background.

As Sharpe was about to reluctantly leave the bridge the satellite phone rang.

“Captain,” he answered.

“Turn the underwater lights off under the garage door when you leave. We don’t want to be seen,” Alexander ordered.

The line went dead.

“I wonder if that man has ever done anything in daylight?” Sharpe pondered as he left his command.

....

Alexander and his crew manoeuvred the Donzi alongside the open garage door. The Boss was not with them. Alexander had no clue where the Boss was but knew very well he was nowhere near Monaco. Not to have asked to speak directly with the Boss Sharpe was clearly going soft. No matter.

The forward crew member leapt onto the garage door with the forward mooring line and deftly wrapped it in a figure of eight around a bollard.

Alexander knew the names of none of the crew. There

was no reason to; it would be their last mission.

Silently a second crew member threw the first the aft line.

"Stay here," Alexander ordered the helmsman. "Kill the engine."

With the engine shut down the only sound was the gentle irregular slap of the ocean against the rocking hull of the Donzi and the subdued hum of 'AZUL's' generators. Alexander stepped into the garage.

"Pass me that," Alexander ordered the crewman behind the helmsman. "Gently," he hissed.

The crewman gently raised a package approximately two metres square by thirty centimetres thick. The helmsman looked rigidly forward unwilling to witness what was going on behind him.

"Grow up!" Alexander growled as the crewman passed the package to him. "It won't kill you." He took the package into the garage. "You, come with me," he ordered the man standing there. Alexander gave the package to the man then led him down the companionway into the engine room. "Put that down and find a cordless screwdriver. Remember where it came from so you can put it back. Find all the driver bits too."

Silently the man did as he was instructed.

"Good. Let's go," Alexander said.

The man followed Alexander through a bulkhead door

into the line of crew cabins. Alexander made a great play of opening and closing cabin doors as if he was uncertain as to which cabin he was looking for. The crew member would in all likelihood be dead before he could ever testify but Alexander, forever cautious, chose not to take the risk.

"This one I think," Alexander said opening the door to a cabin that clearly belonged to a stewardess. It was small but had its own window. There was a photograph of a middle-aged couple stuck at an irregular angle to a mirror above an arsenal of make-up. "Give me the screwdriver," Alexander ordered whilst taking out a folded sheet of paper from inside his jacket. Had he lived the crew member may have thought that the paper had a plan on it. Alexander examined the shell expansion plan. He lifted a pelmet from above the window and noted the shape and dimension of the brass screw behind it. "Leave the package there," Alexander said nodding at the stewardess's bunk, "then go."

The crewman carefully placed the package on the bunk and left the cabin.

Alexander removed two screws from behind the pelmet. With a slight pop the wooden panel stood slightly proud. Alexander managed to insert his fingers behind hit. With a hissing sound the panel came free.

"Velcro," he said. "One billion dollars and it's still Velcro."

He placed the panel on the bed. He looked into the space and, with relief, saw the vertical and horizontal steel frames he was looking for. Certain that he had the right area he checked the shell expansion plan again. Spot on. He felt satisfied having located such a small area in over a thousand square metres of steel.

Alexander placed the plan on the bunk and carefully unwrapped the package. He gently lifted the contents and moulded it around the curvature of the hull at the joint between the vertical and horizontal frames. Smoothing the material with characteristic accuracy he stood back and admired his work. Quietly, he replaced the wooden panel and tightened the screw, then folded up the plan.

Leaving the cabin Alexander was dismayed to find the crewman waiting for him outside the cabin door.

"Here," he said, thrusting the tools into his chest. "Take those back. Put them back exactly where you found them. We never leave a trace."

....

11

18 November 2008
Roadtown, Tortola, British Virgin Islands, Caribbean

The following afternoon I found myself sitting in the small reception area of V.S. Vincent QC, just off Main Street. I was waiting for the great man himself who was running over an hour late. The walls had been painted a bright gloss yellow, the furniture was old, the plastic chair coverings cracked by the heat. The front door was open. A few tourists from the cruise ship of the day wandered past, gazing in, hoping to find something (or someone) of interest to photograph. They stared at me. I stared back. A large black lady sat behind a desk reading a battered novel.

It was early yet. The lawyer would eventually come rushing in apologizing profusely and meaning none of it. He would mumble something about the slow wheels of the legal system. I would smile and greet him formally. There are no first names here. He would then take me to meet his esteemed client who he would have been briefing on what he should say, and more importantly what he should not, for the hour I had been waiting in reception. I love my work, but now and then it can be predictable.

At one hour and six minutes later than our appointment, he appeared all gowns and bogus fluster. He need not have bothered with the act or the costume.

"My dear sir, I am so, so sorry," V.S. lied.

I watched his mouth moving but didn't listen to the rest as I examined him. He clasped my right hand with both of his in an act of hammy sincerity. He was a small man, barely a metre and a half tall. His dark eyes were recessed too far back into his skull and his hands were minute, even for a man of his diminutive size.

As he led me to the conference room I knew whatever V.S. said next would be more lies. I would play along.

My learned, now friend, lead me into a library lined with hundreds of law books. An immaculate young black woman sat poised holding a Mont Blanc pen ready to take notes. This worried me slightly. I sensed off-island education (probably the United States). It was her posture and that pen that meant a good deal more learning than my new learned friend; Too-Bright.

Sitting opposite Too-Bright, perspiring and wide-eyed was an accountant ten years my junior. I knew he was an accountant because the second owner's representative served up to me (the first being the lawyer) is always an accountant.

Nothing to worry about; he reads in numbers, I read in words. In court words are so much more persuasive.

My learned friend introduced me to Mr. Lomas and to Miss. Too-Bright. I was not offered a drink. V.S. droned on. I chose not to listen; I was busy weighing up Too- Bright. I then wondered about the ability of the sweaty, puppet accountant. He repeatedly dabbed his forehead with a wet handkerchief, although the air conditioning system was working and clanking away above his head. The fan motor needed new bearings I decided.

"'AZUL' has disappeared. We expect, and demand, that the Syndicate you represent promptly investigate and pay our client's claim for Actual Total Loss, without undue delay. We will, naturally, cooperate fully in your investigation." I heard Too-Bright say.

"I understand your client's position," I replied formally. "However, as you have just acknowledged, my client has the right to fully investigate this loss."

"Forty people are presumed dead, Mr. Stone. Forty. They have families," said Too-Bright.

"Yes," I agreed.

Too-Bright was expecting more. We had the measure of each other.

My learned friend V.S. stood crossed the room and reached for a weighty law book. The spine was ripped at the top. Whatever speech was to follow I would not be the first to have heard it.

The silent accountant reached for his handkerchief again.

"Mr. Lomas' boss had to go down island," V.S. said opening the book.

"...unexpectedly," added Too-Bright.

I like you Too-Bright. We could get on.

She smiled at me.

Ah. My mistake.

“Mr. Lomas,” I said, “I was sorry to hear of your loss.” This was deliberately ambiguous. I meant the boat; he was thinking of his absent boss. “My office asked you for some documents. Do you have them with you?”

Sweaty Lomas looked at Too-Bright who nodded. Lomas reached down to pick up a scruffy brown satchel, revealing a red-raw nape of his neck as he did so. This isn’t a local; they flew him in. I started to think. It is 1630 now. I got the earliest possible flight from London after the sinking. Either he spent the morning on the beach or he had been on the island a few days. The burn was starting to peel, so the latter. For the first time I looked closely at Lomas. I had seen the sunburn but then realized why he was sweating so much. He was wearing a thick cotton shirt and heavy winter suit trousers.

“When did you arrive in the BVIs Mr. Lomas?”

Lomas looked startled.

“Mr. Lomas’ firm of accountants is well established in these islands,” said Too-Bright, too quickly.

V.S., who seemed unaware that I had worked out Lomas’ hasty deployment from London to Tortola, placed his book on the conference table, flattened his gown and sat down.

“Sir, may I share something with you, something important that I have learned during my many decades in the practice of the law?”

He spoke softly, as if he was running in his voice box.

“Of course Mr. Vincent.” I played along. I knew what was coming.

"There is a belief often held by those who visit us, that we on this island are ignorant of the law. On other islands that may be true, but not here. We are not ignorant of the law of your land either. As you will have seen from the brass plate by the front door I am silk; Queen's Counsel. As a result of this misplaced belief, those of us who have chosen the law as our mistress..."

I admit it. I winced.

Mr. Lomas had stopped sweating

"...or our lover…"

Even Too-Bright kicked a crossed leg at that one, as if we needed to test her reflexes.

"…have studied the complexities of the most infinite degree. You might be wondering what this book is? This book was written by my grandfather whilst he was in chambers in London. He was a small man smaller than me. He lived simply but was held in the highest regard. He commanded respect."

Lomas was still. Too-Bright prepared to feign enlightenment.

I was getting a little bored.

"My grandfather often wrote on matters of commercial law under your legal system. Those writings included many texts upon the business of insurance. Many of those texts were relied upon as authorities in later court cases. This is just one," V.S. said pressing a small finger on the page in front of him. "Are you familiar with the Latin term uberrimae fidei Mr. Stone?"

Tortolan lore dictates that I should have said something. He was being so politely rude that I said nothing.

"It means "utmost good faith"," he murmured, locking his sunken eyes onto mine.

Too-Bright delivered her sigh of enlightenment.

"My clients and I are fully aware of our legal duty to deal with you and your client in good faith Mr. Vincent," I said frostily. "Do you have you the documents Mr. Lomas?" I asked, rudely ignoring my learned friend.

An hour later and still puzzled by Lomas I left the chambers of V.S. Vincent QC carrying five files of ship's papers. I recall walking passed Pussers Pub on the way back to my hire car. I experienced the same feeling as I had in the lounge at Heathrow. I was being watched.

....

For convenience Rachel had billeted me at Treasure Isle Hotel for just one night, there was no point in going further out of the capital Roadtown to one of the resorts in the picturesque bays on the north coast of the island.

I sat in the restaurant staring at the 'Rotary Club' sign listening to crickets and thinking about the disappearance of 'AZUL'. I was the only diner.

My waitress was not born for public service; service with a grimace. Each time she flopped towards me I acted as if she had my life complete. I was expected to do this. I had Lomas' files on the table in front of me. I tried not to look at the cigarette burn (old) and guava juice stains (even older) on the tablecloth. I remembered the relief in Lomas' eyes as he passed the lever arch files to me, as if he had just handed over a bomb.

I started to read the documents in the first file. All of the pages were neatly labelled and indexed. First was the Certificate of Registry. Fine. The Load Line and Classification Society report were next. They were all in order and valid. I hauled the safety manual up from the floor. I knew this would be in order too. I was only interested in identifying the 'Designated Person Ashore' – the DPA – the person called in an emergency. Inside the file, his card was neatly inserted behind a clear plastic window. Somebody had put many hours work into this presentation. This struck me as odd given that the yacht had disappeared only the day before. The DPA's address was in Fort Lauderdale, Florida. I noticed that he was not located in the yachting hub of Southeast 17th Street, as I had expected. He was north. Far north. Almost at the Palm Beach border.

So that's where I would be going next I thought as I replaced the manual on the floor. I will read the manual on the planes, I decided. I flicked through the first file again. Various radio and telecommunications licenses. The stability booklet.

The boy Lomas had been hard at work to get all this together and have time to get sunburned, I thought. Even if the DPA had called the lawyers immediately he heard of the sinking, no Tortolan would have stayed up all night making these, near perfect copies.

Ping. Rachel.

"Your case is everywhere. You're going to be famous. I'll love you anyway."

My waitress shuffled back with a burger, stiff chips and tomato slices that looked just a little too red. I closed the file before she reached the table.

I heard someone take a table two or three rows behind me. I remembered the lounge at Heathrow and Pussers earlier that afternoon. I had an identical certainty of being watched. The waitress stared behind me, patently affronted that she would have to serve two diners in one evening.

I heard a woman's voice, mid-twenties. She had a faint accent that I could not place above the crickets.

I reopened the file. A few receipts from surveyors for special surveys. Then a copy of the insurance policy with Henry Coles' signature at the bottom of the last page.

"Excuse me."

I immediately slammed the file shut. "Yes?" I said harshly without looking up.

"Would you happen to know the time of the first ferry to St. John's?"

I looked up and saw that my dining companion was so expensively dressed I had to doubt that she had ever been on a ferry in her life.

"Sorry, I don't," I said.

"Oh," she said disappointedly. "I thought you might know. I'm sorry to have bothered you while you're working," she added softly. If she intended to make me feel guilty for my ignorance of ferry timetables, she succeeded.

She returned to her table.

I tried to concentrate on the papers in front of me but could not. The papers seemed ridiculous. I felt tired, but more than that – disturbed. Why was she following me? I abandoned my burger, and walked to her table.

"May I?"

She was gazing out to sea.

"Of course," she said without turning towards me.

"Why are you here?" I asked gently taking the chair opposite her.

"Business," she replied.

"No, why are you here?" I asked again.

"Is there anywhere else worth the drive?" she said turning towards me.

"Brandy Wine, I suppose. Eclipse?"

"You're a regular visitor then?"

"Not regular enough to know the ferry timetable."

She smiled. "Why are you here?"

"Business."

"No. Why are you here?"

"That's a question I ask myself quite often," I said

nodding at my untouched burger.

She smiled again. I had already said too much.

"You could be at either of those places too."

"The pool here is nice. Have you seen it?"

And so I found myself sitting by the deserted swimming pool, talking with a spy and total stranger, sipping glasses of warm white wine, occasionally glimpsing our reflection in the water.

"I'm glad to have met you," she said as we walked up the steep steps to our respective rooms.

"I am glad to have met you too," I said.

As I carried on climbing the hill past her room I felt relief. If she was the tail I could expect in this case, she was a great improvement on the norm.

Her name was Francesca.

12

Surrey, England

"V.S. says he's impudent and nothing to worry about."

"I'm not interested in V.S. What's Patrice's take on him?"

"She agrees he's impudent, but says we'd be foolish to underestimate him. He has reputation, influence and a dogged determination," Alexander sighed. "Nothing a bullet couldn't solve."

"Not just yet."

"No?"

"Not yet," I replied looking once more at those sea-green eyes on my monitor. Let's see how great at this game you really are Mr. Stone.

13

1 January 2000
Fort Lauderdale, Florida

Joseph Lamb Jnr stood on the balcony of his 37th floor apartment, coffee mug in hand, looking over the New River to the slumbering City of Fort Lauderdale. Gazing eastwards he sipped on his strong black coffee and watched the sun rise for a new millennium. Not bad for a boy from Ruskin, he reminded himself.

Close to the Florida Gulf Coast, a short drive, but a world apart from affluent Sarasota, Ruskin had only one redeeming feature – the road out. The Lamb family had progressed from a trailer to a six hundred square foot single family home with chain link fencing. Air conditioning units hung by chains from some of the windows. His father had sold cleaning products door to door, when he wasn't cleaning up after Joseph's mother who was a drunk. It was a tough business; there wasn't much cleaning going on in Ruskin. Finality came when a category 5 hurricane barrelled in from the Gulf of Mexico taking most of Ruskin with it including half of the already small Lamb home. Joseph's mother had refused to leave the building despite pleas from a Deputy Sherriff she had been at school with. The last time Joseph saw his mother, she was gulping madly from a fifth of bourbon, shooing him away as he tried to give her a hug.

14

19 November 2008
San Juan, Puerto Rico

I avoided the early morning scheduled flight from Tortola and took a six-seat charter plane instead. Rachel had found that the pilot was flying Beef Island to San Juan to pick up a couple destined for Neckar Island. I had watched the sun start to rise ahead of us, bringing a lazy muted purple over the water and the snoozing flotilla of charter yachts below.

I remembered I had heard nothing from Banksy. Odd, I made a note to call him from Florida, once I had interviewed the DPA.

....

Should an evangelist ever need inspiration to describe the horror of hell, then San Juan airport is it. The first flight leaves daily at 0800, exactly the same time as two thirds of the check-in staff turn up for work. There were people everywhere, shouting, prodding and jabbering in Spanish. Arms flailing, shouting, pointing at each other, shrugging shoulders with outstretched palms. I was looking (admittedly from business class check-in) at around seven hundred such people. The noise was stupefying.

"Enjoy your flight Mr. Stone," the petite check-in clerk said calmly, handing me my boarding pass. How could she remain so cheerful working in this chaos each day?

A man well past retirement age equipped with a wide broom was trying to sweep the floor. He asked no one to move. He swept up to their shoes, retreated, then swept up against the toes of the next person.

Dotted between the Latinos were a few red-faced Americans. One was standing at one of the two open check-in desks shouting and pointing at the ten closed desks. The pretty Latina agent shrugged and smiled. The Latinos behind him became hostile at the time he was taking.

"We are Americans too," I heard someone yell.

"Only when it suits you," he replied.

I scanned the remainder of the crowd. I knew I was being watched but could not see who by. There was no sign of Francesca. That would have been too obvious.

15

Following the death of his mother and the near annihilation of Ruskin, Joseph Lamb Jnr's Uncle Sol, living well in Fort Lauderdale, invited the Josephs to live with him. Lamb Jnr embraced the optimism, ego and enterprise of the city.

Joseph Lamb Jnr had yet to be created. No rush.

Lamb watched the growing numbers of Latin American's setting up homes and businesses in South East Florida. He looked at the Cuban refugees. Well educated, hardworking, diligent, and honest amongst them. If the Cuban embargo ended there would be fortunes to be made. Lamb realized he could not wait that long.

With no state income tax, no penalties for bankruptcy, hire-and-fire at will, and the climate, Lamb saw that South East Florida was destined to boom. At the age of fifteen he decided that he was going to not only get his share of boom, but that he was going to lead it. Certain that his humble beginnings in Ruskin would eventually catch up with him; he had to factor that awful town into his plans. Somehow he had to turn the negative into a double positive. Lamb laughed. How South Florida? Words that sounded fantastic; that on any analysis were absolute garbage.

....

After community college, Jnr got a job working garbage trucks. Success – not failure. He wanted to see how good money was being made. No better way than collecting rich folk's trash.

“He owns a chain of pizza places...” said Jonny the Sage.

Churn. Churn. Macerate.

“We can’t take sofas Madam. You will have to wait for bulk collection.” Jonny again.

“He buys strip malls and then uses another of his companies to lease them...”

Jonny had more sophistication than Lamb had credited him.

“Condos...”

Jnr was staring to become bored.

“Japanese car importer...”

Too risky, many Americans refused to buy Japanese cars unless second hand. Someone else had paid the profit to the bombers of Pearl Harbor.

“Football player...”

Great.

There was one profession that Jonny mentioned regularly with contempt.

“Attorney.”

How bad would you have to be that even your garbage man hated you?

16

19 November 2008
San Juan Airport, Puerto Rico

Sitting in business class window seat '2A' with the first coffee of the day, I watched idly as the passengers embarked. I didn't think any of them would be my babysitter for the flight.

Lomas' documents were in the bag in the overhead locker. Once the curtain between the classes was closed I intended to take out the bulky safety manual and start to read through it. Two and a half hours flying time to Fort Lauderdale would be sufficient.

I looked around business class as the short blue nylon curtains were zipped behind me. There were only two of us in there me and a large man who had started snoring before we pushed back from the stand. He was a row behind but on the other side of the aircraft in '3E'. I was satisfied that even if he woke up he would not be able to read my files from his seat.

I doubted the middle-aged, lively attendant was watching me, but I was wary.

Paranoia can sometimes be justified.

Rachel had sent me a file of press articles from the web and first editions. Based upon the sparse details known of the loss of 'AZUL' the number of column inches was impressive. I marvelled at how so many journalists and their editors never let the facts get in the way of a good story.

My learned friends in Tortola had yet to make any comment. In my opinion they would be foolish to do so.

I watched the sea below us and flicked my eyes to the azure above then opened the second file and pushed back into my seat. This is my life.

17

19 November 2008
Surrey, England

"She's still alive Jack!"

As head of the organisation, customer satisfaction rests with me. Watch and learn. I don't irritate people; I don't e-mail my clients interminable questionnaires. No discount coupons either. Overall, how would you rate our service? Below, above, or at your expected level?

No. Either the target's dead or they aren't.

In this, albeit rare case, our service had been delivered below our client's expectations.

"Jay. She might not make it," I say. "Alexander has been to the hospital with lilies this time."

"She is still ay-live Jack! She should be dead. I couldn't care less what bouquet Alexander bought. Why didn't he kill her?"

Would you mind going for a walk or something? Admitting failure does not come easily to me.

"Send him back to finish the job."

Jay. Trust me on this. Not even Alexander can stroll into an intensive care unit and assassinate a patient without getting caught."

“I don’t care if he’s caught.”

“Yes you do Jay. If he gets caught it leads right back to you. At the moment it looks like a bad accident. The poor girl was in the wrong place at the wrong time. We shoot or poison her and someone is going to make a connection.”

“I have powerful friends. An investigation would be dropped.”

“If you believe that Jay I’m very happy for you. Personally, I don’t. As your oldest friend I’m telling you – don’t make me do this.”

I thought I told you to take a walk?

“I agree,” he said slowly. “Just pray she doesn’t survive.”

“Her injuries are sufficient. By the time she’s recovered the project will be over and she’ll be an irrelevance to you.”

“Very well. But I don’t want you using whoever botched this job on my project again.”

“Agreed Jay. Goodbye.”

We know we won’t be using him again don’t we? We are watching a movie. We are watching the scene where Alexander breaks the hapless assassin’s neck. He was our co-worker; so sad.

18

Fort Lauderdale Airport, Florida

My rental car was in bay 16; a white, American-wide Ford. Anonymous and perfect. I headed out of the airport and pointed the sofa on wheels the short distance north-west onto US1. I love US1. This road runs all the way up the eastern seaboard from Key West to New York City. Parallel to it runs the Intracoastal Waterway, a tame voyage I intend to make once I've sailed the Atlantic outer side. I spend all day with yachts, but never tire of them. There is always something new.

As I drove past the intersection of US1 and Southeast 17 Street, I wondered again why the owner of the largest, most expensive yacht in the world positioned his DPA so far away from this strip.

I drove slowly around the edge of Downtown. The answer struck me by the Saturn dealership. Secrecy; total, paranoid, secrecy. Whoever the owner was, his DPA would not be found in Waxy O'Connor's or any of the other crew bars shooting his mouth off about the Boss's business. Perhaps the Boss lived here? The DPA won't be promising to take young tourists of either sex aboard to show them a good time. He won't be say anything. My guess? The DPA and the Boss went back a very long way.

I kept an eye on the rear-view mirror. I really did not expect to see anyone. They knew where I was heading so why spend the money to tail me?

....

The road snaked left and right until I reached an area of discount stores. Large neon signs lit a small mall that must have once excited the neighbourhood.

I turned left into prime 'sub-prime territory', the catchphrase coined that year. Home values were predicted to halve, leaving those few still paying their mortgages wondering why they should bother. For the lucky ones gleaming pickups stood in the driveways. Mostly old grey rusting 1970's Fords or retired police cars surrounded me. The realtor signs and foreclosure boards almost outnumbered mail boxes. I took another left and found myself in a crescent of small grey identical detached houses. The house I was looking for was at the far end with a high, dense, hedge around it. I saw a black Audi Q7 four-wheel drive, in the driveway incongruous with its surroundings. I drove past, stopped, and then reversed onto the driveway just in case I needed to leave quickly. In the rear-view mirror I saw CCTV cameras on either side of the house. Unusual in Florida, particularly attached to a cheap property such as that.

I turned off the ignition and quickly e-mailed my location to Rachel. Chum's regulations state I should always do this. I rarely do, unless I feel a need.

I felt the need.

As I approached the oversized front door and risible Corinthian pillars, the door opened. This I liked.

Before me was a tanned, tall, slim man in his late thirties with a straight back and square shoulders. Your unsinkable yacht has sunk. Are you proud? He was wearing the regular yachting uniform of knee-length shorts and a polo shirt. I am used to muscular bodies. Some yacht crews have nothing else to do when they have finished the daily wash-down other than workout. There was something more; something military.

"James Johnson. DPA," he said reaching to shake my hand.

"Lukasz Stone," I said warily.

"Come in."

I entered to find an atypical Floridian home which included a Le Corbusier LC4 sofa and two matching chairs. Originals? A Le Corbusier glass-topped dining table, with Harry Bertoia diamond chairs and two Eames chairs. Through the far end patio doors I could see a screened pool hidden by large green shrubs.

"The Boss believes that if I have to live out here, then the interior should be to my taste," Johnson explained as if reading my thoughts.

"And is this to your taste?"

"Of course," he said slowly. "Before we proceed can I assume that our conversation is entirely confidential?"

"I had assumed the Boss's lawyer on Tortola would have briefed you?"

"Please, sit down."

I sat on the sofa. It was an original.

"Mr. Stone, I run yachts. I am not a lawyer. You are here to investigate the tragic loss of life aboard a ship that I had legal and moral responsibility for. I will fully cooperate with you in your investigation."

That was the second time I had heard that phrase in less than twenty-four hours. As for 'moral responsibility' I had my doubts. In my experience and without exception anyone that starts an interview professing faith, morals or philanthropy feels the need to justify themselves. What follows will be lies.

"I fully understand that you have to satisfy your client's shareholders that everything is satisfactory. You will understand that my interest is to find out what went wrong and then to protect the owner's interests," he continued.

Quite a script. Well rehearsed; deftly delivered.

"Mr. Johnson, is our conversation being recorded?" I surprised myself by asking.

"Why do you ask?" he replied guardedly.

"The CCTV, the rehearsed lines."

"Rehearsed?"

"Scripted."

"I think you had better leave."

"So do I. We will continue this with you answering my questions, under oath in Miami. My client's office will make the arrangements with you. I am sure you will come prepared."

I saw myself out.

"This is going to get a lot worse before it gets better,"

I mumbled to myself as I drove south towards Miami-Dade. This time I watched the rear-view mirror, rather more closely.

19

After three years of mornings on the dump truck and afternoons working at a supermarket packing bags, Joseph had saved enough money to put himself through law school. He chose the University of Miami, close to wealthy Coral Gables. With a ready wit, charm and good impeccable manners he was a popular student. He drew the line at excessive drinking, never smoked or took drugs, but yet was the centre of attention at any party.

In his second year he met a philosophy major named Lori. Within three weeks they were engaged. She was a quiet girl with a sincere smile and was delighted to live in Joseph's increasingly well-regarded shadow.

According to plan, Joseph obtained a first-class law degree and was rewarded with his first job at a niche family law firm in Fort Lauderdale. The small firm had long standing society and political connections, with a small but exclusive client base.

By the age of thirty Joseph had made partner. His reputation was as he had constructed it – a lively, intelligent mind inseparable from his integrity. He maintained his limited drinking, never took drugs and was never a philanderer. The firm had seen to it that he was in the public eye and associated with all the most advantageous charities, events and political causes.

At thirty-two with his first child on its way, Joseph Lamb Jnr was openly known as 'The Honest Lawyer', exactly as he had planned.

20

19 November 2008
Miami, Florida

I dialled the Coles Syndicate office number in London and asked for Joe Wallis. I should, by the regulations, have been reporting to Chum every forty-eight hours. This phone call would have to do. I assumed Chum was too busy to talk to me. Despite my lack of interest in insurance I had noticed that when I spoke to them, insurance people listened. That was very inconvenient for Chum, as he had the reverse effect. Besides I really needed accurate and complete information, not just the abridged version that Chum would supply.

"Lukasz! My boy! You are missing the party! Chum has issued orders that we are all to exude 'confidence and happiness'. If we are really good he will bring in sweets tomorrow."

"What's going on Joe?" I asked, through my laughter.

"Let me shut the door." I waited as Joe padded, shoeless as always, across his office and closed the door. I heard the wheels on his chair move as (I imagined) he pushed back and put his feet up on the desk. "Where to start? First thing this morning we had the regulatory guys from Lloyd's in. They are livid. This sort of thing is not supposed to happen anymore. This is so eighties. The Central Fund is exposed etc., etc. You can imagine the hyperbole."

Not really.

"Joe, the Central Fund has enough in it that the whole of Lloyd's could fold and it would still keep paying out like an ATM," I said.

"I know Lukasz, but give them a break. These guys are young. They've got careers to make. It's the closest thing they've ever seen to a scandal."

"Is it a scandal Joe?"

Joe laughed. "All that's your game, my friend. I just insure stuff."

"You didn't write the 'AZUL' though?"

"I answered the phone didn't I? No, that one was Henry Coles. The files have his scratches all over them."

"Have you seen the originals?"

"No, only copies."

"Chum e-mailed me. Coles' gone."

"Seems he forgot to purchase reinsurance."

"I don't buy that."

"Neither did he. We haven't got any reinsurance. Not one-off facultative, whole book quota treaty, not even insured out for Total Loss Only; nothing."

"Who else has been in the office?"

"Charlie Secretan. He's the London broker for 'AZUL's' owners, whoever they are. The business came to him through a producing broker in Fort Lauderdale, can't remember his name. Secretan has been in with Chum all afternoon. He came to see me first. He wants the hull claim paid, reinsurance or no reinsurance. You have fourteen days to finish your investigation."

"Fourteen days! That's impossible."

"Chum has agreed. We will give him an answer on the fifteenth day, third of December; no later. Apparently a lawsuit has already been drafted against us."

"Someone's in a hurry."

"A billion dollars is a lot of 'someone's' money, Lukasz. Clearly they want it back and quickly."

"Does the policy say where they have to sue us?"

"Any 'Court of competent jurisdiction' in the Unites States."

"You know I don't know what that means."

"Where are you?"

"Florida."

"Nice. Does the owner have an office there?"

"Sort of, yes. The Designated Person Ashore lives here."

"That's two connections with Florida. The producing broker and the Designated… what did you call it?"

"Designated Person Ashore."

"They will probably sue us in Florida then. I would if I was them."

"Unless we pay."

"Unless we pay one thousand million dollars within two weeks."

"What if it's Lloyd's Central Fund money?"

"If it's Central Fund money you should expect heavier pressure to pay, not less. Your owner versus Lloyd's in a south Florida court is not something the twelfth floor would relish. Did you see the photographs of the crew in the newspaper last night? Would you want to put those in front of a jury?"

I shuddered.

"We, or rather you, have fourteen days Lukasz." The lightness had left Joe's voice.

"Could you go into the underwriting stats for me please Joe?" I asked.

"Sure." I heard Joe tapping away at the keyboard. "By the way, Chum concluded his meeting with Secretan by saying, "I'm sure there is nothing to worry about. Our best man is working on it now.""

Joe and I laughed.

"Then, "Regards to Samantha and the girls."" Joe's impersonation of Chum was flawless. "The man's an idiot. A dangerous idiot."

"The worst kind," I said.

“OK, I’m in the system. What do you want to know?”

“What’s ‘AZUL’s’ loss record?”

“Erm, new piece of carpet last year, someone spilled red wine on it. Two hundred thousand dollar claim – carpet came from Tibet. Didn’t get an offcut did they? Err, engine damage before that. Manufacturers paid out. Remember those were all with the previous insurers. Finally a claim advised to us but not pursued. Wouldn’t have been covered anyway.”

“What was it?”

“Wrongful dismissal lawsuit.”

“When?”

“About two months ago.”

“Joe, would you send me the file on that one please?”

“For our best man – anything.”

“And Joe…”

“Yes?”

“Encrypt it please.”

....

As the sun started to set, I drove from the InterContinental Hotel to the Rusty Pelican on Key Biscayne. Three young Latinos were attempting to recover a speedboat onto a trailer. Several elderly couples had quietly taken their seats to watch the sunset to the left of the downtown Miami skyline.

A green Ford Taurus had joined me at the Key Biscayne tollbooths and had followed me to the Pelican. The windshield was so heavily tinted that I could not see the driver. The car parked twenty metres away from me, but no one got out.

My phone rang. The screen showed area code '787' – Puerto Rico.

"Stone," I said.

"Good evening Mr. Stone. This is Lieutenant Jorge Rodriguez of the Puerto Rican Coastguard. How are you today, sir?" he asked coolly.

"I am well Lieutenant. How may I be of assistance?"

"I understand that you are investigating the disappearance of motor yacht 'AZUL' off my island on behalf of an insurance company."

"A Lloyd's Syndicate."

"Lloyd's? Good. I am the investigating officer for the Puerto Rican Coastguard."

"I see."

"I understand that you have passed through Puerto Rico twice in the last twenty-four hours. I am, shall we say, disappointed that you did not come to find me."

He sounded more than disappointed.

"I understood how busy you must be with the search and rescue," I lied.

"As you know, Mr. Stone, in this case, regrettably, it is all search and no rescue. I've had plenty of free time to meet with you. No wreckage has been found, not even a sheen of oil," he said quietly.

"I am sorry to hear that," I said eying the immobile green Taurus. The car was too cheap and the approach too obvious for it to be Francesca inside.

"We believe our sonar search has identified the wreck in the Trench. We're not absolutely certain, as there are so many wrecks in there. We believe that most are much smaller than 'AZUL'."

"What is the depth of water?"

"In places in that location it can be several miles deep."

Sonar has its uses. Looking for a large yacht in an underwater scrapyard is not one of them.

"And you are going to send a Remotely Operated Vehicle camera down to examine the sonar target?"

No movement from the Taurus. A feeble attempt at intimidation I concluded and decided to give Rodriguez my full attention.

"Unfortunately our own equipment cannot reach that depth. We have no budget to charter either an ROV from the mainland or commercially here." Rodriguez's tone was softening. I knew where he was heading – towards Henry Coles Syndicate's cheque book.

"How large is the target you have located, Lieutenant?" I asked, puzzled that such a senior officer would give the sonar image any credibility.

"We believe we've the port bow to around the fourth bulkhead – say 1,000 square metres."

From a sonar image? Unless the United States Coast Guard was there when 'AZUL' sank (which I had at that time no reason to suspect) there was no way absent blind luck that they could have correctly identified her wreck so quickly just by sonar. But... But this was the United States Government. What did it want?

"So you were thinking that my client's Syndicate might have a budget for it?" I heard the chilly tone in my voice and instantly regretted it. Looking back I can see that the pressure on Rodriguez to provide rapid answers must have been immense.

Rodriguez cleared his throat and expertly played the ace in his hand, "Or we could federalize the operation, sir."

"No, no," I said much too quickly. Involve the Federal Government and we would be invoiced for everything ten times over and learn nothing of what they found. Rodriguez knew the power in his threat.

"We assumed you would want the yacht back," Rodriguez added implausibly.

As a kit? I inhaled deeply.

"Lieutenant," I said as I exhaled, "the best thing I can do is talk to my people in London first thing tomorrow. They open five hours ahead of us."

"I know, I spent a year at the University of Southampton."

“I have your number. I will call you back.”

“The longer you leave it the further the current will sweep the debris.”

“I am aware of that.”

“I look forward to hearing from you tomorrow. If you need anything let me know.”

“There is one thing,” I said, my confidence building.

“What is that, sir?” Rodriguez asked warily.

“Find out when a British citizen called Thomas Lomas entered the British Virgin Islands. I don’t know whether he entered by sea or air, but I suspect air. You only need to get the records checked for the last two weeks. Do you have those connections?”

“I’m surprised you do not have those connections.”

“I do. But do you want me distracted? You speak to your people, I will speak with mine. I will have the answer waiting for you in exchange.”

“Very good. And Mr. Stone…”

“Yes?”

“Be careful. We believe someone wanted that yacht destroyed. They may well want the same end for you.”

21

Surrey, England

"He's tough," I told Alexander.

"He's only had the first degree," Alexander replied defensively.

Are you listening to this? Our finest man troubled by an insurance guy?

"He's got spirit." I can't help toying with Alexander. "We've been looking into his family."

I hope you don't mind the 'we'? We are in this together, remember? How could you forget? I would be sure, if I was a betting man, that you wake up in the dead of night seeing me hit that key; the moment we killed them all. I have never gambled. I plan. I see risks. I allow for them. Then I execute.

"The mother."

"The mother?" Alexander asked.

"Polish. Resolute. Absent father. She carried, pulled and pushed our boy. He's OK. We should hire him."

"You're joking? He isn't military."

"Is that everything I wonder?"

"You know it is!"

Did you hear it in his voice? He thinks I'm going soft.

"Alexander, you pulled up in a public car park in a Ford Taurus – a green one at that. Of course the guy wasn't intimidated. Use something larger next time."

"I should just kill him."

"No!"

I am starting to enjoy this accomplice. Aren't you?

22

19 November 2008
Hamble River, Hampshire

“Mr. Banks?”

James looked up from his desk in the ‘Crows Nest’, his office high above his boatyard. He looked straight into the barrel of a gun. Behind the gun, barely illuminated by the only light from the banker’s lamp on his desk he saw the image of a toned man dressed in a dark suit, crisp white shirt and dark tie.

“Let’s go,” Alexander said.

Silently, James lead the way down the office stairs keenly aware of the gun aimed at his back.

“What now?” he asked when they reached the ground.

“Don’t worry Mr. Banks. I’m only interested in your latest acquisition. Please, put her back together and sail us out of here.”

“I can’t do that,” James said.

Alexander waved the gun in front of Banksy’s face.

“I really think you can,” Alexander replied.

As James set to work Alexander kept the gun trained upon him. The railway motors started and the boat edged its way down the railway. When the hull reached the crane James said, "I have to get in the crane. You understand?"

"Sure. You have to step the mast."

"Yes," James replied looking once more at the gun. Was it loaded? He looked into Alexander's eyes. It was loaded.

It took twice as long for James to locate the mast in its step than usual; nerves. Alexander watched dispassionately unaware of the delay.

Once the yacht and mast were reconnected Alexander made a phone call that James could not hear.

"Pick me up in an hour." He hung up. "Let's go sailing Mr. Banks," he said.

James manoeuvred the yacht out of his yard. The last time he would ever see it.

23

Fort Lauderdale, Florida

By the start of the new millennium, Lamb's firm was ten partners and thirty associates strong.

He resisted further growth.

"Niche," was the word he used to his partners. "We will retain our niche."

Joseph never changed the name on the practice door or ever added his own.

The South Florida property boom was underway, but Lamb refused to grow his firm to service it. Areas thought down at heel were seeing prices double as mortgages became freely available. Their true value? "Ask me again in five years," he said.

Lamb prospered, but it wasn't enough. The law firm was making money, millions of dollars. The millions, however, took time to collect. In the meantime Lamb had staff to pay, office rents, trial exhibits, a wife. The cash flow was flowing too slowly for him to accumulate wealth at the same rate as on paper he earned it. Even as managing partner Lamb was still working two thousand chargeable hours a year, the same as a rookie associate.

The solution was obvious. So was its illegality.

24

19 November 2008
Miami, Florida

The sun had set.

A hundred and fifty miles south the nightly sundown party was underway in Mallory Square, Key West. The cat man, fire-eaters, jugglers all screaming for the attention of dazed, sunburned and mostly drunk tourists.

Banksy? What had happened to Banksy? Waiting three hours for him to get me what I needed was unheard of. Three days? I dialled his number. Voicemail. I left a message, then I called Evo, Banksy's yard manager.

"Battersea dog's home. The top dog speaking."

"Evo, it's Lukasz."

"Well if it isn't Lord Air Miles."

"Have you seen Banksy?"

"Well. I'm very well thank you Lukasz. And yourself?"

"Sorry, Evo. Long day."

"Ah, no problem mate. You got out of the wrong side of first class this morning?" he asked with more good humour than I deserved. "What can I do for you?"

"Have you seen Banksy today?"

"I haven't been at the yard today. Rachel called earlier about the Mills boat though."

"Why?"

"Why?" Why do you think Stone? She's worried."

"Worried?" I was more concerned about Rachel being worried than I was by why she was worried.

"Lukasz, it's me. As you know, my experience of women is limited to two of 'em. My mum and a Labrador called Trisha. That said I'll take a punt. Firstly, you're investigating something that has danger UXB written all over it. Secondly 'UXB' is written in huge, bold, dayglo lettering that everyone can read but you."

"Evo, please. Just get Banksy to call me. Thanks. Goodnight."

25

20 November 2008
Miami, Florida

I rose at 5a.m., showered and went for a walk through Biscayne Park. Thirty years ago this would have been a no-go area, even on the edge of downtown. Miami was the unrivalled vice capital of the world; then came the clean-up.

I stood by the Miami River watching a small rusty aged freighter, being towed stoically up river by an even more decrepit tug. The deckhand on the freighter was smoking by the wheelhouse door, lazily watching me.

I don't know for how long I stood watching the Miami River, but I remember sensing the warmth of the rising sun on my face; time for work.

As I turned to walk back to the InterContinental Hotel, my phone rang – Evo.

"Evo."

"Banksy, Banksy has disappeared."

"Don't mess around Evo. Banksy's more reliable than the moon."

"I'm telling you. He's gone. So has that Mills boat by the way – but that doesn't matter."

It matters to me I thought and immediately regretted it.

“No one has seen Banksy since you left.”

“So?” I asked confidently.

“So Banksy hasn’t been seen since you left.”

“Have you…?”

“He’s not at home and he’s not on his boat.”

“He’ll turn up.”

“Be careful.”

“I always am.”

“No you’re not. That’s why I said it.”

....

After breakfast I drove to an unmarked warehouse in Southwest Miami, a few blocks from the airport. The dry heat burned off every sound. In the parking lot, four gleaming F350 dual cab pickups sat parallel to four matching box trailers. Only a few of us knew that one of the most advanced salvage teams in the world kept their equipment behind the building’s steel shutters.

To the right of the shutters was a small door covered by high-definition CCTV. I pressed the intercom and waited for a gruff voice to ask me my business.

“Lukasz Stone. I’m here to see Bud please.”

Silence. I gazed around the yard. Click.

Bud was my first choice – worldwide. We worked Australia, Turkey, Singapore, Hong Kong, Tallinn… you name it. We had known each other for ten years. Over the three thousand days he'd proven himself an honest and diligent man, with a sound head for business. His employees trusted his judgment implicitly – essential given the dangerous business they were in.

I was shown through the cavernous warehouses to Bud's office. He was sitting behind his desk alternating his attention between an instruction manual and a mobile phone.

"I could raise 'TITANIC' Lukasz, so why can't I work this thing?"

"Too easy Bud, you're looking for the problems."

He put down the phone and stood to shake my hand.

"Good to see you Lukasz. We were wondering when you'd turn up. Why didn't you phone?"

"It's not one of those jobs."

I moved and sank into the sofa in the corner of Bud's office.

"I heard. We had a call yesterday."

"About 'AZUL'?"

"Ut – ut."

"What about?"

"About you."

"Me?" I asked without surprise.

"You."

I said nothing.

"As you said, it's not one of those jobs."

"Who was calling?"

"Dunno; withheld number."

"What did they want?"

"Wanted to know if you had been in to see us yet."

"You said?"

"We said, "No.""

"I had a call from the Puerto Rican Coastguard late last night. They thought – only thought – they had found part of the hull."

Bud lit a cigarette.

"Heck, Lukasz it's a graveyard in that trench. Forget the sunken sports fishers the Latinos couldn't afford the payments on, there's whole ships down there too. If they're using sonar their target could be older than me."

"Clearly someone thinks it's our baby, otherwise why the call to you?"

"A warning to you."

"They needn't have bothered. I've been tailed since this thing began. More than tailed though. Everyone I've met has been perfectly briefed and solidly prepared. It's like being on the stage during a play, only I haven't seen the script."

"So," said Bud drawing deeply on his cigarette. "What have we got? The Puerto Ricans have got a big hit on their sonar. Big deal. They haven't got the money to investigate so they are pitching it to you. More importantly they don't want the embarrassment of telling the families that all they've found is the side of a hulk that's been down there forty years and a few boxes of bananas. If, however, an insurance company does it and comes up with the wrong result, no one cares..."

"...because everyone hates insurance companies anyway that will just annoy and harden the families resolve against us. Makes the death claims harder to settle," I pitched in.

"You going to pay this claim then?"

"Not my call Bud."

"Please tell me it's not Chum's?"

"Afraid so."

"So what you want from me, if I would be prepared to do it, is a proper seabed survey, an ROV camera search of each target area. It's five miles deep isn't it?"

"Give or take. We'll give. Say three miles at last known position from the Auto I.D. system."

"We can do that with a little help from our chums up

the road."

I knew he was referring to NASA.

"Ballpark?"

"Without lifting anything?"

"Without lifting anything. That would be phase two."

"Without lifting anything and trying, no more than trying, to find as much as possible over that area – ballpark ten million dollars."

"How long would you need to mobilize?"

"I've got a tug in Sint Maarten I can pull off a job. I can sub-con another in Puerto Rico. The ROV will take a few days, maybe longer. You up against it?"

"Yep, Chum has backed me into a corner. I've got thirteen days to finish this."

"And the other side's already years ahead of you."

....

Back at the hotel I called Chum.

"Christian. It's Lukasz."

"Ah, the wanderer."

"Congratulations on your promotion."

"Thank you. It's a shame it's in such circumstances. I

had the deepest respect for Henry Coles. I owe a great deal to him."

I wondered how many times in the last few days Chum had chanted those lines.

"How are you getting on?" Chum asked, just a little too warmly for my liking. I heard papers moving.

"I've read the yacht's papers and, so far, they all appear in order," I replied. "I am taking the Examination under Oath of the DPA in a few hours' time."

I heard the paper shifting stop.

"Isn't that rather heavy-handed?"

"He is heavy-handed."

No reply.

"If we aren't going to take a EUO for a billion dollars then when will we?"

"I see your point. Just go easy on him."

I ignored him.

"I hear that the Puerto Ricans think they have found part of the wreck," Chum said. "What do you think?"

"I think they have found a large target in an area of multiple large targets."

"Are they going public with this?"

"Depends on us. They want us to pay for an ROV."

"What does Bud say?" he added hurriedly, "I assume you've seen him by now."

"He says ten million to ROV the site. Sonar is useless."

"That sounds a reasonable price."

"It's a bargain. The hitch is the mobilization time. The ships are available but the ROV won't be there for several days if not a week."

"We only have thirteen days left."

"So I heard," I said impassively. "The ROV is the only way we are going to know for sure what happened, if we can find her."

"Surely you can work it out without that."

Why talk with this idiot? I wondered.

"In my view there are only two possibilities. One, either 'AZUL' suffered a major structural failure in calm water on an almost unprecedented scale…"

"…we could sue the builder and the designers," Chum said excitedly.

"…or she was blown up."

"I don't like that one," Chum said.

"Neither did the crew."

“Pardon?”

“To sue the builders and designers you would need to locate and lift every piece of debris and hope you find the piece that failed, or at best enough debris to calculate what failed. Remember Bud’s quote is only for looking – lifting is another matter.”

“How much do you think?”

“One hundred million dollars; minimum. Bud’s done it before with downed aircraft but they are lighter.”

“The aircraft were in more pieces though.”

“We don’t know that, do we? Then there are the relatives of the crew to think about.”

“We will worry about them later,” Chum said. “Tell Bud to mobilize; quickly.”

“Send me an e-mail authorizing it and I will mobilize Bud immediately.”

Just before I replaced the receiver I heard Chum’s voice again.

“Oh, Lukasz, I was saddened to hear about your friend Mr. Banks.”

I slammed the receiver back against my ear.

“What about him?”

“He’s dead. Didn’t you know?”

"What?"

"Yes, dead. His body was found a couple of hours ago."

"Where?"

"On a yacht, in the Solent."

"On a boat?"

"Yes Lukasz, on a boat. In fact the very same boat that you told Henry Coles and I was the newly found Mr. Mills boat," Chum paused, and I sensed what was coming next. "In fact it isn't Mr. Mills' boat at all. I don't know what game your friend Mr. Banks was playing but it earned him a bullet in the back of the head. This also leaves you rather exposed. Not only did you not follow procedures, but when questioned, you lied to us. We will be having a formal chat when you return. Joe Wallis has sent you the file you requested. Good day Lukasz."

With that, he was gone.

....

The e-mail from Chum authorizing me to mobilize Bud arrived within seconds. I e-mailed Bud then called Evo.

"You've heard," he said as he answered the phone. It was an accusation.

"Chum just told me. I'm so sorry Evo."

"Not a nice way to hear it," he said softening slightly. "It's all over the TV and radio here."

"He would have hated that," I said without thinking.

"Wherever he is, I'm sure he's trying to block it."

We both tried to laugh.

"The boat has been towed back to Banksy's yard, the yard, for forensics."

"Chum said he'd been shot."

"A single bullet to back of the head."

"They disabled the CCTV, restepped the mast and refloated her?"

"Got Bansky to do it then shot him on the boat."

"That is a lot of trouble to go to," I said.

"It depends upon the point you are trying to make," he said languidly. He paused. "And to whom. What else were you and Banksy working on?"

"Nothing out of the ordinary. He'd bought a few fire wrecked hulls from us, a few stolen and recovered. You guys fix them up. The largest was the recovery of the 'allegedly' stolen Mills boat. She's a little bigger and more expensive than usual but the case was nothing special. Just a boat that didn't want to be found."

"Apparently you two didn't find it. Word on the river is it's the wrong boat."

"How many of those yachts have you seen on the

Hamble in the last two weeks?"

"None."

"Two months?"

"Same answer."

"Two years?"

"Lukasz," Evo said heavily, "I get your point."

"I will deal with the Mills issue when I get back. And I will find out who killed James."

"Will you?" Evo asked, quietly.

"Yes Evo," I promised.

26

17 September 2008
Off Port Hercules, Monaco

"Tell your men to wait outside. You too."

The X room emptied leaving Lamb and the Governor in an awkward silence.

"Do I need to know where the money came from Jay?" the Governor asked slumping heavily into a leather sofa. He crossed his legs, looking intently at Lamb.

"Legitimate professionals. Drink?"

"Could use one; Scotch."

It was the first time that Lamb had poured a drink aboard his own yacht.

"You know my reputation Governor. I do not mix with anyone who could embarrass us."

"Embarrass you Jay," said the Governor, taking his drink. "Nothing to do with me."

So that is how it is to be? Lamb thought to himself. We'll see about that Governor.

"Have you forgotten Amsterdam?"

"I've never been to Amsterdam. My brother took care of that."

Lamb sat opposite the Governor on a matching sofa. The dense soundproofing deadened the air. Lamb felt a cold draught from the air conditioning unit above his head.

"I appreciate your concern Governor, but your money is safe. Lehman's was a surprise to us all."

"Not all," said the Governor swirling his drink in the tumbler.

Thanks for warning me partner.

"My brother says there are many more failures to come. He's not planning on stepping in."

Lamb stood up and walked back to the drinks cabinet. His mind was racing. Was this true? Couldn't be? The Federal Government watching banks fail? The financial system, held together by the slightest of threads in Lamb's view, allowed to fall apart at its seams?

"The Federal Government will not intervene?" Lamb asked, aware that his palms were damp; head pounding.

"Not necessarily," the Governor replied slowly.

"Your view or message from the President?"

"Both."

Lamb felt rising panic.

"I want my money back by the end of the week Jay. You've given me a good return, probably better than those diamonds but the show's over. Any records of my involvement are to be destroyed." The Governor walked to Lamb and patted him on the back. "Understood?"

“Of course Governor.”

“Thanks for the drink.”

It took several minutes for Lamb to realize that the Governor had left ‘Room X’. He was alone. Wholly alone.

27

20 November 2008
Miami, Florida

The file Joe had sent was so small I could read it on my phone. It was a seasonably warm day with no humidity so I had walked back to Biscayne Park and sat on the spiky palmetto grass reading it. The Coles Syndicate had received an e-mail from 'AZUL's' brokers advising that a Natalia Youngs, a twenty-one-year-old stewardess had recently been dismissed. In reply she had retained a lawyer in Tampa who, predictably, brought a lawsuit for wrongful dismissal against the yacht owners.

In my experience a case like that would never reach a courtroom. Some sort of compromise would be reached in exchange for a watertight Confidentiality Agreement. I estimated the cost of paying Natalia off; if the claim was genuine, maybe two hundred thousand dollars, if bogus, a third of that.

The annual maintenance budget for 'AZUL' must have been in the region of one hundred million dollars. Even at the top end of Natalia's verdict range the amount involved was minute.

I rolled over onto my front with the sun pleasantly warming my back. I jotted down some figures using the hotel's scratchy pen and their ribbed notepaper. I quickly reached a figure for weekly groceries aboard 'AZUL' which comfortably exceeded two hundred thousand dollars.

"Why bother your insurer with an embarrassing claim that you could pay off the moment it was made?" I mumbled.

It is said there are only two seasons in Florida – summer and winter. That's untrue. When autumn and spring arrive, they are measured in only a few days. I was fortunate to have seen the autumn of 2008.

"Because you wanted to make sure your insurer was there and listening, didn't you?" I said aloud.

The next page was a reply from Chum telling the broker that 'regrettably' the Coles Syndicate "cannot respond to the claim due to a lack of coverage."

The Chum e-mail was timed at 2314 GMT; clearly an urgent reply. From my rudimentary grasp of insurance I guessed Chum was right about the lack of coverage, but the timing? Nearly midnight – so close to the sinking?

Both e-mails had been copied to the DPA who should have been on his way to Miami for our meeting in half an hour's time. I made a note to ask him about Natalia Youngs.

....

Back in my hotel room, I opened the third file of documents given to me by Lomas. I extracted the crew list. Holding it up to the recessed ceiling light I read it. There she was the penultimate entry, Natalia Youngs. Twenty-one years old. Below her name and date of birth I found a copy of her passport and photo, social security number and mailing address.

I opened the minibar door and took out a diet Coke. So sweaty, peeling Lomas was telling me she was on board when clearly she wasn't.

Let's see what my DPA can tell me about Ms. Youngs before I track her down and hear her story?

The phone rang.

"Your meeting room is ready Mr. Stone and Miss. Planter has arrived."

"Thank you. I'll be straight down."

It had taken several years to find a stenographer who could understand my accent, recognized boating terms and didn't laugh when she heard blatant lies. The first Examination under Oath I took with Miss. Planter, the injured crewman asked her out on a date on the record. His attorney resigned from the case shortly afterwards.

As the elevator doors opened I saw Trixie sitting in the lobby reading a newspaper. Her large black stenography bag laid almost abandoned a metre from her side. She was wearing a black pencil skirt, tailored white top, and the expression of someone who was questioning what they were reading.

I walked up behind her and read over her shoulder.

"Miss. Planter, thank you for coming at such short notice."

She folded the newspaper and stood up.

"You're welcome Lukasz. How are you?"

"Good thanks Trixie. You?"

"Good. The Coles syndicate on the ropes?" she thrust the newspaper into my chest.

"I don't know. I don't keep track of that sort of thing."

"They are talking takeovers."

"Then they haven't met the new client. No one would volunteer to take him over."

She laughed sweetly as we headed to the elevator.

"OK Lukasz, your cases are always the best, but the office said the matter doesn't have a lawsuit title?"

"There isn't a lawsuit – yet."

We watched the LED display lazily show the floor numbers as we ascended the hotel.

"So who do we have today?" she asked breaking the silence. "Will I want to date this one?" she asked still staring at the floor level display.

"I think not. But then I don't know your type."

"I think you do."

....

In our meeting room I poured Trixie a glass of water and placed her customary bowl of cherries close to her seat. Why cherries, I do not know, but if that's what she needed, that's what she got.

The room could have comfortably seated twenty people. The walls were clad in rosewood veneer. It was too cold; I pressed the air conditioning remote control in both directions and could not find the right temperature.

"How many boxes today do you think?" Trixie asked.

"Let's say four."

She piled four boxes of paper tape next to her machine. I know how to work (and fix if necessary) some of the most sophisticated bits of marine kit in the world, but I still couldn't work a stenotype machine.

"So who is he?" Trixie asked.

"The guy responsible for safety on motor yacht 'AZUL'."

"Those poor people. Can you recover the bodies?"

"We are not sure yet," I lied. "Depends on whether Chum will pay for it," I replied.

The phone rang.

"Mr. Stone, there is a Mr. Johnson here to see you."

"Thanks. Please send him up."

Trixie laughed.

"You Brits are just so nice. You say 'please' and 'thank you' for everything."

"Thank you."

A knock at the door. I opened it to find Johnson in a suit and tie. He was carrying two lever arch files.

"Mr. Johnson. Thank you for coming."

Johnson strode in.

"No problem at all. It's captain Johnson actually."

"Sorry," I lied.

He nodded at Trixie and she smiled sweetly. Johnson sat down opposite the seat marked by my closed files. He neatly arranged his two files and pulled a sheet of paper from the top one. I could see that there were notes this time, not a script. Remembering the CCTV I wondered if he was wired. I assumed he was. We won't be going 'off the record' with this guy.

I took my seat opposite him.

"Miss. Planter would you swear the witness in please."

Johnson raised his right hand and duly promised to tell the truth. I would have been disappointed if he had.

We sailed through the formalities of name, address, phone and social security numbers. No previous convictions. No previous insurance claims. No health issues. No prescription drugs. Good. We had a witness.

"Captain Johnson, are you the Designated Person Ashore as required by the International Safety Management code for the motor yacht 'AZUL'?"

"I am."

"Captain Johnson, would you please describe the General Arrangement of 'AZUL', for the benefit of the record."

Johnson opened one of the folders.

"For the record, captain Johnson has brought two lever arch files with him. Is that correct captain Johnson, for the record?"

Johnson glanced at me with contempt.

"I concur," he hissed.

"For the record captain Johnson has passed me a document entitled 'General Arrangement Plan'. Please mark this 'Exhibit A' Miss. Planter."

Trixie reached into her bag revealing quite a lot of leg in Johnson's direction. He didn't move, just maintained a steely gaze on me.

"Captain Johnson would you take me through the general arrangement plan for the record."

"Top deck down?"

"Keel up or top deck down. Either is fine with me."

"'AZUL' is... was… a 200 metre luxury yacht constructed of steel and built in Germany. The top deck was the sundeck with Jacuzzi, barbecue and a huge party area. At the aft end of that deck there were two flights of stairs. The portside led to an enclosed glass lounge, the other to the owner's private deck."

"How did you make sure the guests took the correct stairs?"

Johnson fixed his gaze upon me.

"They knew."

Trixie reached for her cherries.

"Go on."

"Behind that was an infinity swimming pool. It had a glass aft end so you could swim and be seen from the dock as the ship… yacht… came into moor."

"And that deck was called?"

"Although not the top deck, we always called that the 'sky deck'."

"Please mark that on the plan."

Trixie took advantage of the break to eat more cherries.

"Go on," I instructed Johnson.

"Below that, starting from the stern was an area for al fresco dining with the large retractable roof. Curved glass doors then lead into the salon. A dining room was located forward of the salon starboard side with the galley portside. The owner's study was in front of that, then the owner's stateroom, then the remainder of the owner's deck.

"The owner was?"

Johnson halted.

"The owner was?" I repeated.

"I am not authorized to say."

I looked quickly at Trixie. She'd got it. He'd just admitted knowing the owner if not personally, at least his identity. Perfect.

"Continue," I said concealing my pleasure.

"At the very front of this deck was the bridge with the captain's double cabin behind it. Below that the next deck had twenty double guest cabins."

"Twenty? Twenty named?"

"You will find the names within these files," he said gently laying his hands on the top file. "They were all named after postmodernist artists."

"Each cabin had examples of the artist's work?"

"Yes."

"Originals?"

"I believe so."

"Captain Johnson, for the record, I have been to your home in Florida. Your home has genuine, iconic artefacts of early to mid-twentieth century design within it; Eames, Le Corbusier. I cannot believe you cannot recognize a work of art when you see one, even if it is not your period."

He ignored me.

"If those twenty cabins had original artworks from the respective painters, the combined value would have been immense."

"I do not know if they were originals or not."

"Captain Johnson, whether originals or not, were those paintings on board 'AZUL' when she left San Juan on the morning of the sinking?"

Johnson replied too quickly.

"Why wouldn't they have been on board?"

I leaned towards him. "I ask the questions. You provide the answers. I will ask you again. Were those paintings on board that yacht when she left San Juan, Puerto Rico or not?"

"I don't know," he eventually said.

I stood up and walked to the window. I heard a cherry stone hit a ceramic dish.

"Let's move onto something you do know about captain Johnson. Please continue with your description of your yacht."

"The next deck down was the entertainment deck. That was where the forty-seater cinema and multimedia room was located. Using an almost unique design, particularly to the deck above, a basketball court was built into that deck that could be converted into an auditorium."

"Did the designer have to incorporate any other 'almost unique' factors into the design of 'AZUL'?" I asked.

"That is something you will have to ask him," Johnson replied looking away.

"I intend to."

Johnson smirked.

“Change of tape,” said Trixie.

I watched her as she deftly changed boxes of paper tape. I again marvelled at the stenotype machine and thought how antiquated it was for use in the twenty-first century.

“Back on the record,” Trixie said brightly.

“Captain Johnson, before the change of tape, you had remarked that the vessel ‘AZUL’ had an ‘almost unique’ design by way of the basketball court, located on the leisure deck. Is that correct?”

“Yes.”

“You answered by referring me to the vessel’s designer. Is that also correct?”

“Yes.”

I slowly leaned forward and picked up my copy of the general arrangement plan. Taking a pencil and turning the plan around to face Johnson I asked, “So we are here… the basketball court is there, correct?”

Johnson followed the tip of my pencil.

“Correct,” he said to the pencil, not me. He was tensing up. We both knew what was coming next.

Trixie glanced at him, then at me.

Silence can be used aggressively.

Four, three, two… one.

“What is this space, next to the basketball court?” I asked.

Johnson squinted at the plan, as a myopic man who had never seen it before.

“It is on the entertainment deck captain Johnson. Every other space you have identified had an entertainment use. Surely this one had too?”

“I do not remember.”

“What was that space?” I asked him again.

“You will have to ask the designers. Ask the Naval Architect.”

“Who was the Naval Architect?”

Johnson started to smile. He looked like a ferret; he sensed his escape route.

“His name is David Archer. I can give you his contact details,” he said happily.

“I will ask Mr. Archer another time. Right now I am talking to you. You were the man designated, by law, to know everything about that ship. I am asking you again. What was that space captain Johnson?”

“You will have to ask David Archer,” he repeated.

Archer, Archer, Archer. Always Archer.

“I will. But this afternoon I am asking you.”

“Mr. Stone, you have been to my home, you have seen that I appreciate fine things. I have an eye for beautiful things…” he said looking at Trixie, “but I am a technical man, not at all creative. I have no idea what Mr. Archer created that space for. You will have to ask him.”

“I will ask David Archer,” I said, signalling for Johnson to return my pencil. “So please explain the arrangement of the lower deck to me, for the benefit of the record.”

If Johnson was bothered by my incredulity he did not reveal it. He was relieved to have passed the subject to the absent Archer.

“That deck was the crew accommodation, engine room and garage deck.”

“OK, same approach as before, talk me through it, from bow to stern.” I took the pencil and pointed to two spaces immediately behind the collision bulkhead. “I don’t need to know about those. I can see one is running gear for the anchors, the other gear for the bow thrusters and the forward garage door. Is that correct?”

“Correct.”

“So let’s start here,” I said pointing to a cabin.

“That is the first of the crew cabins.”

“How many crew?”

Johnson coughed theatrically then poured himself a glass of water.

How many more areas of this ship does he not want to

talk about, I wondered?

"I should first explain that I understand the Boss is a very private person. Although in no way compromising safety, I understand that the yacht was designed with the Boss's privacy in mind."

Give me a break Johnson, I thought. You know the Boss, too late to distance yourself now.

"How many crew?" I asked sensing weakness.

"Forty."

"Forty?" I asked with fake incredulity.

"Forty. Didn't they tell you?" Johnson answered colouring.

I watched Trixie punch 'forty' into the record.

"Didn't who tell me what?" I asked.

"I thought you had been to the islands?" he said squirming in his seat.

So V.S. and Too-Bright did write your script for yesterday I realized.

"That was the full complement? Fully loaded?" I asked again.

"Forty… as I said… that…"

"Was there a full complement at the time of the sinking?" I demanded interrupting Johnson.

"Yes," he replied.

"Do you have the crew manifest with you?"

Johnson opened a second lever arch file.

"I have the crew manifest here."

"Please pass it to Miss. Planter."

He complied.

"Miss. Planter, please mark this document as 'Exhibit B' and title it 'Final crew list'. Captain Johnson, you handed Miss. Planter a document that you identified as the comprehensive and correct list of crew members aboard motor yacht 'AZUL' at the time of her sinking. Is that correct?" I asked knowing full well how dire Johnson's testimony would look on the transcript.

"Yes."

Trixie attached a yellow sticker marked with a bold letter 'B' to the edge of the document. I watched as she made sure the sticker was straight and perpendicular. She handed the document to me. I scanned it and quickly located what I was looking for. There. There, the second name from the bottom – Natalia Youngs.

I used some more aggressive silence.

"Captain Johnson, for the record I am going to pass 'Exhibit B' back to you." I solemnly passed the sheet of paper back to him. "I have asked you this question before, but I want to make absolutely certain that I understood your answer. As you sit here today, under Oath, it is your sworn testimony that 'Exhibit B' is the full and correct list of crew aboard 'AZUL' at the time of her sinking?"

Trixie's fingers were twenty millimetres above the keys of her machine.

We waited.

I looked into Johnson's eyes. I watched, as I had done so many times before. My witness replayed every word I had just said, attempted to unearth a hidden meaning, conclude that there was none and then say…

"That is my testimony."

I heard Trixie immortalize Johnson's affirmation.

"Captain Johnson, did you create 'Exhibit B'?"

"I did not."

He returned to staring at me.

"Who did?"

"I don't know."

"Where did you get if it from?"

"The owner."

"The owner? The owner personally?"

"No."

"If not from the owner, then from whom did you receive

it?"

"I do not wish to answer that question."

Fine; our friends in Tortola without a doubt.

"Would you please take both exhibits. On 'Exhibit B' please write the job title of each of the crew next to their name. On 'Exhibit A' write their names where their cabins were located. I know Sharpe's accommodation was behind the bridge, so do not concern yourself with him."

I passed both exhibits back to Johnson. I watched as he neatly wrote 'chief stew'. I asked him to use full titles. Without a murmur he corrected it to 'chief stewardess'. I could see Natalia's name at the bottom of the list. When he reached it, he hesitated – only briefly – but a definite pause. Blink and you would have missed it. He then wrote 'stewardess' and marked a cabin on the portside towards aft with her name.

"Thank you captain Johnson. Please examine both exhibits again. Take as long as you need. If you are certain that they are correct, please initial and date the right-hand corner of each page."

....

"What did you make of that?" I asked Trixie later over a diet Coke in the hotel bar.

I had taken a table adjacent to the furthest wall facing the hotel entrance. We could hear the soft clicking of heels on the marble lobby floor, muted by the height of the cathedral ceiling.

"I wouldn't date him if that's what you mean."

"And you know that is not what I mean," I said.

"Who is Natalia Youngs?"

"You saw it then?"

"Of course. And the look on his face when you made him initial each page. Last time someone looked that pained was in a schoolroom in Germany wasn't it?"

I smiled at Miss. Planter then looked away. As I always did.

"What's he hiding?" I asked.

"So far as he knows perhaps nothing? Simply doing as he's told?"

"There's a difference between following orders and the sudden realization you're being stitched up, Miss. Planter."

Trixie took a gentle sip of her drink.

"You haven't spent long enough in the Sunshine State, Mr. Stone. Those who have been here too long know they go hand in glove. The realization is a question of when, not if, it happens to you."

"How do you stand it here Miss. Planter?"

"My secret Mr. Stone."

I smiled. Good answer I thought, but did not say a word.

I suddenly felt tired. Trixie is funny, beautiful and irresistibly intelligent.

"Time to leave Miss. Planter," I said. "I have a date with Jorge."

"Lucky Jorge," she said holding my gaze for a little too long.

"Puerto Rican coastguard."

We stood to leave.

"Who is Francesca?" I asked.

I have no idea where the question came from, but Trixie hesitated. Blink and you would have missed it.

....

I took the elevator back to my room and called the United States Coast Guard, San Juan, Puerto Rico.

"Lieutenant Rodriguez, this is Lukasz Stone."

"Mr. Stone, good evening. How did you get on with captain Johnson?"

How did he know?

"Very well thank you," I replied brightly. "Do you have any information on Mr. Lomas for me Lieutenant?"

"Mr Thomas Sean James Lomas entered the British Virgin Islands two days before the sinking of 'AZUL'," he said flatly.

“Thank you Lieutenant.”

Rodriguez was silent. He was expecting me to tell him whether his information was relevant or not.

That is not how London operates.

“London has authorised the cost of the ROV,” I added quickly before he could probe more about Johnson or Lomas.

“I am pleased to hear that Mr. Stone.”

He did not sound pleased. He sounded wary.

“We will carry out an exhaustive sonar search first. London wants to identify the target area first, and then put the camera down. Those things are expensive.”

“I agree with your approach.”

Too right Rodriguez, London is doing your job for you.

“Being British there is one condition.”

“No publicity.”

“Agreed. London would prefer your agency to take the credit for the initiative.”

“You have my word Mr. Stone.”

The word of a man you have never met before is on a par with a man you have; worthless.

“We have a Coast Guard cutter in the area and I will dispatch another this evening. We will keep anyone approaching your survey ships under keen surveillance."

I almost laughed. Keep who under surveillance?

....

I wrote a record of my telephone conversation with Rodriguez, and went for a walk through Bayside Park.

Later, I ordered room service, showered and climbed into the oversized bed. I wondered about Natalia Youngs, Francesca, and Trixie, but mostly...

28

21 November 2008
Miami, Florida

Every now and then I feel the need to get away from my life. I cannot put it any other way. I wish I could unscrew the top of my head, take my brain out and park it for an hour or two. Other people smoke, do drugs, get drunk or all three. I just have to get waterborne. I hired an old sports fisher from Haulover Park. The hull was older than me, but the new Detroit diesels humming below the aft deck created an almost spiritual experience. I headed out just behind the reef, cut the engines to idle and enjoy – nothing; just nothingness. I watched boats come and go; anxious anglers at the stern, fish captains perched on tuna towers. I just drifted. There I did not need to think.

Two hours later, I returned to Haulover Marina and reversed the boat gently back into her slip. As women went she had given me more pleasure than I could remember for a while.

As I drove back to my hotel in downtown Miami, Natalia Youngs was foremost in my mind. I knew she wasn't on that boat when it went down; so did Johnson. So did Trixie. So did the owner. Most importantly, so did she.

Back in my hotel room I looked over Natalia's details again. I needed to move carefully.

29

Alligator Alley, Florida

The seventy mile journey across the middle of Florida is tedious unless you tune in to Everglades radio. As you trundle across Alligator Alley at a steady seventy miles per hour (planes track you if you don't) the narration on the cheap AM radio station brings the massive slow flowing river of the Everglades to life.

I watched gliding rare tailed hawk, alligators, and gangly white ibis until I exited the western side of the freeway under cruise control, right on time. I then headed north in the direction of Naples.

The serenity of the western Gulf coast of Florida trumps the mayhem of the eastern seaboard. South Beach is fun, in an eccentric way. Key West even more so. The west coast is also where the 'old money' is found. It has a calm confidence. I passed the decay of the redundant Naples fishing fleet, killed off by banned gill net fishing many years before. Their captains received subsidies from the Federal Government to start new ventures. Most are now fishing guides or formed clam farming businesses. I passed a crazy golf course, numerous shops selling tee shirts and arrived five minutes later outside an imposing single family home overlooking the bay. A man in a spotless tan coloured shirt and shorts was cutting grass, while another identically attired cleared fallen palm branches. I parked and walked to the front door, feeling the warm late summer sun directly overhead. I pressed the bell push.

Nothing.

The men looked at each other and shrugged. I rang the bell again.

Nothing.

“No one home?” I shouted over the noise of the lawnmower.

“No,” they shouted back in unison.

I walked back down the driveway and tried next door. At the second ring a woman of about my age answered. Unlike me she was perfect in every way. I was transfixed by her teeth. I have a good eye for measurements and angles, not one tooth was irregular. My wonderment almost cost me.

“Can I help you?” she asked for, I suspected, the second time.

“Sorry to trouble you. I’m looking for the Youngs.”

“Why?”

“I’m insurance. It’s about Natalia.”

“Then you’ll know they are at the hospital,” she said sharply.

“Hospital?”

“For an insurance man you aren’t very well informed are you?” she said angrily. “Natalia is fighting for her life.”

“I’m sorry, I didn’t know. Since when?”

“Since five days ago. Car wreck. Bad one.”

Five days ago? Before the sinking – by hours.

....

16 November 2008

Another rejection; Natalia seethed, as she jammed the ignition key into her Toyota, Corolla. "Damn, Sharpe! Damn …! Damn 'AZUL'."

She slammed the gearshift into reverse and with little attention slammed her foot on the accelerator. Apparently out of nowhere two different car horns blared in her direction. She thumped the steering wheel – "Damn you all!" she shouted.

Her cell phone rang, her father. She flicked it open.

"Another 'no' Daddy," she blurted out, feeling tears welling up in her eyes.

"I'm sorry Nats," Mr. Youngs said gently. "It will come right. You did nothing wrong."

"Right does not always win Daddy," Natalia heard herself whine.

"No honey, not always, but usually. Where are you?"

"Southeast 17th Street Lauderdale. I'll be home in two hours."

"Drive carefully. We love you," Mr. Youngs added.

Natalia stared through the windshield at both of the drivers she had annoyed. They were talking, gesturing towards her.

"Get a life," she mouthed before carefully reversing out of the car lot.

On Interstate 595 just past the Davie Road Intersection she noticed a black F350 pickup appear in her rear-view mirror. Nothing unusual, she thought – this is cowboy territory after all. The truck kept a respectful distance but instinctively she felt something was wrong. She felt small. Her tiny '86 Corolla against that hulk of steel machine.

At the Sawgrass Expressway Intersection, the last before Alligator Alley, the F350 moved over as if to leave the freeway. Natalia felt a wave of relief. As quickly as the truck seemed to leave the interstate it was back, closer, filling more of her mirror. Natalia's instincts told her to pull over at the service area before starting her journey across the isolated Everglades.

"Why should I?" she said aloud. "I have had enough of being pushed around. Come on little car," she ordered, "Get me home."

As she passed the service area, the truck loomed as closely as ever. She pressed the accelerator gently. The truck did not respond for a few seconds, and then accelerated back to where it had been.

Natalia felt her heart rate quicken. So they are playing with me she thought. She looked at her cell phone on the passenger seat. Who could she call? What could she say? Was there even a cell signal out there amongst the alligators and cranes?

She tried to concentrate on the road ahead. She counted

heron, she counted marker posts, looked for any small details that could distract her from the truck behind her. Seventeen northern pintails, eighteen rock doves. Then she saw the truck move to the left side of her vulnerable car. She heard the bang as the truck struck just behind her rear wheel. She watched her hands on the steering wheel fighting to keep the car in a straight line. She saw the grass of the median in front of her face, once, twice, three times as the car rolled. She heard the panels of her car dislodge, metal, plastic, glass. Then darkness.

....

I had noticed before, the longer I spend in the State of Florida, the more hardened I become. Rachel had told me this several times. On one occasion she told me to, "go and have a hot shower and thaw out." That more than depressed me. It drained my spirit. I'm vaguely aware that I'm good at what I do, but if I think about it, I don't know how I do it. Every time a boat sinks, disappears, is arranged to disappear, catches fire, or the like, I turn up and work out what happened. I suppose there are stages in the investigation business which are common to all my cases, but the order in which those stages are completed can be very random and none more random than in fraud cases. Whoever is behind the fraud usually has been planning it for some time. Every year we have a few desperadoes who are easily caught, but fraud is usually well thought out. I prefer it that way; it makes my job more interesting. Mentally I award extra points for ingenuity, provided no one has been harmed. It does mean, though, that my opponent has had a head start on me of weeks, months, if not years. Who pays, if anyone, is not my concern. I did not know at that time whether 'AZUL' was a fraud case or not. I knew that thirty-nine people were dead, another critically ill, a career ruined and Chum had got what he wanted.

....

I parked the car. I passed the security guards and entered the foyer of Collier County General Hospital. A life-sized Ronald MacDonald sat on a bench, his arm wrapped around the top plank as a hefty Latina took a photograph of a small, dark, pretty girl posing under his plastic arm.

I produced my passport and business card at the front desk, was duly photographed by a burly and ungracious security guard and given a security care badge marked 'Visitor'.

Natalia was in a private room on the seventh floor, effectively one of a number of side wards off the Intensive Care Unit. This was not the first U.S. hospital ward I had been on. The television cannot depict how they smell differently to wards in Britain – they have no scent. There was no one in Natalia's room except the patient. There was an eerie stillness, about the room that still raises the hairs on the back of my neck as I write it. ICU should feel safe, secure, positive, but the closeness of death defeats it. This is where our mortality is laid bare. The only sounds were coming from the machinery trying to keep Natalia alive.

A nurse came up behind me. She was more miniature than petite – she was so tiny. How could such vast responsibility fall on someone so small?

"It was a bad wreck," she said softly her bright-blue eyes fixed on her patient. "I saw it on the news bulletins."

"What happened?"

"FHP aren't sure," she said inhaling more air than I thought could fit in her tiny lungs. "Seems she was fishtailed. Her car rolled three times."

"The other car?"

"They haven't found it."

I waited a moment then asked.

"Fishtailing? Isn't that what the police use to stop suspects?"

She laughed lightly, "Sounds so stupid when said with your accent."

"Sorry."

"Don't be. My son watches all of the 'When good cops go bad' type TV. That's how I know what it is. They ram the back of your vehicle then keep the pressure on until you overcompensate with the steering and crash."

"And they put that on television?"

"Of course. It's our right to know how to kill each other. And for those that survive we try and put them back together."

We both stood in silence and stared at the twisted and crushed body in front of us.

"Will she make it?" I asked.

"Are you family?"

"No, insurance."

"Oh," she said stiffening and preparing to leave. "I couldn't say. Her doctors are doing all they can," she said reciting I suspected some verbiage the hospital had taught her by rote to fend off lawsuits. "You want to see her parents? They're downstairs in the family room."

"Thanks. I'll go down."

It is a part of my job that I've met too many people like the Youngs; decent people thrown into torture not of their making. The waiting… The highs, lows and endless plateaus, desperately looking for hope, however slight, of recovery. Brain damage cases are the worst. The waiting takes two years, during which time there are the highest peaks, lowest troughs and interminable plateaus.

Death is easier – they were at breakfast this morning but they won't be home for dinner.

I found the Youngs huddled in a corner close to a water cooler. They were both pale and clearly exhausted. The exhaustion doubles up when a loving couple want to support each other I had noticed. Divorced people have more energy for the fight, sort of several not joint. I was certain the couple hadn't slept for days.

"Mr. and Mrs. Youngs?"

Mr. Youngs looked up. I don't think his wife heard me. My voice was not that of a doctor… or Natalia.

"Yes?"

I stretched out my right hand, which Mr. Youngs accepted.

"I'm Lukasz Stone. I'm an insurance investigator from London."

"Have you found who did this?" Mrs. Youngs asked, suddenly raising her head.

"I'm sorry Mrs. Youngs, I'm not investigating the car crash, I'm investigating the sinking of the 'AZUL'."

"The parents… of those poor people," she whispered.

"Mrs. Youngs, I'm trying to piece together what happened to cause the ship to sink."

"They're saying it was a bomb," said Mr. Youngs.

"There is a lot of speculation at the moment," I said as I looked at him. I have no children, no pets, not even a pot plant. What could I know of what this man was feeling? I thought again of the child downstairs feeling comfortable with a plastic statue of an imaginary protector. "I know this is a traumatic time for you, and you want to get back to your daughter, but could I ask you a few questions about Natalia's time on the boat?"

Mr. Youngs looked at his wife. She nodded.

"Sure. Please sit down. Would you like a coffee?" asked Mr. Youngs.

Why did these tragedies always happen to the good people?

"No, but thank you. I understand Natalia left the boat about two months ago?" I asked sitting down to face them.

"That's right. She was so excited when she got that job," explained Mr. Youngs. "She'd been on a couple of smaller boats, one sixty metre and one of a hundred, but nothing near the size of 'AZUL'."

"We met the captain. He was a very quiet man, but we sensed he was decent," added Mrs. Youngs. "They aren't all like that."

"But things started to go wrong almost from the beginning," said Mr. Youngs, putting an arm around his wife.

"Such as?" I asked gently.

"I think the chief engineer took a liking to Natalia. You wouldn't think it to look at her now, but she is, was, a very pretty girl," said Mr. Youngs.

"I have seen her photograph. She is certainly very attractive. So what happened?"

"It's not the lifestyle we ever wanted for her, but we know it's far from unusual for that sort of thing to go on. What happens on the boat stays on the boat. But Natalia's not like that. She has had very few boyfriends; she has a passion for life. She will settle when she wants to," explained Mrs. Youngs.

The water cooler released three large air bubbles into the blue plastic tank above it.

I was doing some good. They were talking of her future.

"She told me that she told him politely that she enjoyed his company, but she wasn't interested in a relationship," Mrs. Youngs continued.

I looked at Mr. Youngs. I gauged Natalia had told him nothing, relying upon her mother to pass on anything they decided he needed to know.

“How did the chief take it?” I asked.

“Not very well,” said Natalia’s father. “In fact he went out of his way to make her life difficult.”

“Did she talk to the captain about it?”

“We don’t know. The next thing we knew she had been fired and was back home with us,” said Mr. Youngs.

“Then this happened,” said his wife.

“Did Natalia file a lawsuit against the owners of the ‘AZUL’?” I asked rhetorically.

“Yes. She wanted to clear her name. The megayacht community is very small as you know, reputation is almost everything,” Mrs. Youngs said straightening her back.

“She was afraid she wouldn’t be able to get another job. She wasn’t interested in the money...” added Mr. Youngs quite apologetically. I assumed he thought the lawsuit would have been passed to the Coles Syndicate.

“Not my concern Mr. Youngs,” I assured him. “Did Natalia ever say anything about the boat? Any problems with it?”

“She didn’t like the owner’s taste; too bland. But she said she would rather have been banging her shins on sharp modern edges than endlessly polishing gold as she had on the previous boats,” Mrs. Youngs explained.

““‘It’s a commodity not a yacht,” is what she said Mister Stone,” explained Mr. Youngs.

"Lukasz, please."

"But she had her own cabin, which for a junior stewardess was unheard of," said Mrs. Youngs.

"When they fired her they wouldn't let her go down and get her things," said Mr. Youngs with the only hint of resentment I heard that afternoon. "They were boxed up and forwarded onto her. That was unnecessarily hurtful, I think that is what drove her to go and see a lawyer. We aren't combative people."

I thanked Mr. and Mrs. Youngs for their time and sincerely wished them well for Natalia's recovery. They made me promise to keep them advised of how my investigation progressed if it related to Natalia.

As I handed my security badge back to the front desk I now had the first fact of this case. Natalia Youngs was not on 'AZUL' when she sank. Why then, were my opponents (for that is what they became that afternoon) going to so much trouble to convince me that she was? And where did Francesca fit in?

....

Bud called me shortly before I exited the Miami end of Alligator Alley.

"Where are ya?"

"Your end of the Alley. What's up?"

"I'm heading to Tamiami Airport; join me, my plane's waiting. I'll find you a spare toothbrush when we get there."

Twenty minutes later I pulled up alongside Bud's truck in the small car park alongside the runway at Tamiami Executive Airport. He jumped out walked to my car and got into the passenger seat.

"We've got everything except the ROV," he said lighting a cigarette. "I've put NASA on heat, but they're still Government."

"How much are you paying them?"

"Don't worry about it," Bud said tapping his lighter on the 'No Smoking' sign on the dashboard. "Come on client, we've got a job to do."

Bud's jet was waiting for us, with the starboard engine already running. We climbed the portside stairs and the door was closed promptly behind us. I heard the port engine starter whine.

There were four men already on board seated towards the front of the aircraft. As we settled in our seats I looked at Bud.

"What?" he asked struggling to locate the left side of his seat belt.

"Bud, how much do you have on the streets at any one time?"

He found the elusive end. Clamping the two ends together he replied, "If I'm owed less than fifty million on any one day my banker is a happy boy," he whispered.

Once airborne Bud and I walked forward, I was introduced to two senior salvage masters, and two sonar experts. I cannot recall their names but they are on the file.

"Sonaritas, you get an answer, I want the same answer twice. Got that?" Bud instructed them.

Both sonar experts nodded. The salvage masters laughed then asked for beer.

"Go find it boys," Bud said patting the sonar men both on the back.

"NASA send their own nannies with their kit. Fair enough at three million bucks rental," Bud told me as we walked away from the sonar operators back to our seats.

I did the maths – Bud was breaking even. He must have believed that the Syndicate would want to raise 'AZUL', or at least enough of her to make all this effort worthwhile.

"This is the break even part. You want the bits raised, I'm gonna make money," Bud confirmed before I could question him further.

"Have you spoken to the Puerto Rico Coastguard?" I asked as we both sat down.

"Yep, Jorge. Man he was annoyed you didn't call him when you went through P.R."

"Sorry."

"Don't worry about it, we go way back. Drink?" Bud asked.

"No thanks."

"Rodriguez is one of the good guys. I've smoothed it over. You should have called him Lukasz. You can't ignore the Government of the United States of America."

....

The flight to San Juan took two hours. The ocean is so clear by day it reveals coral, reefs, sandbars and tiny islands. My mind was elsewhere, in the Puerto Rican trench, in a hospital in Florida; London.

....

At San Juan our aircraft passed the passenger terminal and United States Air Force base. We were cargo. This was a domestic flight six MIKE PAX with equipment. We taxied to within fifty metres of a helicopter. Its rotors began to turn.

"You OK with helo?" Bud shouted as we ran across the tarmac.

"Sure," I shouted, as if I had another option. I understand the science behind helicopters – and it's all too fragile. A boat would have taken too long. We strapped ourselves in, hovered above the runway before quickly becoming airborne again. According to Chum I was supposed to have a safety certificate for this, I thought, smiling to myself.

Seven minutes later we landed on the aft helo pad of the larger of Bud's two ships. Finally I felt at home. We were three miles out and I could relax.

"Lukasz, this is Jack MacDonald, Master of this fine ship."

As Bud introduced me both MacDonald and I knew Bud was in command. Without another word Bud descended the companionway. I could still hear him talking.

"What we got?"

There was mumbling then silence.

"Hey Sonaritas, come here," Bud shouted summoning his sonar experts. They shrugged then rapidly disappeared down the companionway leaving me under the night sky with MacDonald.

"Tragic," said MacDonald as we watched the helicopter fly back to San Juan.

"Yes," I agreed.

Bud stuck his seventy-year-old head up through the companionway hatch.

"Don't hold your breath, Mr. Stone."

I nodded and smiled. I never do.

....

Following small talk with the captain, I headed below towards the crew mess. I stopped off by the sonar station. Both experts were glued to the screen with Bud in the middle.

"OK guys, night duty. Four hours on, four off. Either of you see anything you wake the other up. If you both agree, wake me. I'd rather be woken than not, right or wrong. Got that?"

Both grunted agreement.

"Flip a coin to see who goes first."

Bud and I took the stairs down to the mess, the slow rumble of the engines increased as we descended the narrow staircase.

Two crew – Spider T and Crill were already there. Spider was drinking rum. They were seated around a crescent shaped, Formica covered table, resting their arms on the fiddle around the edge. Riddled with arthritis Spider was no help as crew but he'd been a lifelong companion to Bud. Going to sea without T was unthinkable. Crill was a small, hunched man of about thirty, with sharp eyes and a crooked, thin nose.

"Say Bud, Crill and I were just saying what we would do with a billion bucks," slurred Spider.

"What's that T?"

"I'd donate at least a half to a good cause," said Spider laughing.

"A brewery," said Crill and sniffed.

No one laughed.

"And the other half?" asked Bud quietly.

"I'd tuck it away until I'd thought of something I wanted."

"That T, sounds like a plan," said Bud pouring Spider another rum whilst blatantly ignoring Crill.

"Dulls the pain hey, T?" said Bud.

"You remember that job in '67 Bud?"

"Couldn't have done it without you T."

I knew Bud had been reminded of the 1967 job at least once a day, every day for over four decades. His patience would last as long as Spider T needed it to.

Crill shifted uncomfortably on the plastic covered bench.

"About ten more miles to check?" asked Crill.

"Maybe," said Bud not lifting his gaze from Spider.

Crill might as well have jumped overboard right then and swam to shore. This was going to be his last night on board. Insult Spider T? Find some other ship.

Bud and I sank into the bench around the crew mess. We were happy. Crill wisely made up some excuse and left. Bud handed me a tin mug and poured in a large shot of rum. He poured himself a larger one. I was the youngest man there by decades – the adopted son.

"Where do you get these kids from Bud?" asked Spider.

"I don't know T. I think they find me. I'm sorry."

"Don't apologize to me. My body maybe wrecked but my mind's still looking out for you."

Bud and T chatted warmly as I started to think.

Maybe it was lack of sleep, the rum, maybe the weight of

this case, or another hundred valid reasons, but the devotion between these two men brought humanity to this case, just as Mr. and Mrs. Youngs had done. I thought of the granite captain Johnson. My leaden learned friends in Tortola for whom this was just another chance for them to demonstrate just how very, very clever they were. Dopey Lomas. Odious Chum.

Beneath us were the bodies of thirty-nine, mostly very young, human beings, their bodies now empty of desire, passions, ambition and dreams.

I felt ashamed. What were millions of dollars compared with the investment in health, education, drive, energy, manners of a parent's love second by second, minute by minute, hour by hour, day by day, year by year? The gardeners that came back day after day to water the roses, thorns and weeds alike. Look after the pennies, and the dollars will look after themselves.

"I will find who did this," I silently promised the dead.

"You OK?" asked Spider T.

"I think I am," I said with a new sense of purpose.

"About time," T said as he raised his tankard to his lips. "You're getting it now."

Bud looked at me affectionately.

"He's OK T, he's one of us."

Forget insurance. I was determined to find who did this.

30

17 September 2008
Off Port Hercules, Monaco

The Chief Stewardess had divided the crew into two before 'AZUL' reached Monaco.

Natalia was dismayed to find she was going ashore on the second night in the same group as the Chief Engineer.

"Would you mind if I changed group?" she asked the Chief Stewardess.

"Yes. Once started it never stops."

The crew had been ordered to the crew mess as the owner and guests arrived by flotilla of speedboats. The same boats were to take the crew ashore. Although the crew did not see the owner and his guests, they could not but help notice the large number of armed security guards scattered around the yacht.

"Say nothing," the Chief Engineer whispered into Natalia's ear as he slipped an arm around her waist.

"I know my job," she said wriggling free.

"I didn't mean that. I meant don't say anything about us."

"There is no us! Just leave me alone!" she shouted above the chatter of the other crew members.

There was stunned silence.

"Nat, come over here," said an Australian stewardess whose name she couldn't immediately remember. "Come with us."

The Chief Engineer found a sycophantic third engineer.

"Don't know what that was all about," remarked the Chief.

"Who knows boss. We all know she fancies you."

"Obvious," said the chief smiling. "How much are you going to throw down in the casino tonight?"

31

22 November 2008
Off Puerto Rico, Caribbean Sea

Aboard Bud's main ship off Puerto Rico, the men from NASA had arrived with their ROV. Bud did not seem impressed with the operators.

"They couldn't find their own feet in a bath tub," he said. "But I love that camera. The quality of the images Lukasz blows me away each time we find something. I've got Spider telling them where to look, it's doing him good. Rum consumption is down by half."

We were sitting once more in the crew galley, chatting over tea.

"I heard about your friend Banks."

Bud swirled his tea in his mug.

"Must be tough."

"Another one to solve."

"Do you think it has anything to do with this?" Bud nodded downwards.

"It's difficult not to think that, but I can't see the connection."

"Lukasz, my friend, you are the connection."

Before I could answer…

"Bud! Bud!" Spider puffed breathlessly, scrambling down the companionway into the galley.

"What is it Spider?"

"An inny-outy."

Before I realized that either of them had moved, I was running up the companionway behind them. If ever I had underestimated my heroes Bud and Spider it was now – they could move.

All three of us gathered around a large colour monitor. Bud was right – the definition was astonishing. The ROV lights had clearly picked up a sheet of steel, two metres square according to the target data at the bottom of the screen. The jagged edge of steel curled upwards, it reminded me of flying over the Alps in winter.

A classic 'inny-outy'.

The force – whatever the cause of the force – was applied from the inside out.

"Bud, this is your ship, your operation and I know this is being videotaped, but can I direct some stills?"

"Be my guest," he said without removing his attention from the screen. I asked the NASA men to photograph every millimetre of the fracture. Each image was timed, dated and its exact location recorded on the still to within the distance equivalent to less than the width of a human hair.

The claws on the camera flipped the piece of steel over. White; white gloss. There was no sign of algae. This could be part of 'AZUL' above the waterline.

We turned the piece of steel back over and spent an hour familiarizing ourselves with it.

"Look… look at that ripped edge again… back up… there… look just there," I said drawing a line just behind the rip. "That was welded to something… something transverse." I grabbed a piece of paper and quickly drew the profile of the yacht. I darkened the area that the piece of steel could have come from. "Look…"I said as I glanced back at the screen that was welded to a bulkhead. "It's been blown away from a bulkhead!"

"You've got it Lukasz!" shouted Spider triumphantly.

I didn't have the heart to tell him we needed more. So much more.

…………………………

Bud and I climbed up and sat on the helideck sipping more tea and stargazing.

"It's none of my business so tell me to shut up…" Bud began.

"Go on."

"If your friend's death is related to this, these are serious players."

"One piece of steel Bud."

"I'm no munitions expert, but I was in Vietnam. Tears that jagged…"

"I know Bud, but that piece was above the waterline."

Bud sat silent for a while, choosing to ignore my foolish denials; a good man.

"You know finding the neighbouring piece is going to be nearly impossible?"

"Yes," I said sipping my tea. "It's coated black with antifouling paint."

"Or grey bilge paint if it's upside down. That camera is good… the best… but finding the piece you need, 13,000 feet down, in the dark…"

"In time," I interrupted.

We sat in silence again.

"You know even if we find it, that one piece, if, what use is it? I can have it analysed for everything – kinetic force, likely explosives, origin of the likely explosives."

"Unless you know from where on the yacht the steel came from you cannot prove the bomb sank the ship," Bud said. "You drew a pretty sketch, not evidence."

"Exactly. She had every certificate from the highest classification and regulatory societies known to man. You should have been able to sail her upside down without spilling your drink."

"So, someone knew the soft spot."

"Could you link all that back to an anonymous owner, in under a week Bud?"

He stood up, emptied the cooling dregs of his tea overboard.

"Nope."

32

Off Puerto Rico, Caribbean Sea

"You've got me floating around with a geriatric drunk."

"Shut it Crill! Do you want to join the others beneath your feet?"

"Well Alexander, it's strange that you should mention that," Crill said.

"Really?" Alexander replied as he poured himself a glass of water. He was at home in his gym. Crill's call had been an unwelcome interruption.

"Really," Crill sneered. "I don't know why I'm telling you, you ungrateful…"

"Tell me now," Alexander ordered.

"That drunk has found a piece of 'AZUL'."

Alexander laughed. "There should be millions of pieces of that boat. Who cares?"

"You will," Crill said clearly enjoying himself.

"Try me," Alexander said with more confidence than he felt. Crill was no fool.

"It's part of the shell plating. It looks to them as if it's half of a piece of plating adjacent to the explosion."

Alexander could hear his own heartbeat.

"Impossible," he said.

"Why should it be impossible?" Crill asked. "Both parts are down there somewhere."

Crill had waited years for this. The Boss would, finally, have to rid the world of Alexander. Crill knew the successor. He had known him all his life.

"Apart from Spider T, who else is on board the ship?" Alexander asked.

"I'm glad you asked, Alexander. Be sure you pass this on. We have the two sonar guys, the ROV experts from NASA, Bud and, wait for it, your best friend forever."

"Stone?"

"You bet," Crill crowed. "He's glued to that ROV screen like it's the best blockbuster he's ever seen."

Alexander hung up and sipped more water.

"Your time has come, Stone," he said.

....

Surrey, England

Of course you and I were not pleased to hear the news from Alexander.

As I told you in the beginning, they will come for you my novice accomplice, not for me.

If you have any chance of escape you must do something about Stone. He already knows too much. If by pure blind luck he finds the mate to that part of steel you are in trouble.

Even as only an accomplice to thirty-nine counts of murder, you will never see daylight again other than through the barred window of a cell. Does that appeal?

What was that? You're making me laugh again. You want us to do what? You are one of us now. We look after each other – mostly. Yes, Sharpe; he was an exception. He'd gone soft on us. You, however, are hardening nicely – because you're threatened.

We will take care of you.

We will take care of Stone.

33

24 November 2008
London

With precious days disappearing fast, I faced the inevitable and met with Chum. I was irritated, but not surprised that he had taken Henry Coles' office, rearranged the furniture, ditched his artwork and fired his secretary. A young woman in her mid-twenties showed me into Chum's stolen office.

"Lukasz. So good to see you," he lied, without turning his eyes away from his computer screen. "Do sit down."

I obeyed.

"Nimrod! How goes the hunt?" he asked giving me his full attention.

"We haven't found the boat," I said flatly.

"Your hunch?"

"I report facts, not hunches."

"First time for everything," he smirked. "So, other than no wreck, what have you got?"

Had Coles been asking the question I would have told him about the piece of jagged steel.

"Christian, does the Syndicate have a billion dollars to pay this claim?"

“Of course not,” he said laughing.

“So Lloyd’s will step in?”

“Of course, it has to. They have been round again today putting pressure on.”

“Pressure, for what?”

“Merger. Apart from this blip our business is good.”

Forty dead a ‘blip’?

“The Leadenhall Syndicate is on the acquisition trail, m and a. You know the sort of thing,” he said haughtily, knowing full well I knew nothing of the sort. “Our syndicate and Leadenhall would fuse up together well. Mango and chutney, Bonnie and Clyde. Turnkey of course.”

I winced.

“Turnkey?”

“Already up and running. You put the key in the ignition, turn it and you are good to go. Vroom! Vroom!”

Is it worse to detest someone, or to loathe them? I’d never been sure.

“We might just be it for the Leadenhall boys. Digits crossed.”

“I understand now Christian. Thank you for explaining it to me.”

He had explained rather more than he thought.

"Not at all Lukasz, happy to serve. Your contract with us would be safe of course provided you can explain the Mills matter, which you are just about to do."

....

Hamble, Hampshire

As the lines of luxury cars parked around the perimeter of St. Mary's Square, the pounding rain began to ease. The clouds parted and the sun appeared. Two lines of school children lined the path through the churchyard. The single bell of the church rang slowly. It appeared to me that the entire village had come out to show its respects to Banksy. There must have been two hundred people standing around. No one spoke. No one entered the church. Whether they believed the press reports of fraud about Banksy or not (and I believe other than a few unwise opportunists in the boat trade the majority did not), they were here. As the church clock started to chime upon the hour, the funeral cortege entered the square.

Call it cowardice or guilt; I could not look at Banksy's coffin. I straightened my back and watched as his broken parents followed their son into the church. Behind them Banksy's younger twin brothers and his sister Rebecca, who Banksy had tried to get me to date in the flattering, if misplaced idea, that I would treat her well. With a slight motion of a gloved hand from the funeral director, we all filed into the church, the bell still ringing above our heads. There was nothing more than a nod, half smile or 'after you' hand movement between the mourners.

Other than the villagers, most of the congregation I had either met at Banksy's yard, or the rowdy Guinness tents at who knows how many boat shows. All of his employees were there, even the office cleaner who rarely saw him.

I saw Henry Coles four rows in front of me. What was he thinking? Was he thinking that I had put Banksy in danger, which ultimately cost him his life? There was no sign of Chum but, honestly, I would never have expected him to attend.

Small electric heaters high on the walls glowed orange trying to keep us warm. The chill of the morning felt appropriate to me. The winter sunlight was filtered to grey as it passed through the large arched windows.

The Parson spoke well. He gauged correctly the genuine loss that everyone in his church felt. I added him to my short list of the humane. He said something to the effect that although he only knew Banksy by sight, judging by the affection of the congregation he wished he had known him better.

Had I caused Banksy's death?

Thinking back to my epiphany on Bud's boat, I realized I was now investigating forty deaths. Forty-one if Natalia Youngs did not pull through. Banksy's case should take priority, but then I had so few days left before the 'AZUL' deadline imposed by her owners and endorsed by Chum ran out.

I became aware that I was being watched. I was sitting at the end of a pew, on Banksy's starboard side. I was being watched from port. During a prayer I turned to my left and glimpsed Francesca staring straight at me.

"…for eternity. Amen."

"Amen."

We all stood as Banksy left the church. His mother was leaning heavily on her husband. He looked stoically ahead.

The road to the cemetery was closed more by the number of us, than by the two police motorcyclists dispatched to stop the traffic. I saw Francesca walk swiftly back into the square in the opposite direction to the cemetery.

Four rows back from the grave Henry Coles stepped next to me. "We need to talk," he whispered.

"I don't know what happened," I replied.

"Not about this," he said, nodding towards Banksy. "It's about 'AZUL'," he explained.

"I only have twelve days left."

"Then what I have to tell you may save you a lot of wasted time," he said calmly as he passed me an envelope. "Don't open that here Lukasz and watch your back. So far you haven't got in their way."

"Really?"

"More by luck than judgment. But yes, really."

"Where can we meet?"

"The Cricketers. Do you know it?"

"Yes."

"Four o'clock. My new number is in there. If you need

to use it don't call it from any of your phones. Use a call box."

Banksy's coffin was lowered into the freshly dug grave. The part I hate most was happening – the family throwing earth onto the coffin. Does this comfort anyone?

I knew I would be expected to go back to the Banks' family farm afterwards but of all the warnings I had received in the last week, Henry's concerned me the most. Who were my enemies? Chum? The owners? Francesca? Mills? Too-Bright? Who were the people following me working for? I, foolishly, wondered how dangerous they could be. I had just seen the answer to that lowered into a hole in the ground.

I walked slowly back to my car parked in a side street near the square. Checking that the street was empty, I opened the envelope Henry had given me. Inside were two sheets of paper; a copy of an insurance certificate and a copy of a reinsurance contract. "Subject matter reinsured: M/Y 'AZUL'."

....

Who is Francesca?

....

The silence in the Crow's Nest was eerie. Whenever I had been in Banksy's office before there had been constant noise and bustle. At times, particularly in the spring, all of the phones would be ringing simultaneously, Evo and the other yard workers would be running up and down the stairs laughing with each other on their way in or out from seeking Banksy's opinion or instructions. Banksy would be seated in his large, black leather chair with full view of his yard – he missed nothing. Now all was hushed. I shuddered.

I pulled back Banksy's chair and turned on his banker's light. Although the mahogany desk (removed from a yacht I guessed) was chipped and scuffed, the papers that lay on top of it were all clipped together in piles and neatly arranged.

I sat down and gently picked up the first set of papers. A Broom European motor yacht, in the yard for a new engine. Next to that a Jeanneau sailboat in for work on the keel bolts after hitting a rock. The further ten sets of paperwork were of no interest either. I drummed my fingers on the desk, spun round in Banksy's chair and looked at the row of filing cabinets behind me with growing depression. I looked at my watch. I had time to tackle at least two cabinets before I needed to leave to meet Henry.

I walked to the bank of cabinets and started opening them from portside. The code Banksy had used on the drawers was indecipherable. I then realized that the first cabinet was for purchase and work orders; the Mills boat had been neither. The second cabinet seemed more relevant. It was full of handwritten notes Banksy had made on yachts that had passed through the yard. I flicked through the files, reluctantly passing notes on some classics I would love to have read. Camper and Nicholson's, Fairey's, even an original J-class sailing yacht! But I was on a mission and I also had a tight deadline to meet Henry. The files were ordered by name of the owner, but after a few minutes I realized Banksy didn't know Mills' name. She wasn't filed under Coles, so I opened the third drawer down and located 'L'. Sure enough under 'Lloyd's' there were six yachts all sent to Banksy by me, the middle one was Mills'. I pulled out the file which was understandably very thin. Under a brief handwritten description Banksy had written "Hull I.D. number .... Query if 'Golf' was 'zero'?" He had initialled and dated the foot of the page.

I was surprised that whoever murdered James had neither removed the file nor returned for it. The Crow's Nest office had been a designated crime scene until the previous evening. There was still time for the murderers to return. I quickly took the file to the desk, photographed Banksy's notes and carefully replaced the file in the cabinet. I ran down the Crow's Nest steps and sprinted across the yard; next stop – Henry.

....

After the leaving the yard I took the back roads to reach 'The Cricketers' pub, stopping in field gateways to see if I was being followed – I wasn't. With half an hour to spare I parked by the church, closest to the rival pub 'The Chequers'. I then started to walk the quarter mile back to the meeting point. Outside the Post Office I sat on a bench and checked my e-mails. Among the fifty or so that had arrived during Banksy's funeral, two got my attention. The first was from Chum, marked 'top urgent' reminding me I only had twelve days left to complete the 'AZUL' investigation, with a postscript that we needed to meet immediately to discuss the Mills matter. I did not reply. The other was from Natalia Youngs' father.

"Lukasz, Natalia is conscious but unable to speak. Will keep you advised. Best, Dan."

"Dan, so glad to hear your good news. Thank you for letting me know. My very best to you all."

....

Of all of the meetings so far in the case, the planned meeting with Henry was the one that worried me the most. Although Henry was no longer my boss, and, as far as the insurance industry was concerned he was finished, he was the only person I knew who knew my job as well as I did. He'd never done my job – never wanted to – he just 'got it'. Instinctively he knew the wheat from the chaff; what was worth the fight; those fights that took more energy than they were worth – like eating celery.

He was always courteous enough to treat whatever I told him as valuable. It was only later I realized he was letting me run ahead, sniffing around, in what he already knew was there. Perhaps my job would have bored him. What I really admired, wrong phrase, unsettled me, through no fault of his own, was that he usually knew what I was going to say before I said it.

I'd heard all the terms 'LMXs', 'Spirals' over the years but never asked what they were. Henry cut surgically through all of that. Three decades of experience – or intuition? You learn experience. You are born with, or without, intuition.

So how had he ended up disgraced and redundant? I never believed a man of his ability would have forgotten something as fundamental as reinsurance for our biggest risk and the papers in my jacket pocket proved me right. I never understood why he hired Christian, the 'Chum' of his syndicate either.

As I approached the glazed double doors of the saloon bar of 'The Cricketers' I could see Henry seated on an oak carver chair flitting between a broadsheet crossword and gazing through the bay window. I paused just in time to see him throw his pen down. I gently opened the doors, and produced a fake cough. He turned and smiled appreciatively. We both knew I had seen his frustration.

"Can I get you a drink?" he asked.

I understood the great offence that would have been taken if I had refused, even more so if I had offered to pay.

"Thank you Henry. Which of those fine ales is the best?" I said nodding at the pumps.

He smiled faintly with a slight shrug of the shoulders.

"I'll ask. You sit down."

I sat opposite his newspaper and empty chair. Upside down I could see Henry had not answered the easy clues, let alone the cryptic. Following a soulless chat with the barmaid which I could overhear he returned with a pint of something that was probably brewed using twigs and small mammals.

"Here," he said placing a pint in front of me. "It's called Poachers Trap or something. She, Chantelle, said that it's good but she prefers a Breezer."

I looked over at Chantelle who was watching us.

"I bet she does," I said. I took a sip of Poachers. It was warm, treacly and really rather nasty. I shrugged at it. We both laughed, really laughed.

"So..." I said, suddenly nervous drawing on another Poacher.

Our barmaid, possibly having pulled her first ever pint, put on some music. Pan pipes – great. Henry gave me a momentary look which said in capital letters, 'Don't ask me how I am'.

"What happened?" I asked.

He asked, "Were you followed?"

"Tonight? No."

"First time?"

"Until now," I said nodding towards the bar. "They've got a lot of people and some budget, I'll give them that."

"Do you know any of them?"

"Do I have to keep drinking that?"

"Sip it. Don't let on you know she's your tail."

"I know one of them. She says her name is Francesca. She was in the church this morning; slipped away before I could speak to her."

"I am pleased that you agreed to meet someone who bankrupted the syndicate and brought Lloyd's to the front," Henry said.

"You were very a naughty boy Henry. Now you are sitting on the naughty stair."

Henry leaned towards me with an evil twinkle in his eye that I wanted then, let alone when I reached his age.

"No, no, no, Lukasz. You've got it all wrong."

"Really?" I asked enjoying the game.

"I was very forgetful."

“What did you forget?” I asked.

“I forgot to buy eight hundred and thirty millions dollars of reinsurance.”

“I suppose you had odd socks on at the time. You forgot?”

“So I was told as I was handed the cheque.”

“By?”

“By Mr. Christian... “Bye, bye Henry”.”

Our barmaid was having difficulty hearing us over ‘Bridge over troubled waters’. Thankfully we left the pub, the pan pipes, the Poacher and the worst tail yet.

“Nice jeans,” Henry said extracting a bottle from under an outside table.

“Wasn’t up to much was she?”

“Doubt they will use her again.”

“We’d remember the jeans.”

The Poacher was poaching.

“We?”

We headed towards the sea wall. Easy to find, just follow your nose – salt in the air. As we walked towards masthead lights we heard fractious movement in the hedgerow.

"Remember safe sex kids. Don't go near the blackthorn, it hurts," Henry called out.

I heard a girl laugh, then her boyfriend told her to shut up. True love – in a ditch.

We sat on the sea wall watching the moon reflected on the river.

"If you can remember, can you tell me what happened?"

A silence would have been better. Particularly as that is what the question created.

"Sorry," I said eventually.

"Not at all. I was just wondering where to start?"

We listened to the crackling sound as the retreating tide sucked the water from the mud.

"At the beginning please Henry. Start at the beginning."

34

Joseph Lamb Jnr's law practice was intentionally diverse. The prime business, however, was built up around a solid book of business representing top-flight property developers gorging themselves in their never-ending hunger for prime land and real estate. As these men grew in stature and wealth they asked Joseph's advice, usually on one of Florida's better golf courses, as to where they should invest their money. Initially Lamb found this puzzling – I am a lawyer, not an investment strategist. Why ask me? Then he realized, they trusted him, Joseph Lamb Jnr the Honest Lawyer.

Lamb decided to hire more attorneys to take care of the land deal business so he could channel his time into investment strategy. All went well. A tie-in with an old college buddy, then a well-known trader on Wall Street, facilitated some rich, fast rewards for Lamb's investors. The more they made, the more investors came to him. Eventually his investment business was being blessed by actors, musicians, socialites and politicians. Old Money. New money. Who cared about the age of it? Money, cash.

Joseph's face appeared in the society pages of all Southeast Florida magazines every week. He knew the Governor of the State of Florida. He met the President. The photograph of the pair adorned the rear wall of his office facing the door.

Then came the luxury yachts. Everyone wanted one. It became a competition over length, price did not matter. In 1985 the term "superyacht" was coined. Back then eighty-five foot yachts turned heads. Within ten years a yacht double that size was needed to arouse any interest. Lamb Jnr found he had a connection with the sea. Each yacht deal took place twelve miles off the Florida coast in international waters. He loved the voyage out, the party atmosphere when the deal was done, and the trip back. With his partners bonus he bought himself a new fifty-foot cruiser. Lori enjoyed it.

It was then that he learned about yacht insurance. Unlike automobiles, it seemed that if you agreed the value of your boat with your underwriter it was fixed; forever. Fixed... Joseph Lamb Jnr couldn't believe it. Have a claim and the actual market value of the boat meant nothing; you got paid out the agreed value. If the values dropped and you lost the boat, then the agreed amount was still paid out. What kind of invitation to commit fraud was this? The insurers were taunting every no-good out there to get themselves a boat and sink it.

Joseph struggled to believe this 'agreed value' notion was true. Weren't they just inviting cheats? The more he read, the more he became convinced. And so it was that the Honest Lawyer devised a plan – a plan that would take time to execute. He had planned before in creating the facets of the man Joseph Lamb Jnr. That plan had been a billion dollar success. Could he do it again?

35

23 January 2003
The Doral, Miami, Florida

April in South Florida is a pleasant time of year to do business. The 'snowbirds' have flown back home to the north; the temperature is mid-sixties, early seventies and the deluge of humidity has yet to arrive. As Joseph Lamb Jnr took his table at the Doral Golf Club looking towards the fairway he thought again how far he had come since Ruskin. Only two hours by road but a world away from Miami, Ruskin must surely still drag its way through each year with dreary inevitability. Places like Ruskin don't change. How could they?

"Mister Lamb, your guest has arrived," announced the impeccably groomed Latin waiter. Cuban? No, Puerto Rican. Don't mix the two, they hate each other. Lamb's guest bounded towards him. If pressed Lamb would have said he was around twenty-seven, twenty-eight. He felt depressed. There is no money in this; I should have stayed in Broward County this afternoon.

Lamb stood to meet his young guest.

"Mr. Lamb, thank you so much for seeing me, and driving all this way," he said hand outstretched.

"It's no problem at all," Lamb said shaking the offered hand. "A lovely day for a drive. Please, take a seat."

Joseph's excitable new friend waited for him to sit first.

"It really is a privilege sir. I heard you speak at the hospice charity ball. Compassion with humour, if I may say so?"

If you must, Lamb thought. That speech had been written by an associate Lamb recalled.

"Well thank you," said Lamb modestly. "But we are here to talk about you, Drew."

The waiter returned. Joseph ordered water, his guest a cola. Lamb worried that caffeine would push his already excited companion into some form of mania. They both ordered chicken Caesar salads to start, followed by pasta dishes.

"Mr. Lamb I have been told by close friends that you have been running a successful investment scheme for several years."

You should choose your close friends more wisely, Drew, Lamb thought.

"Well yes I have actually Drew," Lamb said smiling coyly. "It started small and I never intended to grow it, but it has grown quite considerably. My investors seem very pleased and that is, of course, what matters."

Have I have used that line before? Lamb wondered. Is it stale? He looked at Drew – the face of a gullible angel. Still, it was time to think of something new. Taking no chances Lamb changed the subject.

"Do you play?" Lamb enquired, nodding towards the fairway.

"Yes. Do you?"

"Very badly. There is so much business done out there I never really get to concentrate on my game."

The salads arrived.

"I would really like to invest with you sir."

"Please call me Joseph," Lamb said from behind an oversized pepper mill being wound by the waiter.

"Caesar without pepper would not be right," Joseph's young guest said as he commenced a surgical separation of the pale cheese from the chicken. "Lactose intolerant."

"I see. I'm sorry," Lamb said startled that even a sycophant such as this would risk sickness or death, just to gain his favour.

Once the potentially lethal Parmesan had been quarantined on a side plate, Joseph asked, "How much were you thinking of investing Drew?"

"I don't know. Joseph," he replied cautiously, clearly uncomfortable using Lamb's first name. "Please advise me."

"We have a minimum deposit amount, as you can imagine."

"Of course."

"What were you thinking of investing to start with?"

Lamb assumed the answer would end talk of business for the day.

Nervously Joseph's guest laid down his cutlery gazed out onto the fairway and in the voice of a child answering a maths test said, "Seventy-five million dollars?"

Lamb Jnr paused, his fork halfway to his mouth. How much?

"Is that enough… Joseph? I could go in with friends if that's too little?"

Lamb wiped his mouth with his napkin.

"I think seventy-five million dollars will be fine Drew," Lamb assured him.

Even seventy-five million had to be accounted for.

"If you don't mind me asking Drew," Lamb asked, "That's a lot of money, an awful lot of money, particularly for a deposit. How did you come by it?"

"Computers," Drew said as if the answer was obvious. "My friend, Joshua, and I developed a binary code at college."

Good. He has an equally rich, comparably foolish friend, thought Lamb.

"We had so much fun developing it. We are writing a book about our voyage and our experience."

Lamb picked at lettuce rather than laugh; experience? Have you ever been to Ruskin, Drew?

"We sold out about a year ago. The money is just sitting around not doing much."

“Well we better set that lazy money to work,” Lamb said.

The young man laughed. And laughed. Drew and Lamb chatted about family and friends, hurricanes and fishing. Joseph asked the young man about his invention and, while pretending to listen, worked out what he was going to do with seventy-five million dollars. The entire fund was capitalized at five hundred million over fifty investors. This kid was quite something.

“Oh I see. That is really very clever.”

Lamb said sensing Drew had finished.

“Simple really.”

Indeed you are Lamb assessed.

“Tell me. What rate of return are you looking for?”

The kid looked blank. Lamb chose to help him.

“How about we say a minimum of, say, thirty per cent for the first year?”

“You can turn it into over a hundred million that fast?”

With your mouth I can. Go and tell your friends. Just tell Joshua if he is your only friend. Preach it, boy!

“Don’t see why not,” Lamb assured him.

“I must tell my friends about this.”

That’s the idea, thought Joseph Lamb Jnr, Attorney at

Law.

....

As the espresso cups were cleared away Lamb asked, "Do you have any questions?"

"Only one."

Lamb was worried. He suddenly regretted asking the question.

"Go on," he said airily.

"What's the Governor like?"

Lamb laughed.

"Younger than he looks on the TV Drew."

....

The following day, during his daily morning balance checks, Lamb Jnr saw with pleasure the arrival of seventy-five million United States dollars into his bank account. He then personally booked a flight to Tortola. Travel reservations were always arranged by his assistant Jean – not this trip. He reserved a room at Long Bay Hotel. He was not interested in pool or beach; he wanted to be as far from Road Town as it was possible to stay. He had obtained a credit card under a false name and address from a gullible mid-western bank several weeks before. He used it to make the reservations. He would settle the bills in cash.

"Jean, I'm taking a few days off to prepare for the

Lauderhill trial. Would you please make sure I'm not disturbed," Lamb said into his office intercom.

"Of course Mr. Lamb," she instantly replied.

He would have to lie to Lori too – the first time. It would be worth it to them both he reasoned. Lamb Jnr then drove to Sawgrass Mills outlet mall in Sunrise. As he parked his Mercedes as far away from the entrance as possible he puzzled over the name of the city. Sunrise? Almost the most westerly city in Broward County. He needed costumes; Hawaiian shirts, shorts, sandals, hats, anything to make him look like any other another American tourist. He felt uncomfortable looking in the fitting room mirror. He could not meet his eye. Lie to Lori? It will be worth it. It will work. Security. No harm done. Prudence. No option. No Ruskin.

....

In Tortola, the meeting with the accountant and the lawyer went perfectly. Within two hours Azul Yachts Incorporated had been formed, with the essential total anonymity of ownership. Within the following twenty-four hours, a bank account had been created into which Lamb Jnr transferred seventy-five million dollars. Contented, Lamb Jnr flew back to Florida.

....

David Archer left the north-east of England in the early 1980s as the shipyards began their terminal decline. A qualified naval architect and ship engineer he found himself on a ship bound for Florida. Once there he never left. Sipping a beer, the first of the day, at the Quarterdeck on the beach road, he could not recall why he had not returned home.

"Let me get this right Mr. Lamb. You want me to design the largest yacht in the world?"

"Yes."

"Why me?"

"Because, and forgive me, I'm not a naval man, I believe that a two hundred metre vessel is a ship not a yacht."

"Aye, it is."

"And you design and build ships."

"Yes, but since I've been here I haven't designed anything over fifty metres."

"Are you saying you have forgotten how to build ships?"

"Never."

"Good."

"So what's the deal?"

"Can you come to my office tomorrow? You'll need to sign a confidentiality agreement."

"Why?"

"It's confidential."

Both men laughed.

"Where are ye?"

Lamb pointed inland up Las Olas Boulevard. "The tall one. Top floor."

"Figures," Archer said as he finished his beer; the first of the day.

....

"Mr. Archer is here to see you Mr. Lamb."

"Jean, pick up."

"Yes sir."

"Is he sober?"

"So far as I can tell sir, yes he is."

"Good. Send him in."

Archer strolled into Lamb's office, wearing a polo shirt which bore the motif of his last yacht. Lamb recognized it. It left for the Mediterranean ten years ago and never came back.

"Mr. Archer. Good to see you again. Please take a seat."

Archer had noticed the picture of the Governor.

"You two close?"

"No closer than that," Lamb lied.

Lawyers, Archer thought.

"So where do I sign?"

Lamb Jnr passed Archer a single page document.

"That it?"

"Yes."

"Bit short isn't it? I thought you were a lawyer," Archer said signing the agreement without reading it.

"We get bad press."

"So, Mr. Lamb…"

"Joseph."

"No, no, no. Mister Lamb, sir or Boss. You pick. Now, what do ya need?"

"A very large yacht Mr. Archer," said Lamb leaning back in his chair making an arch between his fingers of both hands.

"Oh aye. The hull I can design in a heartbeat but what styling are ye after?"

"Nothing radical."

"Nothing radical? Are you sure? Boss, you want the largest yacht ever built and you don't want anything radical?"

"I'm concerned about resale values Mr. Archer. I'm sure she won't be the largest yacht in the world for long," Lamb said.

I don't care if it is luminous pink with wings, just build me a boat, Lamb thought.

"So you want a standard displacement hull. Nothing fancy like a dreadnought bow?" Archer asked optimistically.

"No. Nothing radical. Just nice lines, the prettier the better," Lamb added realizing that something of the project had to keep Archer's attention away, albeit fleetingly, from alcohol. "I understand that prettiness is difficult to achieve in a boat of this size, but just do your best."

"Do you have a stylist in mind?"

Lamb had not.

"Have you worked with anyone you think would fit the project?"

"Aye, a chap in Holland."

"Is he discreet?"

"They all are at this end of the market. Have to be."

"Good. Please retain him."

"Done."

"Mr. Archer, you will be my only point of contact for this project. If anyone has a query over, let's say the guest bathroom marble, the radar arch, the lighting for the bridge – they come to you. Understood?"

"Understood."

"If absolutely necessary you come to me and we will find an answer to the problem."

“Understood, but you have only asked me to design the boat.”

“Would you like a coffee?” Lamb said reaching towards the intercom.

“No thanks.”

“Would you have a problem staying on after the design stage?”

“After I’ve designed her you want me to oversee the build?”

“Would that be a problem?”

Archer scratched his left cheek and looked at Lamb. “Not at all. She is a large yacht but still only a small ship.”

“Exactly.”

“How many decks?”

“Five.”

“Power?”

“I’ll leave that to you, and the range.”

“Range won’t be a problem,” Archer said laughing. “We’ll have plenty of space for fuel tanks in this one.”

“Thank you for raising the subject of space,” said Lamb sternly. “In addition to accommodation for forty guests, I want all the crew to have their own cabins with daylight. But,

Mr. Archer, and I insist on this – no more than forty crew."

"Forty?" exclaimed Archer, all trace of mirth gone. "Only forty? For the size of ship you are talking about. That's not very many."

There was uneasy silence as both men glared at each other.

"Work the calculations would you please Mister Archer. I'm certain you can do it. That is why I chose you," Lamb lied. "This is to be a private boat. My deck must be completely soundproofed. In my line of business I have many sensitive and private conversations."

"Not a problem. I assumed you would want a cinema. That will be soundproofed so one more area won't make much difference."

"Two other areas."

"Two?"

"Yes, two. I want you to incorporate a soundproofed room behind the basketball court."

"Oh aye, now that's the sort of job interest I like."

"Some of my acquaintances require privacy."

Archer was not famed for perception, but he would later recall the ambiguity in the intonation of Lamb's voice as he said the last word.

"Where will you be building her Mr. Archer?"

"How far are you prepared to travel for your regular inspections Mr. Lamb?"

"I will not be inspecting her, regularly or otherwise. That's your job."

"If you want a fast job then a commercial yard in the Far East," Archer said concealing his amazement. "If you want a quality job it will have to be Germany for a boat of this size."

"Germany it is. That means accounting in Euros."

"Yes."

"Shall we put a budget on this equivalent to six hundred million U.S.?"

"I can design to that. I will have to meet with my chap in Holland and the Germans first before confirming. As you want traditional styling scaled up, no new trial designs, materials or finishes, I think that amount should be plenty."

Joseph Lamb Jnr had heard the same from property developers over the years. He had no doubt Archer was sincere, albeit sincerely wrong. 'AZUL', the cloudless sky, would be built over budget. Lamb would hold a secret one hundred million back. He would make Archer beg for it while reminding him of this conversation.

"I will put you in funds initially of ten million U.S. dollars. The funds will come from an account in the British Virgin Islands," Lamb passed Archer a slip of paper. "This is the accountant you are to send the invoices to. He will arrange payments. Mr. Eversley is very helpful and very efficient. Any concerns regarding money, don't hesitate to call him."

As Jean showed Archer out, Lamb felt confident he had the right man; overqualified for the job when sober, defective when drunk. And that defect was just the qualification Lamb was going to need.

36

By the summer of 2004, a mere eighteen months after Lamb's meeting with Archer, the keel of 'AZUL' had been laid at a yard in Hamburg. Security was tight. The yachting press knew nothing other than Project number 893 being built in shed nineteen was rumoured to be the first two hundred metre yacht ever built. The second rumour was that the yacht was being built for an American owner. Alarmed by the accuracy of the second speculation, Lamb arranged for Archer to be put in funds to bar-hop in Hamburg until the new yachts owner's nationality changed.

"I do not care what nationality, Mr. Archer. Just change it and make sure you are consistent."

Archer did a good job. Scuttlebutt changed direction on ownership to the Middle East – a plausible assumption.

Lamb Jnr had, on paper, made a return for Drew of fifty per cent. Drew withdrew two million for annual living expenses and reinvested the remainder with Lamb. Easy.

During the sweltering heat and near miss hurricanes of 2004 Lamb amassed a further five hundred and fifty million dollars. Along with the Governor's money, Lamb was free to start enjoying his creation. He was insured. He was assured. Nothing could go wrong.

Carpe diem.

Seize the day.

And anything else he could get his hands on.

37

"Ladies and gentlemen, it is the greatest honour for me to introduce to you a man who needs no introduction – Joseph Lamb Jnr. Managing partner of Woods and Woods he will present the thirteenth Woods & Woods Fort Lauderdale Community College Scholarship award..."

"Ladies and gentlemen, our speaker this evening is Joseph Lamb Jnr, managing partner of Woods & Woods, lawyer, philanthropist and bad golfer..."

"Joseph Lamb Jnr, a well-known Fort Lauderdale lawyer and president of Doors for the Homeless said that the problem of homelessness in South East Florida was now so severe that his law firm would be donating half a million dollars to the cause. He encouraged other businesses to do likewise..."

"Joseph Lamb Jnr (left) opening the new Woods & Woods Hospice Wing."

38

10 March 2005
Hamburg, Germany

"What do you mean he doesn't want to see it?" Jan asked.

"He doesn't want to see it. Says he's too busy. He's the Boss," Archer replied.

Both men were sitting at their desks in the project control room at the Hamburg yard. The desks were reminiscent of a schoolroom, only some of the dubious jokes printed from e-mails and pinned to the walls suggested otherwise. Large tinted picture windows gave a panoramic view across the shipyard's dry docks. 'AZUL' was the only yacht in the yard. A couple of destroyers, a bulk carrier and two oil tankers poked their bridges over the top of the dry dock walls. It was cold; miserably cold. A general arrangement plan of 'AZUL' dominated the left-hand wall of Johann and Archer's office. Alongside it was a coloured chart with columns gradually growing from left to right indicating building works to be completed against forecasted completion dates. Green columns were on target jobs. Red showed overdue tasks. There were only three of the latter. The build of 'AZUL' was, mainly ahead of schedule. Choosing traditional designs and build methods had helped enormously, albeit boring, was paying off Archer thought.

"What kind of man commissions the largest yacht in the world yet has no interest in its progress? I don't understand."

"Perhaps he just wants a huge surprise when she's finished."

“Or an awesome shock when he realizes it’s not what he wanted.”

Archer stood up clearing some used coffee mugs. “I’m going down to the shed. The portside fairing must be nearly finished by now.”

Jan returned to his computer screen. Archer could hear him sniggering as he took the two flights of stairs down to the yard – another dirty joke.

39

17 October 2005
Fort Lauderdale, Florida

Of all of the events in the South Florida calendar, Joseph Lamb Jnr kept his lowest profile at the world's largest yacht show. FLIBS: Fort Lauderdale International Boat show. As a lawyer increasingly involved in the sale and purchase of ever-growing yachts he had to attend. His diary was always full with existing and prospective clients and entertainment offers from the yards. Offers he declined.

As the owner of the almost complete largest yacht in the world, he required anonymity. Four years into the build the rumours about the yacht's ownership had intensified once more as the project neared completion. Lamb lived in fear minute by minute waiting for his cover to be blown.

The weeks leading up to the 2005 boat show were particularly tense. As the show boats arrived, there was no other topic of bar talk but the ownership of the 200 metre new build about to be splashed in Germany. That the project was on schedule (albeit over budget) was inconceivable, even with German efficiency and tight project control. Lamb decided to fly Archer to the Fort Lauderdale show, leaving Jan to run the final stages of the project. A beer fund was created. If Archer had kept quiet this long, Lamb reasoned, he could be trusted to keep it up. Under no circumstances were they to meet. If they saw each other across Bahia Mar Marina or elsewhere, they would not know each other. Understood?

On the evening of 17 October 2005 Lamb paced into his den, anxiously chewing cashew nuts. He turned on the TV and crashed into the sofa.

"The National Hurricane Center in Miami has just announced that Hurricane Wilma has formed southwest of the Caribbean island of Jamaica. The storm is well organized and is postured for development."

Lamb Jnr stared at the screen in disbelief, halfway through a cashew. Could it be that this storm could stop the yacht show? He called Archer in Germany. He was in a bar and clearly drunk.

"Mr. Archer. It's Joseph Lamb."

"Good evening sir."

"We have a major storm heading our way. I suggest you don't come over."

"Aye aye captain."

By 19 October 2005 Wilma had become the strongest tropical cyclone on record. Winds topped 185 miles per hour.

Lamb told Jean to call his boat show clients and labour concern for their safety. A few diehards took a little persuasion; the show month was the highlight of the year for them; drink, strip bars, drugs. Jean wrote herself a speech explaining that if the storm hit there would be night-time curfews, no open bars, no air conditioning – for weeks.

It worked.

“Certainly Mr. Lamb Jnr can conduct the meeting by conference call at 10.30 tomorrow. Thank you for your understanding.”

Lamb understood that thanks to a lady named ‘Wilma’, the paramount secret of the ownership of ‘AZUL’ was secure.

40

25 November 2008
City of London

I surfaced from Bank Tube station, heading with the flow in the direction of Lloyd's. It was raining; there had been delays on the Waterloo and City line. The three minute journey had taken thirty. The mood was savage. A lost tourist with a wheeled suitcase was the first victim.

Ping. I stepped into the doorway of a clothes shop. A missed call from a number my phone did not recognize. One voicemail received, I retrieved it. Despite the oversized doorway, angry young office girls were miming anger as if I was blocking their path to heaven. A bad day in the City.

I listened.

"Hi Lukasz, this is Francesca. I hope you don't mind me calling you. I got your number from the Internet…"

Women like Francesca say 'web', this was another script. A hurriedly written, poorly directed, 'B-Movie' production.

"…I know that you know our meeting… encounter… at Treasure Isle was not accidental…"

Why change 'meeting' to 'encounter'? To infer sex… This was being recorded at both ends. We were the only guests… witnesses… at Treasure Isle.

"I do not believe you know why our encounter was arranged."

‘Encounter’… twice… once more than the reality. And why make herself sound coerced?

“I would rather say nothing further on an answerphone…”

There she goes again. No one has used ‘answerphone’ for thirty years.

“Perhaps we could meet again? I would like that. You now have my number. I would like to set the record straight. Goodbye.”

I quickly rejoined the crowd. I did not want my surveillance reporting that I appeared interested in the message.

So I had been watched at Waterloo. As soon as I entered ‘The Drain’ they contacted Francesca and her controller. Her message had to be recorded. Had I replied there would have been questions. Neither the script nor her controller allowed for that.

………………………………

“Are you going to save us from Chum?”

I was in the lift heading for the Coles Syndicate office on the eighth floor. The questioner was Rachel, my syndicate contact, self-appointed adviser and sometimes conscience. Her weekends were legendary, but never interfered with her work. Even when she fell off a table, dislocating a knee she hobbled into the office as if nothing was wrong.

“How am I to do that?” I asked leaning back against the outer glass of the lift.

"If you find out its fraud then we don't have to pay. Lloyd's will insist on a real underwriter, won't they? Not Chum." Her aqua-blue eyes flashed at me in defiance.

I was pleased that Rachel had waited for the lift to empty at the sixth floor before explaining herself.

I smiled. "It's a nice idea Rachel, but there's a lot at stake on this one," I said as the doors opened, and we stepped out. She turned to face me, barring the card reader that opened the main office door.

"I know that," she said sternly. "I don't just arrange your hotels you know."

"Shall we?" I said nodding towards the door raising my swipe card.

"Shall we not? There was a call for you yesterday."

"I don't remember seeing an e-mail from you."

"That's because I didn't send you an e-mail."

She nodded back towards the door leading to the toilets. I smiled again, wondering where all this was heading. My instinct was Rachel had good instincts. I stepped with her into the foyer between the ladies and gents toilets, I said nothing and waited for her to continue.

"It was a woman. There was something about her. I just didn't think you'd want the call on file."

"Did her name begin with an 'F'?"

"Yes."

"She left me a voicemail this morning."

"If you want I can send you a missed call e-mail this morning. Say I've just remembered… or my knee was playing up."

I looked into her eyes. Sincerity – not something I see that often; certainly not often enough.

Does this job damage you, or do you have to be damaged to do it?

"No, Rachel. You made exactly the right decision."

I held the foyer door open for her.

As she moved parallel with me she gently asked, "Is she attractive?"

"To a point," I said.

……………………………

Meeting Room 6 had been turned into Chum's 'Operations Room'. All of the documents I had sent back to the office had all been neatly arranged on desks. The pictures on the wall had been changed, some black and white painted stripes by a Spanish artist I had never heard of.

"What are those worth do you suppose?" I asked Rachel thinking of the modern artwork alleged to have been aboard 'AZUL'.

"I don't know. Chum rented them. Apparently they signify 'progress'," she replied.

The two lever arch files of documents provided by the obnoxious Johnson had been dissected and refiled with their counterparts from my learned friend in the BVIs. What a cast of characters. I suspected Rachel would have checked both sets against each other; something I had already done over several nights in hotels, but I was grateful to have my comparison verified.

"They match," she said.

"Thank you for checking. Even those?" I asked jabbing a finger at the crew lists.

"Yes."

We both knew that '6' had been chosen as the operations room because it was adjacent to Chum's office – the walls were thin.

"It's OK, he's not there. He's over at the Box at Lloyd's."

I looked at my watch. "Lloyd's? It's only eight o'clock? There will be nobody there."

"He has another meeting with 'AZUL's' broker. There will be one or two people passing by. Word will get round far quicker than if the room was full."

I realized that both Rachel and I were staring at Natalia Youngs' name as she said this.

"You hate the way those Lloyd's men think, don't you?" I asked.

Rachel walked towards another file marked 'EUO Transcript'.

"They're not men Lukasz. Not when they're in there. They are boys."

She brought the file to me.

"What about the women?"

She sighed. "Women know how to work boys, Lukasz. You know that," she said referring I thought to Francesca.

Rachel opened the file, and turned to the pages of the Johnson's transcript where he talked about the crew list. We both silently read again the part where he confirmed a full complement of crew, thereby including Natalia Youngs.

"Isn't there something in our policies about insureds lying? Doesn't that get us out of paying?" Rachel whispered.

This was not a conversation we could have had if Chum had been next door. I opened the adjoining door (without knocking) to check Chum had not slithered back in unnoticed.

"There is, but – I don't think it's enough."

"How come?"

I was staring at the page, trying not to think about the dead crew.

"We would have to prove the owner was complicit in the lies."

She moved the papers away, so that I had to look at her.

"So who is the owner?"

"A company registered in the British Virgin Islands."

She looked at me as she would an insolent child.

"Lukasz, a company is owned by someone. Who owns the company?"

"The BVI registry thrives on anonymity. We may never know."

"I bet Francesca knows," she said.

Women know how to work boys.

....

For the first time since this case began I had a table large enough to spread out the key documents, side by side and quietly consider what they were telling me. So many cases have been unravelled by the smallest of details – an e-mail with an attachment – the attachment never printed, 'never received', a forged official document with one digit missing or replaced, a general arrangement plan that did not match the yacht in some critical aspect. Small details – tiny. That's where the Devil lives.

Before me I had the general arrangement plan, the schematics of wiring, plumbing and engineering. I'm quite good at figuring out how all of this fits together, but it takes time. Time was what I didn't have. I picked up the phone in the corner of the room and called Harry Randall. Harry was a naval architect, naval engineer and, most essentially, a good sound man.

"I was waiting for you to call," he said gruffly. "What took you so long?"

"I've been rather busy."

"So I hear. Quite the little superstar at the moment, aren't you?"

"Fancy lunch?"

"Only if it's on you and the usual place. Bring Rachel if you want, but not that oily rag."

"He's at Lloyd's."

"Good. Keep him there."

"What do you need from us?"

"Get me the shell expansion and general arrangement plans, frames, bulkheads, and anything else diagrammatic. Make sure they are all signed by a classification society surveyor. In fact get Rachel to blow those signatures up, in case I need to challenge a few people. Bring them with you, don't e-mail me. I've heard this case has quite a high mortality rate."

"Do you want the other schematics?"

"No. Let me work out where the vulnerable bits of the ship are first, and then I'll look at those."

I had given up years ago trying to correct Harry's 'ship' for 'yacht'.

"Harry, do you know a David Archer?"

"I knew Archer years ago. We worked together, but that was before he went to Florida and before he hit the drink."

"What did you think of him?"

"Probably about the best naval architect I ever worked with. Took no chances, over engineered everything – in those days you could, speed and fuel weren't an issue."

"There was nothing radical in the design of 'AZUL'. She was supposed to go on forever, with no regard for cost."

"Then Archer would be your man."

"But that was before the drink?"

"You've got it."

....

'Le Deli de Jour' off Petticoat Lane, is neither French nor a delicatessen. Ordinarily Harry Randall would have avoided the place purely for the attempted deception. However, the finest lasagne and chips in the City was to be found in the bowels of 'Ladaj' and, more importantly, privacy. As Rachel and I descended the steps into the basement, I felt a pang of guilt taking her there. If she was bothered she didn't show it. She rarely spent her lunch break with her colleagues. I occasionally saw her in the summer reading in the gardens at Tower Hill. Other than that whatever she did, and whoever she did it with, was a mystery.

"I'm guessing we are not having snails?" she asked on the last stair.

"Not intentionally, no."

Harry was seated at a middle chair in a table for six. He stood as he saw Rachel. Had I been alone, he would have just grunted.

Shaking hands he said, “I’ve bought the table for an hour, so we can spread out. That’s fifty you owe me.”

“One billion dollars and fifty quid,” I said.

“I suppose we’re buying the lasagne too?” added Rachel.

“Of course,” Harry said smiling. “Show me what you’ve got while you two look at the menu. Sit up that end.” Rachel and I dutifully sat where indicated at the far end of the table allowing Harry to look at the shell expansion and general arrangement plans. He had walls on two sides and his back to the other diners. In the unlikely event anyone came in who knew us their view was blocked on all sides.

I tried not to look at Rachel as she read and reread the menu.

“So Mr. Lukasz,” she said feigning interest in the all-day breakfasts. “So far this year you have been to Miami, to Fort Lauderdale, to Old San Juan, to Tortola, nearly to Palm Beach and Monaco… or was it Monte Carlo?”

“Both,” I replied watching Harry at work.

“And did you eat in all of these places?”

“I did.”

“And you, finally, bring me where?”

“To a small piece of France.”

I felt a well-aimed toe find my right shin.

"Frame 73," said Harry.

"What about it?" I asked.

"Rough, ready, and never to be repeated?"

"Never," Rachel and I said in unison.

"Frame 73, portside, adjacent to bulkhead 17. I'll have to do some calculations. That's the weak spot."

"How weak?" I asked.

"Not very, if it was built the way Archer designed it."

"Is 'weak' the right word then?" I asked.

"Probably not. Just from this, I'd say the frame and bulkhead joint just there would be the most critical to the ship's structural integrity."

"In other words, knock those out and the ship would sink?" asked Rachel.

"Not only that," Harry said. "She would sink very quickly. How much time do you have?" Harry asked gently folding the plans as if they were drawn on the thinnest parchment. "And, more importantly, how much lasagne?"

....

By the time we had finished with Harry, the rain had stopped. We walked back towards Rachel's office, and stopped at a coffee shop. I bought Rachel a sandwich. She had done her best to find something on 'Ladaj's' menu, but it really wasn't her cuisine. We sat in a couple of high-backed throne-like leather armchairs, facing each other.

"So, King, you're running out of time," said Rachel, deftly catching a piece of falling lettuce. "What are you going to do about Francesca?"

I knew it was unlikely that Rachel would come any closer to talking about the case in public than that.

"I can't work her out."

"Have you tried?" Rachel asked looking directly at me. She returned her sandwich to her plate. Clearly she expected a detailed answer.

"Aren't I supposed to ask the questions?"

"Not where women are concerned. You don't know the right questions to ask, do you?"

"She turned up in Tortola. Before that I think she was sitting behind me in the airline lounge at Heathrow. She is now trying to suggest, on the record, that something happened in Tortola."

"Which it didn't?"

"No."

"And who would care anyway? This is London after all. Hardly Profumo is it?"

I felt no surprise that Rachel knew British history of the 1960s.

"No it isn't, but getting friendly with someone who is

close to the owner you are investigating, is not best practice."

"Good enough for James Bond."

"Bond isn't real life Rachel. Believe me, this is."

Rachel resumed eating.

"So, your Majesty, what do you suggest?" I asked.

"Rough, ready and never to be repeated?" she said mimicking Harry Randall.

"Never," I confirmed.

"Call her. Tomorrow. They're watching you, or rather us, right now?"

"Yes."

"Let them. Tomorrow's fine."

....

As soon as I opened the main office door for Rachel, it was obvious the atmosphere had changed.

"Mr Christian's back," Rachel murmured.

I laughed.

"Your idea?"

"Never."

I left Rachel to return to her desk and I headed back

into room 6. Had Henry Coles still been at the helm I would have gone into his office to see him. I sat back down and started to read the 'build file'. That was the file that contained all of the correspondence between the yacht designers, builders, suppliers and Archer. What I was looking for were any change orders – c.o.s – alterations to the Archer design requested by the owner during the four-year build. Rachel had helpfully separated the thousands of e-mails, drawings and photographs chronologically. She had also started (at my request) to look for c.o.s as she went through the documents and marked them. It was a monumental task, but I could see at least twenty marked pages with her neat notations on each sticker. I got as far as the second 'c.o.' before the connecting door opened and in marched Chum.

"Ah, Lukasz, I heard you were in today."

"I am," I said without looking up.

"Meeting at Lloyd's today. Twelfth floor. Need you there."

"What time?" I asked looking up warily.

"An hour's time. They want a 'sit-rep'."

Situation report; Chum knew nothing about yachting other than a few phrases he had learned from Bud, Henry Coles, and myself. Of all the phrases the parrot had learned, 'sit-rep' was his favourite.

"Fine," I said.

Chum turned towards his office, then halted. It was intended to be dramatic but he simply looked indecisive. He turned back and slumped into a chair opposite me.

"Lukasz, we need to talk."

What, again? Can't you talk to Mrs. Unstead-Matthews?

"Christian I would love to," I lied, "but I have so little time left," I said pointing to all of the files and boxes with sweeping movements of both arms. "Just look at it all."

"Lukasz, where are you going with all of this?" he whined painfully.

"Where I always go."

"Where is that?"

"To the end."

"Even if that affects your position with the Syndicate?"

I looked at Chum and weighed him up. He was a fool, but as Henry Coles had found out, a dangerous one.

"Is that a suggestion you should be making so close to our meeting with your controllers at Lloyd's?"

Chum leaned across the table.

"The regulations say the underwriter shall have no influence on the payment or declinature of a claim. The underwriter has gone. This underwriter is here. I'm your client," he hissed.

Backing away he said loudly enough to be overheard in the main office outside.

"You have eight days Lukasz. If you are not finished by

then Lloyd's will take this case over, lock, stock and barrel. You will look a total fool. Now, let's talk about Mills."

....

Although the rain had stopped hours before and Lloyd's was barely a five minute walk from the Coles office, Chum had ordered a black Mercedes to take us there. The journey was taken in silence. We pulled up under the arched glassed canopy, bemused waiters looking on. I had hoped not to be recognized; Chum the reverse. Access to the twelfth floor is by key only, or by taking the lift to the eleventh floor and walking up the stairs.

"Are you going to be OK with this?" I asked nodding towards the tubular staircase, a striking part of the Lloyd's design when viewed from the outside. Chum ignored me.

I had put a tie on for the occasion. I could feel my collar rubbing as we were admitted to the waiting area on the twelfth floor. I understood enough of how Lloyd's works to know that this was going to be a tense and heavy meeting. Unfortunately I did not know anything about the committee we were about to face. Who had which interests to protect? Who held what on the others? I realized I would have to do what I always did and figure them out as we went along. Had Chum told Rachel about the meeting beforehand, she would have Googled them all and reported to me at lunch. Clearly Chum wanted me unprepared and off guard. We'll see about that Mr. Christian.

We were led into a cherrywood panelled room with round windows. In front of us were three men and a woman – Chum knew them all. He introduced me warmly to them. I cannot recall their names; I make my own. The woman turned out to be in the Chair. She appeared flustered. Perhaps she too was unprepared?

"We are sorry to have brought you here at such short notice Mr. Stone, but Christian told us you were in London today and we thought it best, given the high profile of this unfortunate case, that we heard first-hand exactly how your investigation is progressing," she said far too quickly. I felt out of breath listening to her.

"Would you please tell us who you have met with so far?" asked a man of no more than five feet in height seated to my immediate right. He had a goatee beard, but no hair on his head. The beard was a poor substitute – his head looked upside down.

"I have met with the owner's lawyers in Tortola. I have taken the Examination under Oath of the…"

"The what?" asked Breathless.

"Examination under Oath. A series of questions on the record, quite commonplace," Chum assured her.

"Is it 'commonplace'?" asked Goat.

"Is an Examination like this commonplace?" asked Breathless trying to regain the Chair.

"Routine for extremely large losses such as this," I confirmed.

"Would you say such an Examination implies a suspicion of… guilt?" asked a quiet man to the Chair's right. He looked and sounded like a man blessed with a brain and charm. That was the one to be wary of; he could have made a fine assassin.

"Not for losses of this size, no," I said firmly, hoping to halt the inquisition.

"The brokers have complained that the Examination under Oath of Mr. Johnson was heavy-handed and added some questions about the validity of this loss," said Charm.

I learned years ago that you will never catch a Lloyd's underwriter using the 'f' word – fraud – in public. As a result they have developed their own expressions and a thesaurus of alternative words, some very feeble, to replace it.

"I will admit that my first meeting with the insured's Designated Person Ashore did not go well," I volunteered.

"How come?" asked the remaining panellist, an American.

"I met him at his home and quickly realized I was being recorded without my consent. I ended the meeting."

"Why was that a problem?" asked the American on cue.

"In my view recordings should be on the record, in the open and the testimony transcribed."

"An Examination under Oath in other words?" said Goat.

Well done, I thought. "Exactly," I replied.

"Are we entitled to see the transcript?" asked the American.

"That is a decision for my client."

As if woken from the deepest sleep of his life, Chum jumped, realizing that he was being asked a question. He and I were pondering the same thing for once. What was in that transcript; my questions – his answers that was upsetting someone? Whoever that 'someone' was they were upsetting Lloyd's.

"Sorry. What was the question?" Chum asked.

"Are we entitled to see the transcript?" asked the American.

Chum was dumbstruck. He turned to me.

"Are they?" he asked weakly.

I looked directly at Chum just long enough for the committee to get the measure of my loathing for the man.

"Christian, I am just an investigator. I hold no position on the board of your agency. If I were to guess, I would say that as your regulator Lloyd's has the right to see whatever it wants to see, provided it is treated as confidential and doesn't leave this building."

"Of course," said the American, convincing no one.

Personally I wanted them to read it. Strike that, I wanted to drop copies of it all over the Lloyd's trading floor until someone told me what was in it that someone feared so much.

"We will study it very carefully. We will send Mr. Unstead-Matthews' secretary our contact details so that she can e-mail it – encrypted of course," said Breathless.

Back in the needless Mercedes, Chum was regaining his

composure.

"What the hell is in that transcript?" he demanded.

"You're welcome."

"What?"

"You may have missed it but I saved your 'credibility' in there."

"Forget that. What is in that transcript Lukasz?"

"You've read it. You tell me."

"If only I knew."

41

25 November 2008
Nelson's Dockyard, Antigua, Caribbean Sea

Alexander tied the second lace on his Sebago Docksider deck shoes and looked at his reflection in the mirror above the dressing table. A light breeze ruffled the curtains behind him. He straightened the collar of his stark white polo shirt and picked off a dark, stray cotton from his neatly pressed chinos. He could not look himself in the eye.

Outside the hotel, having ignored the permanently cheerful receptionist he slipped on a pair of sunglasses. He patted his left trouser pocket, although he knew very well that the pistol was there. He then walked a short distance to a slip occupied by a Grady White motor boat. Both outboard engines were already lowered in the water. Opening the baitwell he found the ignition keys and started both engines. Alexander would have preferred to have carried out the operation by night – he was a natural night worker like the driver of the night bus, or a kebab shop owner, except his customers never saw him at work.

Alexander threw off the mooring lines and slowly manoeuvred the boat away from the dock and out of the marina. In open water he pulled a piece of paper from his back pocket and he punched a set of coordinates into the GPS. Turning the wheel slightly to port he opened up both throttles until the boat was riding comfortably on the plane.

From half a mile off, Alexander saw his target. The white hulled fifteen metre sailing catamaran sat calmly at anchor off a sheltered cove. As he got closer he saw a tall brunette wave in his direction, she did not smile. Alexander gradually pulled the throttles back and then turned the engines off as he came alongside. He threw a mooring line to the brunette.

"Any trouble?" Alexander asked.

"None. He had a heavy night last night. He's in the saloon sobering up."

"Needn't have bothered on my account," Alexander said jumping expertly from the Grady White over the gunwale of the higher catamaran. "Wait for me in there," he ordered her nodding towards the motor boat.

Alexander walked to the stern of the catamaran and descended the companionway steps into the saloon. Alexander had never met Lomas but, as the brunette had said, a red-faced overweight dressed in a crumpled Virgin Gorda tee shirt and too-short Navy shorts was seated at the crescent-shaped dining table tightly gripping a mug of tea. A younger man was cooking bacon in a pan on a grill.

"Who are you?" Lomas asked.

"You," Alexander said to the chef. "Wait for me in the boat."

The man turned off the gas and without looking at the quizzical Lomas, ascended the companionway steps. Alexander heard the man's muffled footsteps across the deck and Lomas saw his feet as he climbed over the side of the yacht.

"Who are you?" Lomas asked again. Despite the alcoholic fug he found himself in that morning Lomas was alert enough to realize that Alexander was not good news.

Alexander looked around the saloon.

"My name is Alexander, Mr. Lomas. I work for your client," he said smiling. "Please, relax."

Lomas viewed the stranger uneasily.

"Have you enjoyed your time on board?"

"Very much, the crew has been great. Actually I think Jodie rather likes me," he confided.

"Jodie?"

"The brunette girl," Lomas explained.

"I'm sure she does. Our mutual client wanted to thank you for your performance in Tortola; very convincing."

Lomas, be it through alcohol or his natural state, was confused. "Performance?"

"Of course," said Alexander. "Virtuoso."

"Well thank you." He was still confused but sensed that disagreeing with this 'Alexander' would be unwise.

Alexander sat at the stern end of the table. He could smell the stale alcohol on Lomas – Alexander never drank. He felt nauseous but needed to win Lomas's confidence. He moved closer.

"Tell me," Alexander said conspiratorially, "What did you make of Mr. Stone?"

Lomas looked intently into Alexander's face, searching

for the correct answer. The crippling hangover struck him again with full force. There was no answer.

"I didn't form an opinion," Lomas said after some delay.

"Come now Mr. Lomas, you and Stone are both Englishmen. You must have met Mr. Stone's type before?"

"Yes I have," Lomas agreed.

"Good," Alexander said patting Lomas' clammy hand. "So tell me about him."

Lomas blew out his cheeks sending a waft of foul breath over Alexander.

"Well I'd say he doesn't suffer fools – at all. He seemed more interested in Patrice than V.S."

"I understand that she is a very attractive woman."

"She is. Very," Lomas said, relieved to have an opportunity to agree with Alexander.

"Perhaps she likes you too?" Alexander said smiling.

"I don't think so," Lomas said seriously. "She was very stern with me."

"So Mr. Stone. You'd say he is one of the good guys?" Alexander probed.

"I would say so," Lomas said cautiously.

"Good. Good. So would I," Alexander agreed.

Lomas was puzzled. None of the conversation between Alexander and himself couldn't have been held in front of Jodie and… And? Lomas couldn't remember the name of the chef.

"Have you spoken with Mr. Stone since your meeting with him, V.S. and Patrice in Tortola?" Alexander asked.

"No!" Lomas said a little too emphatically.

"Are you certain Mr. Lomas?"

"Certain. Nothing. No conversation, e-mails, texts – not that I even have his number."

"That's great Mr. Lomas. Really great," Alexander said in his most comforting voice, the one he reserved for such occasions.

"Patrice was very specific. Even if Mr. Stone called me I was to say nothing. Just refer him immediately to her."

"Has Stone contacted you?"

"No, ask the other two," Lomas said nodding in the direction of the Grady White.

Alexander saw perspiration on Lomas' forehead.

"I believe you Mr. Lomas. Calm yourself."

"OK," said Lomas, clearly still worried.

"Nice boat," Alexander said.

"Yes," Lomas replied quietly.

"'AZUL' was something else," Alexander said. "You should have seen her."

"I would have liked to."

"Too late now," Alexander said. "A shame it had to end that way."

Lomas's confusion was mounting at the same rate as his fear.

"End what way?" Lomas asked and instantly regretted his question.

"Nothing," Alexander replied.

There was an uneasy silence between the two men.

"Mr. Lomas," Alexander said breaking the silence. "Where did you get the crew list from?"

Lomas stared at Alexander. For the first time that morning he had perfect clarity. He tried to work out why Alexander needed to know. There seemed to be no wrong and thereby dangerous answer, so he told the truth.

"I copied it," he said confidently.

"You copied it?" Alexander asked through a half smile.

"Yes. I copied it," Lomas replied laughing seizing gratefully upon the lightness of Alexander's tone.

"What did you copy it from?" Alexander asked.

"From a previous manifest. I found one from September

when the boat was in Monaco. Or was it Monte Carlo?"

"Makes no difference," Alexander said reassuringly. "Listen, I think if we're quick some of that bacon could still be warm. Would you mind?" Alexander said nodding towards the stove.

Lomas slid around the forward end of the table and lumbered towards the stove.

Alexander shot Lomas in the back of his sunburned neck.

"One more to go," Alexander said to himself as he calmly walked up the companionway steps. "You're next Stone."

42

26 November 2008
Terminal 5, London Heathrow Airport

The following morning I was back in the lounge at Heathrow. Rachel had taken a duplicate set of the 'build' file and I had started reading again from where I had left off before Chum had interrupted me. Nothing had caught my attention. There were the usual early changes to generator specification and change of marble in the master bathroom, all dealt with by Archer. Although it would be years before 'AZUL' was completed sourcing materials such as marble took months. My phone was set to silent, but I saw Rachel's number displayed, along with the picture she had programmed into it yesterday – Tattoo from 'Fantasy Island'. Yes, Boss.

"Good morning Rachel."

"Hopefully, Chum was in a foul mood last night. What happened at Lloyd's?"

"His friends don't trust him."

"Can you blame them?"

"No. So they caught him out."

"Did you save him?"

"Yes but he didn't like it. Has he given you the addresses to send the encrypted EUO transcripts?"

"Yes, I will send them on Monday. He asked me if you'd said there was anything odd about the EUO."

"And you said?"

"No, Mr. Unstead-Matthews, Lukasz said that Trixie had her cherries as usual," she replied, using the clueless voice she reserved for such occasions.

"He left it at that?"

"No. He asked if I'd seen anything odd in the transcripts. "I wouldn't know 'odd' Mr. Unstead-Matthews.""

"Has Archer confirmed his appointment with me?"

"You have a choice of two slots. You can have drunk o'clock tomorrow night, or sobering up Monday morning."

"Where am I meeting him?"
"Mario's office, Cordova Road."

"He will have to drive then. Hopefully that will keep him sober."

"From what I've heard this man's problem is so bad, he'd just not turn up or call in sick."

"Did he say if he would have a lawyer with him?"

"No."

"OK, let's take the sober up time appointment. Make it noon Monday. I need to see Bud first."

"It will be so Boss. Harry Randall called. I think he worked late on this. He sounded very tired, and hungry," she said with mock sympathy. "Like he needed a hug."

"And we know who he'd like that from don't we?"

"You mean it wasn't just for fine dining that you took me along yesterday?"

"Most women would have taken set breakfast number six and felt themselves pampered."

"I am not most women, Lukasz," she said.

I paused – probably for a second too long.

"What did he say?" I gulped, blaming a coffee I didn't have.

"He said, "You can't hold me to it, but I'm eighty per cent certain frame 73, bulkhead 17 is the weakest point,"" she said aping Harry. "He then started to tell me why, but I said that was best discussed with you."

"Would you call him back on Monday please and ask him to transpose the frame plan onto the general arrangement plan, and work out which spaces, salons, or cabins appear around F73/B17. Tell him he is officially retained on the case. If he needs outside engineers to assist, he can have them. Once he has agreed to all of that give him Rob Hargreaves' number at Failure Reconstruction in Marseilles."

I could hear Rachel's breathing as she cradled the phone, writing all this down.

"Yes, Boss."

"And when you've done all that, please shred the note you've just written. When Chum comes in, tell him I have retained Harry Randall and watch his reaction. Don't say anything about Hargreaves, I want Chum to think we are thinking…"

"We?"

"We are thinking that this was a design flaw. If that's covered by the policy it will bring a smile to his face."

"Creepy."

"Sorry, you're going to have to endure it."

"I have a question Lukasz and it's quite a serious one."

"I can't right now, I'm busy. And, anyway you haven't got a dress."

She giggled.

"What is it?" I asked softly. My voice gets sharper when I'm thinking aloud. I don't hear it but I see it on other people's faces as they back away.

"It's all very well knowing which is the 'soft spot' on the ship, particularly when it is not very soft at all, and presumably Harry and Rob together can work out the amount of force that would be required to blow a hole large enough to sink 'AZUL' as quickly as she did, but isn't this all really rather academic? You've got one piece of steel, from who knows where lying several miles underwater."

"It's enough to get David Archer off the hook, which is exactly where I want him to be. Whoever did this is going to blame him. Given his problems he is the softest part of this ship, not the steelwork. Let Chum think we blame him too. I want to see how far that dye spreads."

“Got it. One last thing.”

“What?”

“Francesca. Call her. Today.”

“Yes, Boss,” I replied.

43

18 May 2006
Hamburg, Germany

"Does the sun ever shine here?" Johnson whispered in Sharpe's direction, shifting his hands in his pockets.

Standing tall above the congregation of crew, designers and yard workers gathered around dry dock 28, Sharpe withdrew his gaze from his latest command and considered the trim, tanned, depressing man beside him. I doubt the sun ever shines within ten miles of you, Sharpe thought.

"What does the Boss make of his yacht?" Sharpe asked coolly. "I assume he isn't here?"

"Of course he isn't!" Jonson responded with a laugh, a metallic rattle. "To my knowledge he's never seen 'AZUL'."

Sharpe looked down the line to his left and saw the architect Archer laughing with Jan the project manager. Both were filled with good spirits. Sharpe, although faintly disgusted by their behaviour, would rather have been standing with them than with Johnson.

"We've done it Archer, you nasty little man. We've done it."

"Aye, no thanks to you, cloggy. Didn't see you do a scrap of work in years."

"Gin?" Jan asked needlessly, handing Archer a soft drinks can.

"Go on then."

To Sharpe's right he looked down the row of his crew. Justin, the Chief Engineer had managed to station himself, yet again, next to Natalia the little American Stewardess – one to watch; closely. Sharpe made a mental note to discuss this with the Chief Stewardess.

A band started to play a tune Sharpe didn't recognize. They had been placed near the staging that led up to the bow of 'AZUL', this was Sharpe's cue to climb the steps and join Johnson and the builder's management at the top of the stage. As he climbed the stairs Sharpe puzzled over why he felt foreboding rather than elation. It made no sense; he had been appointed master of the largest yacht in the world. Competition for the job had been formidable, yet he had done it. Every trade magazine, newspaper, television and radio station in the world wanted to interview him, yet he would happily have walked away from the yacht right then, in full view of the media. The sound of a champagne bottle smashing on steel startled him. It was his time to speak – but what to say?

44

London Heathrow

In the time before my flight was called I read through to c.o. thirteen that was the last one Rachel had marked – I was on my own from thereon. The flight heading west was two hours longer than the return so I would have the task of reading all of the c.o.s completed by landing. Any documents unread I would finish that night. It was essential I had read them all before heading from Miami to Fort Lauderdale, for my meeting with Archer.

I called Francesca.

"Lukasz, hi. I wasn't sure I'd hear from you."

The voice of the jilted lover irritated me.

"Thought I'd call before I got on the plane."

She was trapped. Should she let on that she knew where I was? She had already admitted that our 'encounter' was planned, or should she pretend she didn't know, and get caught in another lie? I did not feel inclined to help her out.

"I wanted to explain about Tortola… to meet." It was a clumsy reply, but the safest in her circumstances. "Where are you at the moment?"

"Where do I need to be?" I replied.

....

I ordered a light breakfast before calling Rob Hargreaves. Rob is a specialist in taking the broken, waving his magic wand and returning it fixed – on a computer. He is a failure analyst. His failure is an inability to communicate with any other human being other than by numbers. He is socially inept, overbearing and irritating. He also has an unrelenting, inexhaustible obsession with minutiae. Just the skill I needed for the job.

After breakfast, having read through change order eighteen (alternative wood for the drawer fronts in the crew galley) I picked up the lounge phone in front of me and called Rob's mobile. As Rob's phone started to ring, a young waiter cleared my plate. I noticed he read 'AZUL' on the front of my closed file. I watched where he went next as the French dial tone purred in my ear. Who would he speak to? It was a young upgraded couple.

The yacht was not the headline news of a week ago.

Rob answered.

"Rob, good morning. Lukasz Stone from London."

"Mister Lukasz Stone. Bonjour, bonjour. What time is it there? Oh, early. How are you?"

"I'm fine Rob, not much time to talk. I'm at an airport."

"I quite understand. How can I be of ready assistance?"

"You have heard about the loss of the 'AZUL'?"

"Of course, it was quite big news here. Two of the crew were French, or Belgian, or maybe just residents…"

"Rob!" I interrupted forcefully. "I'm sorry, I don't have much time. My client insured her."

"I see. Just one client?"

"Yes."

"How unusual, I would have thought…"

"Rob, have you or your colleagues accepted any instructions from any other parties who may be interested in 'AZUL'?"

"No."

"Owners, builders, designers, families of the crew, anyone?"

"No."

"Are you certain?" I asked foolishly.

"Of course I'm certain." he said coolly.

"Can you be overheard?"

"I can, but I will shut the door. Hold on for ten seconds."

I heard Rob walk across a room which sounded to have a very high ceiling.

"OK, tell me what you want," he asked when he returned.

"We have very little to go on. From everything I have seen so far this ship was well designed and well built. There's no obvious reason why she sank, or why she went down as quickly as she did. Harry Randall has identified an area between Frame 73 and bulkhead 17 port side that, due to the layout, is the weakest."

"Randall owes me money."

"Put it on my bill. It's the weakest point on the ship Rob, not weak. Harry will call you on Monday and send you the steel spec's, dimensions and layout. I want you to calculate the force necessary to sink this ship from the inside out, in the area I have described."

"Randall owes me money," he repeated.

"Rob, whatever it is, put it on my bill. I want you two playing nicely together. There are a few other things. Firstly, all of this is confidential for the next seven days. If anyone asks, you have heard of the case but you have not been instructed."

"Not been 'formally' instructed."

"No Rob. You have not been called, e-mailed, faxed, winked at, written to, formally or informally instructed or blown kisses through the air. Agreed?"

"Agreed," he said reluctantly. Hargreaves would lay awake for weeks if he thought he had missed this instruction.

"Just for seven days. Then you can talk all you want."

Although I would not recommend it I thought.

"I don't like it," he said petulantly.

"Neither do the families of the deceased," I snapped. "Can you do it or not? Seven days – two days of which are a weekend."

"I can do it."

"Thank you Rob," I said warmly.

The waiter had served a flamboyant Mediterranean businessman, Greek I guessed, and two less than trophy wives. Apart from some flirting, not initiated by him, he had said nothing to anyone to identify me. Whoever was my tail of the day had been here before.

....

Rachel.

"Your 'friend' Francesca called," Rachel told me flatly. "She couldn't get through on your mobile, so she called the out-of-hours service."

"She's not my 'friend' Rachel."

"She wants to meet you at 'Mangos' on Ocean Drive tonight. Sounds friendly to me."

"It's full of tourists and unattractive drunks dancing on tables."

There was a very nasty silence.

"There is nothing wrong with dancing on tables," I said, rather too quickly.

"So it's the drunk you don't like?"

"That's fine too."

I was not aware we had married since our last conversation.

"What time does she want to meet?"

"Ten p.m. She is staying at the Delano, although why you need to know that when…"

"When I've got her mobile number," I interrupted quite firmly.

"She's too old for you anyway."

"Rachel, Francesca was charming in Tortola because she was being paid to be charming and she wanted something. According to my mother, some women can be like that."

At last – a laugh.

"It's as well she told you because you would never have worked it out for yourself. You only think in boats, boats and more boats."

"There is only one thing I want from Francesca."

"To know why she's the drunk aunt who turns up at every wedding."

45

Miami, Florida

There was a comprehensive list of things Chum did not know. Although he was aware of Harry Randall's retention he believed Harry was studying the drawings of 'AZUL' frame by frame with the builders in Hamburg. Rachel really must try to be more accurate when she speaks with him. He did not know that Hargreaves had been retained at all; I had 'forgotten' to tell him. Chum knew that I was meeting with Archer. Chum also knew that Archer had a drink problem and would be an unreliable witness, if (and a very large 'if'), the 'AZUL' claim ever went to court. What Chum did not know was that the collective work of Randall, Hargreaves, Bud, Spider and I could negate any chance of Archer ever being called to testify, if the ROV located many more pieces of 'AZUL'. Such oversights often occur when short deadlines are imposed. Chum also did not know that I was in contact with Natalia Youngs, and her parents. Even Rachel did not know that. I trust Rachel, but there is a limit, despite her willingness, to how much I will put her in.

With eight days to go, Chum and whoever he was colluding with, as far as I could tell, were where I wanted them. His certainty of the outcome of my investigation must have been growing by the day. He would have assumed that my report would conclude that a sudden structural failure led to the rapid loss of 'AZUL'. It would recommend payment of the claim for Total Loss, negotiation with families of the deceased, and removal of the wreck, if required by the Puerto Ricans. Given the depth of water that wasn't going to happen. It would further recommend, in another neat section, filing lawsuits against Archer and the yacht builders.

Chum would take the report to Lloyd's in another black Mercedes; Lloyd's would release funds from the Central Fund. The Coles syndicate would be forced to merge with a larger syndicate, (probably Leadenhall) for which Chum would appear as Active Underwriter. The income capacity for the enlarged Leadenhall Syndicate would top two billion dollars making it the largest at Lloyd's. The profitable, lean business built by Coles would transfer too. Chum's salary would increase to seven figures and his annual bonus would be even larger, plus share options. The remuneration I could stomach, but the thought of walking into the Room and seeing Christian Unstead-Matthews sitting at an Underwriting 'Box' on the ground floor and becoming the most influential underwriter at Lloyd's, I could not. Ring the Lutine bell.

Lloyd's rarely intervenes in the investigation of a claim. It rightly forms committees to ask questions and ensure fair play, but it rarely intervenes. Had it done so then, and halted the investigation, frozen the facts as I knew them, Chum would have been humiliated; the top job would have been lost, probably forever. But that was not enough, I had given undertakings to Natalia's parents, Banksy's parents and although they did not know it, the crew of 'AZUL' to find out who caused the sinking of 'AZUL' and why. All of these thoughts brought me back to Francesca. As I walked through South Pointe Park towards Ocean Drive, I was still no nearer knowing who she was, or who she was working for. Washington Avenue was gridlocked as usual, my tail would have to give up if he or she was in a car, or join me on foot. Perhaps meeting Francesca let me off the leash? If Francesca was working for Chum, the brokers, the feisty committee or the owners she knew enough of the structural failure story to report the facts as Chum knew them. Something in my stomach told me that the meeting was not going to end the way I expected. Cautiously I entered the barn that is 'Mangos'.

Two short, stubby Latinas with poor complexions were dancing on the bar, with more confidence than ability they gyrated to some generic Latin beat. Below them delighted oversized and overdrunk middle-aged tourists leered over their mojitos. I tried not to think of Rachel's table dancing. She would have made a much more attractive job of it – at least until she fell off.

I could see Francesca, seated at a table on the balcony – good choice. If you have to have an awkward conversation with someone, then make sure there is something else for you both to look at rather than each other; avoid eye contact. If she saw me approach she didn't show it.

"Francesca?" As she turned to face me, it appeared she had aged since I saw her last. How long ago was that? A week? Ten days, maximum. She looked exhausted.

"Lukasz, good to see you," she said standing, lining up to kiss my cheek. I intercepted her by grabbing her right hand and shaking it a little too vigorously. The Latinas weren't the only ones performing to an audience, I was certain we were being watched.

"You wanted to see me," I said coldly as we sat down opposite each other. A waitress, considerably more attractive than the dancers, approached us.

"Two diet Cokes," I said purposefully.

"My idea, but your meeting?" she said as the waitress walked off.

"Something like that," I said thawing slightly. "Sorry."

"You don't need to apologize. I'm grateful you agreed

to meet."

"Did you think I wouldn't turn up?"

"It had crossed my mind. But I thought curiosity might win."

"So, what is this all about? Who are you, and what do you want?"

"My name is Francesca Jenkins, just as I told you in Tortola."

"And what are you?"

"I am a financial analyst."

"No you are not."

"I am."

"Francesca, financial analysts don't trail strangers around the world."

"I haven't trailed you around the world…"

Here we go. Lying has a three-part formula. Firstly, the look; Francesca was doing it – an intense stare into my eyes that lived a little too long. Then self-justification – religion, morality or philanthropy – chose one, any one.

"I pride myself on my high ethical standards." Morality – two down, one to go.

Lastly the alibi.

"Besides, I have been far too busy to be worrying about you."

The unholy trinity.

Our waitress returned with our drinks. The music had changed as had the dancers. As I paid, I watched Francesca over the waitress' shoulder, she looked tired and miserable.

"Let me level with you 'Francesca'," I said looking down to the dance floor. "I'm generally regarded as a patient man. I have to be. I live my life listening to lies. If I absorbed even half of what I hear, I believe it would do me no lasting good."

Whatever Francesca had expected I could see from her dumbfounded look that what I'd said wasn't it.

"You, however, have no such concern. You, you revel in deceit."

"I…"

"Don't interrupt," I advised. "You revel in deceit," I repeated.

She did not interrupt again.

"However, you have one thing in your favour."

"Which is?"

"You are so inept at deception it's almost an embarrassment watching your efforts."

"So you will help me?" she asked unashamedly, leaning

towards me in what, I assume, she though was an attractive way.

"I realize that you don't quite understand what you're dealing with."

She laughed.

"I don't mean me, I mean them. Have you been counting the bodies?"

She tried to laugh again but no sound came out of her mouth.

"Have you?"

"Counting what?" she said with a smile on her mouth but not in her eyes.

"You're an embarrassing amateur Francesca and you're likely to get yourself and whoever you're working for killed. My guess, by the end of the week."

"You what?"

"You heard," I said. This was my time to lean towards her. "Clumsy tails, the coincidence meetings, even getting a stenographer involved!"

"Trixie and I…"

"I don't care! You're an amateur!"

"I have something to tell you."

Finally, truth.

What she told me was much closer to the truth than I had expected. Her client, (anonymous), was a wealthy man in his mid-twenties. He had created a binary code, converted it into a commercial product and then sold his company for a substantial sum.

"He is a surprise when you meet him."

"I have not agreed to meet anybody Miss. Jenkins. What is so surprising about him?" I asked.

"He is quite unassuming, articulate with a gentle manner until he feels comfortable and then he is, well, rather excitable."

"Great."

"I don't think he fully understands the magnitude of what he has achieved at such a young age."

"You sound impressed. It's just maths, surely?"

"He has a hundred times my wealth."

"Even of a 'financial analyst'?"

She smiled, "Even of a financial analyst."

"Do you want to know what I think?" I asked pushing the glass of Coke to one side and leaning towards her.

"I'm not sure I do," she said playfully, regaining some of the Tortola composure.

"You are going to hear it anyway. I think there are two types of 'financial analyst'. I think the first sort look for lucrative future investments for their clients. You know the sort of thing, a poor yield Blue Mountain coffee bean harvest means the price will rise; supply and demand."

Francesca said nothing, choosing to sip warm, flat Coke through a straw.

"You are not one of those."

Another sip.

"And then there is the other kind. I'm afraid my portfolio is not extensive and the markets not my thing..."

"Other than yacht markets."

"Other than yachts, but I assume there must be another type of financial analyst. The sort who is called in when investments have either gone badly wrong or an investor is afraid that their money is in danger."

"Correct," she said placing her glass firmly on the table.

"And you, Francesca Jenkins, or whoever you are today, is that type of financial analyst."

"Correct again."

"So, now I know your name and what you do. What I do not know is why you have been following me and what you, your client and your financial analysis have to do with me."

"If I am right, rather a lot," she said confidently.

"How come?" I asked flatly, sitting back in my chair.

"How about you bring your meeting to a close," she said leaning towards me, "and we open mine? Have you been to Casa Casuarina?"

"The Versace place?"

"Yes."

"Not that I recall."

"Let's go," she said.

....

"Joseph Lamb... Joe Lamb... Joseph Lamb Jnr... You must have heard of him, everyone has heard of him."

"Mr. Stone is not from around here," Francesca reminded the wide-eyed binary magnate, who was sitting awkwardly on an oversized sofa next to me.

"Why make them this size? My feet don't reach the floor when I lean back... or if they do I'm leaning so far back I'm staring at the ceiling. All you can see are my nostrils... look...," he demonstrated. I looked at the weary Francesca. She shrugged and smiled. I thought I had a runaway paymaster in Chum – but this? Before I knew it he was back on his perch looking intently (and at far too close quarters for an Englishman) into my eyes.

"You must have heard of Joe Lamb. He's a philanthropist."

Now I was interested. Philanthropy's a top-grade cover for all kinds of sins.

I stood abruptly, purposefully knocking my host back into the vexing sofa; I stood with my back to Francesca and her client staring at the redundant hearth in this dark oversized room. Why build a room this large before the use of air-conditioning, knowing the windows would have to be slits to keep the searing summer heat out? Privacy? Secrecy? Is there a difference?

"Some believe the world requires more philanthropists," I said to neither of them.

A moment passed as I sensed my host and Francesca deciding who would answer.

Eventually:

"Unless it is just a front," my host said rather slowly.

I turned to face him.

"Do you think it could be?" I asked.

Francesca blanched. Fortunately for her my sarcasm was lost on her latest less than analytical client.

"I had begun to suspect, which is why I hired Miss. Jenkins. She is very good."

I turned tactfully back to the hearth. You owe me, Miss. Jenkins. I will call in the debt.

"You two must have your reasons for suspecting that this 'philanthropist' is up to something. Clearly you suspect it is with your money," I said turning back to face them. "However, before you go on let me remind you both of two things. Firstly, the laws of evidence and legal disclosure in this state mean that even as a foreign national, I can be subpoenaed to testify in court about anything you tell me. Secondly, I have no idea what your 'philanthropist' has to do with me. I have only a matter of a very few days to conclude a tragic, complex and high-profile loss investigation. For the second time tonight I am asking you, Miss. Jenkins, to explain what connection, if any, your work has to do with mine, otherwise, I'm leaving."

Then my host began to speak. I endured more commentaries on various defects of life, beyond sofas, but I let him speak as he wanted. Tired, short of time, patience, and a body count that could go higher and include my own, logically, I should have left. This wasn't a reasoner.

....

A thousand million United States dollars seemed a lot of money to me. If Francesca and her client were correct, the amounts involved and the implications were immense.

....

Marilyn Monroe was seated next to me. She was necking a bottle of Budweiser. I watched the flexing of her Adam's apple with each substantial gulp.

Behind Marilyn a man dressed only in a loincloth sat eating a hamburger, a python wrapped loosely around his neck.

Two tables back, Fred Astaire and Ginger Rogers sat silently over two cups of café con leche. Ginger's make-up had run where she had been crying. I guessed that Fred was terminating the partnership.

Three Latinas in microskirts were smoking and laughing outside. There black men were beside them trying, in vain, to convince them that they were in the music business and the next big thing.

All in all, a regular night for 4a.m. South Beach, Miami, Florida.

In between the shows put on by the local population I was trying to think through the implications of what I had learned from Francesca and her bizarre client. Marilyn stood up and demanded another beer sung in a perfect baritone voice.

What Francesca and Drew had described was a classic Ponzi scheme. I had little interest in finance but I knew about financial scams, that is, after all, my job. Ponzi himself was a charmer and a chancer, his scheme was brilliant in its simplicity. Convince wealthy individuals that you have the ability to make vast returns. It was to be kept a secret; the scheme was only suitable for the wealthy. Inevitably they would invest. Equally inevitably they would tell their friends who would invest too – except there were no investments. The last in paid the returns for the first in, or the first withdrawals. This all worked well during the boom times, but those times were over.

Ginger Rogers started to cry.

Marilyn burped.

Python man fed his snake a morsel of burger.

I sipped my double espresso.

What had Francesca's client to do with my investigation?

The three Latinas entered the café giggling amongst themselves at the expense of the three hapless black boys. They were hugging themselves clearly cold from being outside; they ordered a burger to share between them.

I could not afford passengers I already had an impossibly tight schedule. To be distracted by a man whose own naivety and greed had lead him to his own misfortune hardly seemed to be a priority. The crew of 'AZUL', Natalia Youngs and Banksy had done nothing wrong. They played no part in their deaths or injuries other than to unwittingly get in the wrong way of the wrong people at the wrong time.

My head said that I should ignore Francesca and her client. My gut feeling was the opposite.

"Always gut feeling Lukasz," I heard my mother say. "Always."

46

27 November 2008. Thanksgiving Day Fort Lauderdale, Florida

I arrived at Mario's office an hour before Archer was due. Despite the holiday, Mario would have been at his desk for hours talking with London, massaging egos, dispensing advice at only three hundred dollars an hour. A former Coast Guard officer he stood straight backed beckoning me to come into his office while he soothed advice down the phone line.

I sat in a club chair opposite his desk as he finished the call. From his immaculately ordered desk he had a panoramic view across the canal that runs along the south side of Southeast 15th Street. A Cigarette powerboat was moored at Brownie's dock below, a mechanic working on the engine.

"Yours?" I asked nodding in the direction of the boat as Mario replaced the receiver.

"Not exactly, we arrested it yesterday. He is making sure it doesn't go 'walkies'. How are you Lukasz?"

"Tired... Mario, and this chair is so uncomfortable."

"That's the idea. None of my people stay any longer than they need to. Clients get the comfortable chairs next door. They can stay as long as they like – they pay by the hour."

"Thanks for seeing me today. It's supposed to be a holiday for you."

"No problem. Glad to be of assistance. It's an important case. I don't think anything else has been talked about at Waxy's since she sank. Eventually the unthinkable had to happen. How much has Bud located?"

"Not to be repeated, even to Chum?"

"Scouts honour," he said raising his hand.

"Not much. Bud has found one half of what looks like a critical piece of steel plating."

"As your friend and lawyer, I can tell you half a piece of evidence will buy you time, but not a defence."

"Not this time Mario. I have five days."

"What? Why so short?

"Chum says the owners have set a deadline. They've already drafted suit papers."

"So soon?"

"For what is being claimed as an accident these guys were prepared Mario. Every document I have needed, every person presented on time, and well prepared. I've never known a case like it. We are in an international business. In every case there is always some document or key person missing. Not this one. Everything's produced exactly when required."

We watched the mechanic lower the pneumatic struts of the Cigarette's engine hatch.

"That's not going anywhere," Mario said.

"Rather like my investigation."

Mario looked at his watch.

"You want to tell me about it? You've got time before Mister Archer arrives."

"Sure. Thanks."

"Give me a dollar."

I handed over a bill.

"There, now you've retained me as your counsel. Anything you tell me and any advice I give you is covered by Attorney Client Privilege. Please begin."

Mario started to make notes.

I started from the beginning, the Mills yacht, the ruination of Henry Cole, the promotion of Chum, sweaty Lomas, Francesca, Banksy, the binary tycoon, Joseph Lamb Jnr and Archer.

"Do you know Lamb?" I asked Mario.

"Sure, we're often on opposing sides of sale and purchase deals on superyachts."

"How is he to deal with?"

"My firm has never had a problem with him."

"Never?"

"Not once. If we ask for a document it is always

produced, and quickly. If there is urgency or a deadline he is always helpful and punctual."

"Has he been in big yacht law for long?"

Mario smiled. "Joseph Lamb Jnr invented the law of large yachts in this city. If a buyer or seller can afford him, he is the lawyer most favoured by owners. This city would not be the large yacht fulcrum of the world that it is today without Joseph Lamb Jnr."

"How much does he charge?"

"One thousand bucks an hour."

"An hour? In Florida?"

"An hour. But that's not what makes him exclusive."

Still reeling from Lamb's hourly rate I asked, "What makes him exclusive, Mario?"

"He vets his clients. I don't know him well enough to ask why. He has been in the business so long that perhaps he got caught out with some cash in his Client Trust account that was being 'washed'."

"The large yacht business has always had that problem. Money laundering goes with the trade," I said.

"Right, but he also has a client criterion that is an open secret."

"What is that?"

"If you made your money through drink, drugs, clubs,

arms or tobacco do not apply to become a client of Joseph Lamb Jnr."

"You will be refused?"

"Worse than that," Mario said, laughing. "You are likely to find yourself under investigation by some heavyweight government agent or another. Mr. Lamb Jnr has very powerful friends."

"I was told that philanthropy is a large part of his life."

"Famous for it; Broward General has just opened a new Intensive Care Baby Unit, paid for largely by Lamb. Not the law firm – Lamb personally."

I started to evaluate the biography of Joseph Lamb Jnr when Mario added, "It's strange. Lamb has the reputation of being the most honest, caring, almost puritanical man in South Florida."

"What's strange?"

"You are the second person to have asked about him in two days."

....

Archer arrived, and on time. I left him in reception as I took a call from Lieutenant Rodriguez.

"Good morning, Mr. Stone. How are you sir?" he asked perfunctorily.

"I'm doing well thank you, Lieutenant. How can I help you?"

"Mr. Stone, it has been several days since I last heard from you. You seem a little shy in speaking with me."

"I apologize Lieutenant, I thought when we last spoke our agreement was my employers would initiate and pay for a careful and extensive search of the seabed in private. That is what they have done and the search continues."

"Mr. Stone, your silence has made my superiors nervous. They think you are hiding something..."

"Lieutenant, we are examining a huge expanse of very deep water, littered with shipwrecks. We discussed this before."

Rodriguez cleared his throat before asking, "Are you expecting me to believe that following a week of exhaustive searching by some of the biggest names in the salvage business, and NASA, you have seen nothing of interest? NASA, Mr. Stone. If memory serves, they put man on the moon, probes on Mars. How difficult can this be?"

I had no answer for the Lieutenant other than more bluster.

"It is miles deep Lieutenant."

"Mr. Stone, let me level with you. I understand that you see me as a government official who gets paid to do a job, with no risk. Whether I sit in an office, enforce rules, or just polish the Coast Guard Cutters, I get paid, I go home at night, I go to sleep and I do it all again the next day and so on, until one day I'm awarded a medal and retire with a government pension. My employer will never go out of business. There is no commercial risk to my work. Job security is complete from day one. You on the other hand, I imagine, are only as good as your last investigation, and what an investigation this is. Your client is entering into a forced merger, Lloyds has had to step in and forty people insured by your client, are dead. This is not the time to ignore the United States government, Mr. Stone."

"I..."

"Whatever the reason for your silence, Mr. Stone, I leave it as a private matter between you and your client. However, I am calling to advise you that the patience of the United States Coast Guard in Washington has run out. Through the United States Embassy in London, the United States Coast Guard has served a desist order on your client. You have until midnight tomorrow night to hand over all records, including any images of any sort, captured by the surveillance equipment you have been using. From midnight tomorrow this operation will come under the direct management of the United States Federal Government. Your insurance company will receive an invoice in due course. Do you have any questions, Mr. Stone?"

"Yes, Lieutenant Rodriguez," I said calmly. "Just one."

Having expected an argument, or at least a threat of litigation against the Coast Guard, Rodriguez asked softly, "What is your question, sir?"

"Why are you so interested in Joseph Lamb Jnr?"

....

David Archer did not look as I had expected. He had the red, puffy complexion of a man who drinks too much but it was his diminutive size that surprised me. And his hands – small, with thin, short fingers and immaculate fingernails. I expected a man who builds large ships from steel to be, well, larger.

"Mr. Archer," I said, extending my hand towards him. "I'm Lukasz Stone."

Archer appeared distracted.

"They never get it right."

"Who doesn't, Mr. Archer?" I asked softly afraid he'd been drinking.

"Artists," he said nodding over my right shoulder.

I turned to look at a small print, no more than six inches square. Before I had realized he had moved, Archer's small fingers were pointing to the waterline of the Norfolk Wherry in the painting.

"That boat is sitting on the water, not in the water Mr. Stone. And here's another thing...," he said beckoning me to stand close to him, which I did. No smell of alcohol. "Look at that," he demanded, pointing to the end of the boom. "That line look right to you? Does it?"

I had to agree it did not.

"That line would be taut, rigid with sails that full. You could tie a man up with the slack that 'artist' has left in that."

If I can keep you sober, I think I am going to like you, Mr. Archer, I thought.

Mario had given us his boardroom. Archer was clearly uncomfortable in his surroundings.

"Bit different to a shipyard."

"I imagine so."

"You've been in enough shipyards Mr. Stone, you know so."

"Please call me Lukasz."

"They had us sit on beams in the yard, and even if we went to the office it was age-old plastic chairs, white at the seams."

"You have an eye for detail, Mr. Archer."

Archer fixed his sharp eye in my direction.

"Have to, Mr. Stone… Lukasz. When I'm designing, let alone building I'm thinking of the lives depending upon me, depending on me to get it right. There's no second chance at sea."

None at all for the crew of 'AZUL' I thought.

"Would you like coffee?"

"No thanks. Caffeine is bad for the liver."

Perhaps he wasn't quite the drinker he was rumoured to be?

"I prefer to enjoy damaging my liver, as no doubt you've heard."

I let the comment pass.

"Thank you for taking the time to meet with me."

"She's the only one I ever lost, you know."

"Sorry?"

"'AZUL'... she's the only one I… designed I ever lost. And I built her too."

This is a decent man, I thought.

"Mr. Archer… David... has anyone suggested to you that the loss of 'AZUL' may have been your fault? Your design... your build?"

Archer fixed his gaze on the wall.

"Let me tell you this can be a cruel city, Mr. Stone," he said bitterly. "I have heard every rumour going. People I thought of as friends... long-standing... friends… you know?"

"I do."

"I'm sure that man Johnson has been doing me no favours."

"Do you know captain Johnson well?"

Archer sniffed and straightened himself in his chair.

"Well enough. I build ships to Brunel standards. I'd still rivet them if I could. What would Johnson know of that?" he replied.

I paused and considered his answer.

"How did you get involved with 'AZUL'?"

"I got a phone call," he said proudly. "Quite unexpectedly from a friend in a shipyard in Germany, Hamburg to be exact. I hadn't spoken to him for years, in fact I think our previous conversation might have been an argument... possibly worse. I don't remember exactly."

"Who was your friend?"

"He's called Bill Henderson."

"What did he ask you?"

"He said that he had been approached by a wealthy investor who was looking to build the largest yacht in the world. I thought he was joking."

"Why?"

"I was expecting a punchline… or insult."

"Did he insult you?"

"No."

"Clearly it wasn't a joke."

Archer stretched his back.

"Anything but."

"David, remind me, what size was the largest yacht at the time?"

"At the time, the largest was about 120 metres in length, although not necessarily in volume."

"And how large did this 'investor' want to go?"

"He said 200 metres."

"Quite a jump."

"Not for a naval architect used to building ships. The monstrous length made it easier to design. I'm sure he knew, or guessed, that others had yachts planned or under build at around the 175 – 180 metre mark. At these sizes these aren't yachts they are ships. I build ships."

"But the cost?"

"When you get to that size what difference in cost does ten or twenty metres make?"

"Say fifty million."

"Exactly. Nothing, is it?"

"So why call you?"

"The investor had asked my friend for a recommendation for a naval architect who could also not only design but supervise the build. He recommended me."

"Didn't he want the job?"

"He said he was leaving Hamburg for a new build in Viareggio and wouldn't be free for three years."

"Did you believe him?"

"I believed he was involved with something in Viareggio, more likely a woman than a yacht. Besides, they couldn't build something that size in Italy. It would have to be Germany. He couldn't run both projects. He's into sail boats anyway."

"What was the specification for 'AZUL'?"

"I remember it was remarkably detailed. Most of these yacht builds start with little more than a few ideas. The owner had spent a great deal of time, probably years from what I saw, deciding exactly what he wanted. It was as if he did not want to be bothered with it during the build. He wanted me to take care of everything, which was fine by me."

"Had you encountered that before?"

"No. Far Eastern clients place the order today and expect the boat tomorrow. This owner placed the order and all but walked away."

"Extraordinary."

"Unique. Depressing in a way. Have you read the build file?"

"Yes."

"Apart from the size of the leviathan, what impressed you the most?"

"The small number of c.o.s. I think there were no more than fifty."

"Forty-eight."

"Unheard of in a new build even a third of the size of 'AZUL'. The man knew what he wanted."

"Yes, but..."

Archer hesitated, reluctant to continue.

"David, you have come here voluntarily. You do not have to say anything, or tell me any more than you want to."

"It's just... well... I don't know your background but you clearly have an eye for yachts and I suspect a passion."

I smiled, "If they stopped paying me I would still turn up for work."

Archer smiled. "When I was in the shipyards they did stop paying me and yes, I still turned up. They paid me in beer at the end of each day. Probably not such a good thing on reflection..."

"You were saying about the change orders... the owner's wishes."

"Oh, yes. There were less than fifty change orders in four years, and none of them of any more significance than a bolt or two. You know how many bolts there are in a two hundred metre ship Lukasz?"

"No, but you do. As the architect and builder the lack of change orders must have made your job easier?"

"It did, but it didn't feel right."

"How do you mean?"

"It felt as if the whole ship had been planned not as a yacht but as a commodity. Even the c.o.s that did arrive, just papered the file. The file grew as if it was going to be read and marked for realism. People spending that sort of money want to be involved. They want to dream and see the dream when they wake up. Do you know? They want to see their money creating ideas they have lived with for years. They have passion. Aye, arrogance too, but mostly wide-eyed passion. This man? Nothing."

"For such a groundbreaking yacht, the plans don't show anything new or radical."

"The owner wanted a classically styled yacht. No bones to me, that's the designers brief. No flairs, no axe or dreadnought bow, no fancy colours just plain, classic, lines."

"Were you required to put anything into the build that struck you as at odds with that?"

"Not really. She had five decks. The fourth deck up was distinctly the owner's – private access, private swimming pools, owner suite, that sort of thing; the usual. Apart from the dimensions, nothing unusual. Much of her was soundproofed of course."

"Of course," I said remembering the space Johnston refused to talk about.

"Johnson told me about a secret soundproofed space. What was that?"

"That was an obsession that's what that was!" Archer said laughing. "At least once a week, every week I was asked about that space; 'Room X'. Is it soundproofed? Yes. Are you sure? Yes. Are you certain? Yes. Are you totally certain? Yes, yes, yes."

"Anything else that was radical?"

"There's nothing radical about paranoia. The only radical thing was that she was designed to operate with a crew of only forty. That is a very small number for a ship of that size. But then she was never going to be used for charter and had limited guest accommodation. It was an advanced idea at the time for each crew member to have their own cabin, but given the low crew numbers and vast size of number one deck, not that surprising."

"How was the project managed?"

"I rarely spoke with the Boss. Most of my dealings were with an accountant."

"Where was he based?"

"In the islands somewhere, Tortola I think."

"Most of them are."

"Money arrived in a German bank account and I spent it. I accounted for every euro. Money was never an issue – never short, never late."

I decided to gamble.

"How did you get on with the Boss?"

"He was the easiest owner I had ever; ship or yacht."

"Really?"

"Oh, aye."

"How come?"

"I only had to meet him once."

"Could you identify him?"

Archer paused, laughed, and said, "Shall we go and look at that Norfolk Wherry again?"

I laughed too.

"Seriously. Sure I could recognise him... but he had me sign some paperwork on day one."

"A confidentiality agreement."

"Aye, one of those."

....

"Did Lieutenant Rodriguez hand over his dollar?"

"The United States Coast Guard has an army of lawyers Lukasz. They don't need me," Mario replied. "How'd you know the other enquirer was him?"

"How else would he have known I was here?"

We were standing in the doorway of Mario's office.

"Want to come and see my Cigarette boat?"

"Sure."

We took the elevator to the ground floor in silence. As we approached the Cigarette a small lizard scampered away as we clumped along the wooden dock.

"I need you to understand something, Lukasz – me-to-you. When I told you that Lamb has friends in high places I should have been more specific."

"Go on."

"Lamb is president of the Florida Bar Association. He has held the post three times. He's head not only of the Ethics

Committee, but personally chairs each hearing of lawyers accused of unethical behaviour. He is on more charitable committees in this city than you have time for me to name. He's friends with half of the commissioners of Broward County, but more than all of that his closest friend..." Mario paused.

"Is...?"

"...is the Governor of the State of Florida."

"Brother of the President of the United States," I murmured.

The words of Henry Coles following my first ever death threat many years before came to mind. "Their power rarely extends beyond their own shores, Lukasz."

I was standing on their shore.

47

Miami, Florida

I called Bud.

"Don't worry about it, Lukasz. We've been expecting it for a couple of days. Rodriguez arrived here shortly after he had spoken to you. He's a worried man. I think he will be demoted for not keeping an eye on us. Shame, he's a good guy."

"Where did the order come from?"

"High level D.C. that's all he said."

"They are taking over at midnight tomorrow?"

"Yep. We lost the images of that steel plate. Can't remember where we put them."

"Thanks. Please send copies to my private e-mail account."

"Sure. Hang on a minute, Lukasz." I could hear Spider's voice in the background. "I'm going to put you on speaker Mr. Spider wants to tell you something."

There was a click followed by, "Hey Lukasz, we've got some news from the seabed. We've found the other part of that steel plate."

"You are certain?" I asked, immediately regretting it. "Forget that question. It's Spider, I know how long he's been in the business."

"Tell Chum he owes Mr. Spider another very large bottle of finest rum," Bud said.

....

Ping. A text.

"Call me in accounts. R."

I obeyed.

"Chum took me to a hearing at Lloyd's. I've just got back. He said it was to take notes, but the real reason was for me to report back to you. They aren't happy, Lukasz, not happy at all."

"What happened?"

"The chairwoman was OK but I think she is outnumbered. The man with the goatee – he hates you. He accused you of using the investigation to further your career."

"What career?"

"He criticized virtually every page of the transcript and then demanded Chum have the EUO destroyed."

"Rather too late for that the DPA has signed it. It's evidence; it's testimony; it's staying on the file."

"Lukasz! You are irritating some very powerful people."

"It goes with the job."

"Which is exactly that – just a job. In less than a week you have alienated the US Coast Guard, probably the United States government and now some of the most powerful and rising stars at Lloyd's. Let's not even mention your strained relationship with your client." She paused and we both wanted to hear if she would say what she was thinking.

"And then there was Banksy."

48

Fort Lauderdale, Florida

In the departure lounge of Fort Lauderdale International Airport waiting for my flight back to Key West my phone rang. The caller was identified on the screen as Mr. Youngs. I took a deep breath.

"Good morning Mr. Youngs," I said scanning the gate area looking for a private area to talk with him.

"Hi Lukasz, how are you?" His voice was flat.

"I'm fine thanks. How is Natalia?"

"That's why I'm calling. I should have called you yesterday. Her mother and I have been discussing her wishes."

I had found a space between the glass walls and a pillar.

I said the only sincere thing that could be said, "Mr. Youngs, I am so sorry."

He laughed lightly.

"No Lukasz, nothing like that. We don't really have a common language, do we? Natalia is conscious and recovering slowly. She is still at the hospital and will be there for some time yet."

"Mr. Youngs, I'm so relieved."

"I know you are. You insurance guys get a bad press but you have always been courteous to us."

There you are, Rachel – I haven't irritated everyone. The Youngs like me.

"Mr. Youngs, you mentioned Natalia's 'wishes'."

"I will be honest with you Lukasz. We tried to keep the sinking of the yacht from Natalia. Many of those on board were friends she had known from the boats for years. Two were at college with her. There are no televisions in ICU so we thought we would have time to tell her gently later. Regrettably, text messaging, being what it is..."

"Even in the ICU?"

"Can't live without text messaging, these girls. Of course the next day when we visited her there was quite a scene. She wanted to know what we knew and so we had no option but to tell her what had happened. Naturally that led to you."

"Is she prepared to meet me?" I asked gently.

"Lukasz, there is something I need to tell you. A few days ago we received an anonymous letter, postmarked Fort Lauderdale. In fact to describe it as a letter is inaccurate. It was a clipping from an English newspaper, an article on the murder of a Mr. Banks. Enclosed with the clipping was a photograph, not from a newspaper, but taken presumably by whoever sent the clipping."

"What does it show?"

"It shows you standing by the graveside talking with a tall, well-dressed gentleman. I do not know who he is, but by your posture I would say you know him well. Can we assume that the late Mr. Banks was a friend of yours?"

"Yes, he was."

"And can we also assume that the yacht Mr. Banks' body was found on had some connection with your client and an investigation being carried out by you?"

There are rule books in my office regarding confidentiality – I really must read them.

"Yes, Mr. Youngs, Banksy, Mr. Banks, and I had recovered a yacht matching the description of a yacht alleged by its owner to have been stolen. The yacht was located and recovered in England almost to the minute that 'AZUL' sank."

"Was sunk, Lukasz?"

"I am sorry, Mr. Youngs, I really cannot talk about that."

"But you are prepared to let my daughter talk about it?"

I started to formulate an answer but stopped. Was I just using Natalia and her honourable parents?

"Natalia is our only child, Lukasz," he continued. "If Natalia's accident, the sinking and the murder of your friend are linked, then Natalia is the only survivor."

"I am not going to try and persuade you or Natalia to meet with me that has to be a decision for you and your family."

"And what a decision? If these tragedies are linked then someone wants Natalia dead. Whether you meet with her or not, as soon as she leaves the hospital she is in danger again. As we see it, she has no option but to meet with you and hope she can help you prove a case against whoever is behind this – before it's too late. How long do you have?"

"May I see her later today? I have five days left."

"I will check with the hospital and call you back."

....

Back aboard the salvage ship Bud showed me the new piece of steel.

Bud, T and I crowded around the screen. I asked, "Can you put the picture of the first piece side by side with this?"

"Sure."

"When you merge them, it's a perfect match," explained Spider steps ahead of me.

"We work with a guy at NASA who has experience in explosives. We have sent the images to him for analysis," said one of the two NASA operators behind us.

With two clicks of the mouse, Bud had the two pieces of steel aligned. The fracture pattern showed a sharp, what would have been vertical, fracture where the plate had come away from the frame. Horizontally there was very little left of the plate. It had been serrated by the explosion.

"Someone really knew what they were doing," I said, to no one in particular.

....

Report writing is the only part of the job I could really live without. The travel, the long hours, long days, lack of sleep and meetings with the shiftiest people on the planet seem to have no lasting effect. I'm in good health and all my vital signs are where they should be. Choose a job you love and you'll never have to work again – Confucius. But report writing could easily be the death of me. It was with relief that my 'AZUL' report (all four sentences of it) was interrupted by a phone call. The screen told me that it was from a phone at the office, although I did not recognize the extension number.

It was Rachel. "Lukasz, if you're ever asked why you were called today, it was a query with your expenses."

"Accounts lines aren't recorded?"

"Are your expenses that sensitive?"

"No."

"Exactly. You have two messages. Firstly, Chum is now the speaking clock. I am to tell you, that as of 9a.m. today, you have five days to say pay, otherwise Lloyd's is taking over."

"What's in his diary for today?"

"He's stopped using it."

"Let's assume that he will be speaking with, if not meeting, his friends today. He has nothing new to leak. Don't go out of your way to see him, but next time he struts past your desk, tell him you've spoken to me. I am working on my report."

"Are you working on your report?"

"Barely, Chum knows how much I hate report writing and will come to the correct, incorrect, answer that to draft a report I must have reached a conclusion."

"Then he doesn't know you at all."

"The second message?"

"Henry Coles. He was specific that you not call him back."

"So what's the message?"

"He wants you to meet as soon as you return to the UK. I will make the arrangements."

....

Naples, Florida

Someone had placed a three metre Christmas tree in the hospital foyer since my last visit. It was adjacent to the burger place, and over decorated, with more silver baubles to port than starboard. It had dropped a few needles already onto the outstretched arm of the gaudy plastic figure reclining on a bench. A medic in a green two-piece was sitting on the bench eating a large burger evidently, with little enjoyment.

I was signed in, my photograph taken and passport checked. I hoped the security guards were as vigilant for all of Natalia's visitors.

I took the elevator with a porter and an elderly lady in a wheelchair. Christmas carols were being played through invisible speakers in the ceiling. We travelled in silence. The porter and his patient exited at the fifth floor. I carried on to the Intensive Care Unit on the eighth.

I was shown into a different room to the one I had visited previously by a petite Latina with a wary demeanour. I was relieved to see far less machinery in Natalia's new room. Mr. Youngs was sitting at the side of Natalia's bed stroking her hand. She appeared to be asleep.

"No more than half an hour Mr. Stone," the nurse told me. "Agreed?"

"Agreed."

As she turned to leave Mr. Youngs saw me and stood to shake my hand.

"Lukasz, good to see you. How are you?" he whispered.

"Good thanks. How is she?" I asked, nodding towards Natalia.

"She is holding her own," he said proudly. "The medics are surprised by her progress. She has a strong spirit."

"Is now a convenient time?" I asked.

"As good as any. She has been asleep for an hour or so, so let's see if she is alright to talk."

I watched as Mr. Youngs sat back down with his daughter, held her hand and gently said her name. I felt uncomfortable; then guilty for putting these people through this.

I remembered the promise I had made to the dead. As sick as Natalia was, at least she was alive.

As Natalia started to wake I saw a pair of brilliant blue eyes start to focus upon me. She attempted a smile.

"Natalia, this is Lukasz Stone. He is from London."

"A Brit," she said, the smile breaking through her drowsiness.

"A Brit," I agreed returning her smile. "Thank you for agreeing to see me."

"They were my friends," she said the smile disappearing.

"I will leave you two alone," Mr. Youngs said. He put a hand on my shoulder as I sat in the chair next to Natalia's bed. "No more than half an hour Lukasz. I will see you shortly."

Mr. Youngs left the room, gently shutting the door behind him.

"What do you want to know Lukasz?" Natalia asked mischievously, her blue eyes set upon me.

"Are you sure you are alright to talk?"

"Positive. Fire away."

"How did you get your job on 'AZUL'?"

"She was my third boat. I had worked on a sixty metre Feadship then an eighty metre Amels. We cruised the Med during the summer and the Caribbean in the winter. We were based at English Harbour in Antigua. Do you know it?"

"Yes."

“There was an intermittent fault with the crane they used on the eighty metre to lower the tender. It would sometimes stick halfway down leaving the thing hanging there. Before I got into yachts I was a gymnast. Not that you would think it now,” she said looking around the room.

“Go on.”

“We found that if someone pulled slightly on the tender when it stuck it would restart the motor, but that involved climbing up the almost vertical garage door. I was the only one of the crew who could do it. Anyway one afternoon I was performing my stunt…” she shifted in her bed and winced.

“You OK?”

“Yep. So I was performing my stunt and a man came up to me and asked if I would like a job on a larger yacht.”

“What did you say?”

“I said, “Sir, if this looks easy then I’m doing it wrong. Sure I’m interested.””

I smiled.

“It didn’t put him off. He balanced the bag he was carrying on an electricity post and waited for me to finish. Then he asked me again.”

“Who was he?”

“Said his name was Johnson. Not long on charm.”

“I’ve met him.”

"Lukasz, can you pour me a glass of water please? The drugs make me so dry."

I poured her a glass from the plastic carafe on the side table.

"So what was the job?" I asked handing her the glass.

She struggled to sit up. "I am so dented," she said. "It was position of junior stewardess aboard a large yacht. I remember nodding at the eighty metre and reminded him I already had a junior stewardess job on a large yacht."

"And he charmed you with?"

"He said, "That is not a large yacht." So I thanked him for his time. He immediately replied in that way of his, "Miss, our yacht is the largest in the world. Have you heard of project 'AZUL'?"

"What did you say?"

"I didn't 'say' anything, I sort of squealed, "What? 'AZUL'?" He said that it was, then removed his bag from the electricity post and handed me an employment contract. I would like to say that I read it but it was just a swirl of words. Me? Little me on the world's largest yacht? I signed on the dotted line then walked back onto the Amels and quit; simple as that."

I was stunned by her naiveté.

"Did Johnson say anything else?"

"Only that they would not need my acrobatic skills, I think he thought it was funny."

“Figures. So you joined ‘AZUL’? What did you think of her?”

“Did you know that the owner was not even at the launch? All that time and money and he’s a no-show – very odd. I was on the shakedown cruise from Hamburg and immediately felt uncomfortable. I had only crewed two boats before, but the boat was so impersonal it was more like a ferry than a yacht.”

I glanced at my watch.

“You must have met the owner?”

“I don’t think I did. The ownership was secret. I assumed the captain knew who the Boss was. Johnson certainly did. We had very few visitors, and only a few cruises.”

“What happened with the Chief Engineer?”

She groaned.

“Are you asking as insurance or as an investigator?”

“There is no policy coverage for your unfair dismissal claim so just as an investigator.”

“He seemed a nice enough guy. I had seen him in Waxy O’Connor’s from time to time and around the Quarterdeck. He always seemed to end up sitting or standing next to me. I was polite but never encouraged him.”

“Are you sure?”

“Positive.” Her brilliant eyes glared at me.

"OK. So what happened?"

"Oh, Lukasz it was terrible," she said weakly. "He just got more and more brash. It was embarrassing. All the other stew's saw it. I spoke to the Chief Stew. She tried to speak with him but it made no difference. It came to a head one evening when I just lost it and screamed at him…"

I waited for her to continue.

"I just screamed at him to leave me alone."

"What happened next?"

"He complained to the captain and I was let go. The best job in the world for me, ruined by a man who couldn't accept "No"."

"Are you well enough to speak for just a few minutes more? I promised your father and the scary nurse it would only be thirty minutes."

She laughed. "She is quite fierce but she means well. I'm fine. Please, go on."

"Clearly the boat wasn't being used very much. Did you recognize anyone who came on board regularly other than the crew and Johnson?"

"No."

"No one?"

She lay back down and I could see she needed to sleep again. As her eyes started to close she said, "There were two men. One quiet, slick, handsome; I wouldn't have minded his attention. The other? The other… his smile was all wrong," she said drifting into sleep.

....

I saw the black Chevy Blazer as soon as I left the hospital. The shining rims, black privacy glass, the sheer size of the thing. During my meeting at Casa Casuarina I had realized that I had not been followed solely by the Binary team. Their surveillance had been limited. They hadn't sent the green Taurus to the Rusty Pelican. Only Francesca was at 'Mangos'. I had concluded that the clumsy surveillance was hers, and it ended at Casa. That just left Lamb. If this was intimidation, it was, today, working.

I turned off the main highway into the nearly empty parking lot of a Home Depot. The Blazer followed me. I parked and watched the Blazer – nothing. The privacy glass shielded the occupant, or occupants from sight. Thirty seconds, forty, then a minute. Nothing.

"Lukasz, you are irritating some very powerful people." I heard Rachel's voice in my head.

I waited another minute, and then decided to dial 911. I regularly work with the emergency services but had never called upon them to assist me before. The female dispatcher took an immediate dislike to me.

"How may I assist you, sir?" she asked frostily.

How to explain?

"I am being followed and feel threatened."

"Who are you being followed by, sir?"

"I don't know."

"Are they on foot or in a vehicle?"

"A vehicle."

"License plate?"

"I cannot read it. They are too far away."

"Would you mind moving a little closer to the vehicle, sir?"

"I would very much mind moving closer to the vehicle."

"Please do not adopt that tone with me, sir. I am only doing my job."

I took a deep breath. Still no movement from the Chevy.

"I am sorry. This is a rather stressful situation."

"What sort of vehicle is it, sir?" she asked, clearly believing she had won a victory over the British.

"It is a black Chevy Blazer, silver rims, tints... the tint is so dark you can't see through it."

I could hear her typing.

"Nope."

"Nope, what?"

"No vehicles of that description reported stolen today."

I had lost count of the number of meetings, flights, miles driven and hours of sleep missed in the last two weeks. I remember feeling instant exhaustion.

"Ma'am, I am not calling to report a stolen vehicle. I am calling to ask for assistance. I have good reason to believe that my safety is being threatened. I will explain everything to the officers when they arrive. Would you please send someone to help me."

I cannot recall what she said. I recall seeing the brake lights. Then came the reversing lights... then the sound of shredded metal, plastic and glass – impact.

49

28 November 2008
Mid-Atlantic Ocean

I woke up with a jolt at 39,000 feet, just east of the Azores. At least I think that's where I was. The turning aircraft symbol on the screen in front of me was so large it filled most of the Atlantic Ocean. I leaned forward reading the names of obscure cities – anything to take my mind off the pain. And the humiliation.

And so it was here that I realized what should happen next. I should shower and breakfast at Heathrow. I should take the car provided by the airline to the Coles office. I was in no fit state to drive my own. I should face the wrath of Rachel at around 0800, or, worse still, her playing nurse. I should participate and cooperate in Chum's inquisition. I should be open about my investigation into 'AZUL'. I should tell him about Mills. I should tell him about the final forty-eight hours in America. Later on I should be hauled before the Twelfth Floor Grand Jury at Lloyd's. All of these things should happen.

I raised a hand to my left cheek, cut by some part of the dashboard of the wrecked car. I felt tired and nauseous. My heart rate felt high, as my body tried to repair itself. Most of all I felt vulnerable and very, very small. Probably the onset of shock, but I was vulnerable and very, very small.

As I laid back into my flying bed, in the gloom, I started to list my known enemies. In no particular order – Chum, Jorge Rodriguez, the United States government, the owner of

'AZUL', probably the Lloyd's Grand Jury and Mills. There were undoubtedly other foes I had yet to meet.

I then listed my team: table-dancing Rachel, an alcoholic naval architect, an irritating failure analyst and a grumpy London engineer who required cheap but plentiful bribes of lasagne to keep him working. Not a particularly formidable army with which to wage a war. Supposing I survived the day (which seemed unlikely) I should meet with Harry Randall and Hargreaves in Marseilles tomorrow.

I should make a big fuss of Rachel today.

All of these things should have happened.

And so it was with a sense of detached pleasure that at Heathrow I watched my feet walk from the arrivals exit towards the lift. I watched my right hand reach up for the up call button. I smiled despite my cuts and bruises. Outside I saw my feet stride towards the ticket sales desk with more energy than I felt I had. I heard my voice, confident, edgy, purchase a ticket.

I was alive. Others had not been so lucky. How did I know I was alive? Because I was finally starting to get angry. Very angry.

....

"He's not following the plan," Alexander said.

We can see that for ourselves, can't we? Got to say Stone looks quite badly damaged.

"You should have let me finish him off."

“No!” I said sharply. “We are enjoying this.”

We are aren’t we?

“Tail him. Closely… but he lives.”

I feel alive, don’t you partner?

Thank you Lukas Stone.

……………………………

At the end of the jet bridge I picked up a complimentary newspaper. My body was aching for more sleep but I knew it would have to wait. Besides I wanted something to read while the other passengers boarded staring at the dented man in business class.

I had not turned my phone on since landing. I wondered about messaging Rachel and decided I should.

“Hi, won’t be in today. Dr. says rest.”

I was certain that is what a doctor would have said.

‘AZUL’ was nowhere to be found in the first ten pages of the newspaper. In a simple paragraph on page eleven I read:

“ST.JOHN’S, ANTIGUA, THURSDAY. The Coastguard reported today that a 50 foot charter yacht four days overdue from Antigua was located adrift off St. Kitts and Nevis. One crew member aboard found dead below decks. No further details given.”

I didn't think much about the story. Probably another drugs or human trafficking run gone wrong; I had investigated two or three. The plan was simple but effective. The gang followed a formula until we caught them off Cuba. The U.S. Coast Guard liked me in those days. The gang would target a small yacht charter business out of season. They would wait until a poorly paid local was manning the office then charter one of the larger yachts for three weeks. He would ask for a driving license. They'd live in London – no one drives in London. Passport? They would hand over a fake. Security deposit? Cash. The lad knows he is supposed to only take credit cards, but it's a big earner for the time of the year, and besides the boss is down island, out of contact, with his other wife. He takes the cash. Off goes the yacht for twenty-one days. It's breezy – you can sail a long way in three weeks. The yacht never returned; scuttled once it had served its purpose.

I felt my phone vibrate. Looking at the screen I saw it was a text from Rachel.

"We are going to have words, so make sure you get plenty of rest. Too-Bright from Tortola called. She needs to speak with you; Lomas is dead."

As the safety announcement commenced, I folded up the newspaper and stuffed it into the pocket in front of me. I looked out of the window beside the controls. The rain was turning to sleet. The air bridge started to move jerkily away from the aircraft. I could see the operator through a plastic window. He stared at me, stopped the machine and raised his right hand. He raised his thumb, and then stretched out two fingers, forming the shape of a pistol. Without expression he flicked his fingers as if shooting and mouthed the word 'bang'.

"Lastly ladies and gentlemen, we wish you a safe and pleasant flight."

50

Marseilles airport, France

I located a payphone in a quiet alcove. Dialling Mr. Youngs' number I turned to face the airport concourse. I assumed I was being watched again, although I drew some satisfaction from the knowledge my nemesis must have been surprised at Heathrow. Florida is six hours behind France so it was a very early call, but the conversation could not wait. Mr. Youngs answered on the third ring.

"Good morning Dan, I'm sorry to call so early. It's Lukasz Stone."

"Good morning Lukasz, it's no problem at all. We were just talking about you. How are you today?"

"Bruised but alive."

"I guess the police got pretty heavy with you at the hospital."

"How is Natalia?" I asked changing the subject.

"Still at the hospital."

"You need to keep her there. There has been another fatality with an 'AZUL' connection."

"Not another one!"

I heard Mrs. Youngs asking what was wrong. "It's Lukasz, there's been another death."

"Who this time?" he asked me.

"One of theirs, an owner's man. I met him in Tortola. He produced a crew manifest with Natalia's name on it. They failed to kill her so they murdered him instead."

"Will these people stop at nothing?"

"It appears not. Mr. Youngs my investigation and the insurance payout has a maximum of five days to run. I cannot stress strongly enough, you must try and keep Natalia at the hospital for as long as possible."

"Should we tell the police?"

"That's the last thing you should do. Whoever is behind this has hefty connections. If you can afford it, some form of private security for Natalia may help."

"Thank you for telling us Lukasz."

"One last thing Mr. Youngs, I know it's against your nature but should you or Natalia be contacted by 'AZUL' people go along with whatever they want you to do. Lie if you have to. They know we have met so don't deny it."

"We couldn't lie."

"Mr. Youngs this is life or death. Looking around you, you must see more of the latter than the former. Do whatever's necessary."

Mr. Youngs was silent.

"You and your family have been more than helpful.

I have everything I need from you and more. No heroics, please," I added.

"OK," he sighed.

"Please send Natalia my regards."

"I will. Be careful."

That old phrase again. The time for caution, if ever there was one, was long gone.

....

I was shown into Hargreaves' laboratory by a starched, trim woman of no less than a metre and a half in height. I felt the temperature drop. Rob was behind his desk, mouse in hand, lecturing Harry Randall opposite him. Randall's expression is best described as murderous. Randall fixed his gaze on me – it would take more lasagnes, more chips, even more Rachel to settle this one. Randall stood and walked towards me.

"Doctor Hargreaves has been enthralling me with a lecture on the facets of 15mm steel and the torsional load on a transverse steel frame," he hissed.

"I thought you knew all of that?"

"So did I. I've only devoted thirty-five years to building with it, sailing with it and now am going to stick some right up the good Doctor's…"

"Rachel says "hello"."

Randall paused, then, thankfully, laughed.

"She is lovely, if only…"

"I know. If only you were twenty years younger."

"I wasn't going to say that. If only I was another man."

I let that pass and headed towards the inevitable.

"Rob, how are you?"

Doctor Hargreaves stood to shake my hand without lifting his eyes from the screen. As a result his hand waved around in mid-air until mine docked with his.

"Good Lukasz… you're early… that's it… good," he said to his screen.

Harry and I took the two chairs in front of Hargreaves' desk at right angles to each other.

Assuming Hargreaves was engrossed, I asked Randall, "So what have we learned?"

"Some things. Some useful; some not," said Hargreaves.

Randall folded his arms.

"I'm putting my rates up. Did I tell you?" Harry said.

"No, from when?"

"Last Thursday," he said nodding again towards Hargreaves.

"Rob, I know you are a perfectionist, but as I think I

mentioned, time is short. Can you tell me, succinctly, what your conclusions are?" I asked.

Doctor Hargreaves turned his head away from his screen, reluctantly, but still had one of his eyes on it. Randall reached behind the screen and removed the power cable.

"The patient is speaking, Doctor."

Hargreaves moved as if to admonish Randall, and then thought better of it.

"Let me start by recapitulating the known assumptions. One is aware that time is restricted, however, to make calculations we must have assumptions."

Randall had had two days of this.

"Go on. Speed up," Randall spat.

"The colonials have, with the use of their, Remotely Operated Vehicle incorporating an optic device, identified two pieces of steel which, I am instructed to assume, are from the hull of the motor yacht 'AZUL'. I am further instructed to assume that 'AZUL' was built exactly to the design and drawings provided to me."

There are few things more painful than talking with Chum. This was one of them.

"Lastly, I am instructed to assume that the pieces of steel were located between Frame 73 and Bulkhead 17, on the port side."

"Do you agree with all of those assumptions, Harry?" I

asked, to his pleasure and Hargreaves' annoyance.

"I do and as instructed I transposed the frame and bulkhead plan onto the general arrangement plan…"

"Which is of no relevance to me," Hargreaves said.

"But it is to me," I said firmly, silencing him. "What have we got Harry?"

"From the top deck down I found the forward end of the Jacuzzi and the forward end of the sky lounge. Below it the main salon, and below that – spanning above and below the waterline, crew cabin number four."

I pretended this information was a surprise.

"Do you know whose cabin that was?" Randall asked.

"One of the stewardesses, I think. I will have to check," I lied. To suggest to either Randall or Hargreaves that they had confirmed a suspicion would compromise their future work.

"So Rob, if we take all of the assumptions I gave you, and the location of the explosion, what can you tell me about the explosive force required to sink 'AZUL'?"

"If Mister Randall would be so kind as to plug me back in, I will show you."

…………………………

Following the meeting with Randall and Hargreaves I called Too-Bright.

"Hello Mr. Stone."

She sounded defeated; scared.

"Good morning. I understand you wish to speak with me."

"Yes. It's about Mr. Lomas."

"He's dead, I heard," I said a little coolly. I wanted to add, "He was one of yours. Little foolish to lose him," but thought better of it.

"Are you returning to the islands any time soon?"

"I had no plans to. As you probably know I had an accident arranged for me in Florida."

"I didn't know. I am sorry," she said tearfully.

I believed her. I waited.

"Mr. Stone, it is a peril of my profession that one is sometimes privy to information that one would rather not know. We are trained for this. However sometimes it is just too much… too much." Her voice was breaking.

"I understand," I said softly.

"I think… I think Mr. Stone that you have seen glimpses of what you are dealing with here. You have seen some of the evil, but not all."

"Does anyone within the 'AZUL' camp know you feel this way?"

"No, not one. I can act."

"Why are you speaking to me now? You know I'm on a tight schedule imposed by your office."

"I was not supposed to find out about Lomas. My boss was at one time a great legal brain. He now lives by reputation. He is sloppy."

"Can you get to St. Martin for tomorrow evening?"

"Yes."

"Meet me at the Boudreau Restaurant, Baie de Marigot at eight please."

I messaged Rachel.

"Doctor says more rest needed. Tell Chum not to panic. I'll be back Monday. Hope you're OK."

Randall and Hargreaves had both asked me to dinner. Sensing I would spend the evening keeping my two experts from each other's throats, I went back to my hotel, ordered room service, showered and went to bed. Rest at last. Not peace.

51

Ruskin, Florida

There are no steel mills in Ruskin.

There are no watermills in Ruskin.

There are no cotton mills in Ruskin.

There are no windmills in Ruskin.

There are no Mills in Ruskin.

Not anymore.

52

29 November 2008
St. Martin, French West Indies, Caribbean Sea

I arrived at the Boudreau an hour early. Sipping a soda I looked out across the bay of moored boats and started to think again of my investigation. An investigation with a maximum of four days of life left in it – perhaps a greater number of days than remained in my life? I had no yacht. That is always unhelpful from an evidentiary standpoint. I had two pieces of neighbouring shredded steel that in the view of my experts were adjacent to the critical bulkhead. Not only were they adjacent to a key bulkhead but, my experts would testify, that the two pieces showed an explosion from within the yacht, not some kind of design, build or material failure. Not a much favoured limpet mine under the hull.

So, 'AZUL' was blown up. It was against such things that the owner bought his insurance policy. Pay the man, Chum.

So what of motive? Firstly, I did not know for certain whom the owner was. Lamb seemed most likely but penetrating the BVI company registry and in less than a four days? It was never going to happen.

I started to hypothesize. Assume the owner is Lamb. I watched a returning charter yacht navigate by touch back into her berth. Lamb; who was Lamb? Publicly a prominent philanthropist, moralist and lawyer, politically connected at the highest level. But why blow up the 'AZUL'? On the flight from Marseilles I had read through the accounts file. From what I could see 'AZUL' was insured, (for what Lamb, or whoever the owner was), for only a few hundred million more than he had paid for her. Some incentive, I reasoned, but a lot of trouble to go to when weighed against the risk of getting caught. Francesca had raised well-reasoned questions about how Lamb's investment scheme worked. I had promised to call Francesca if I discovered anything dirty. Everything was clean.

Too clean.

I pressed against the back of my chair.

What did I have? A sunken boat, an insured accident and no plausible motive for fraud – not much for nearly ten days work. Wouldn't it just be easier, safer, to concede and pay the man, before anyone else got hurt? What of the thirty-nine dead crew members, Natalia, Banksy, Lomas and Coles? I had made promises to them all. Could I face any of them and say, "Sorry and all that, but it was just all getting a bit too dangerous."? I'd had the opportunity to avoid danger since the first day of this case. None of them had that luxury.

Keep going Lukasz.

....

I saw Too-Bright before she saw me. Whatever I thought of her in Tortola, there was no denying she was glamorous, even beautiful in a haughty way. She was born for superiority and it rested lightly upon her. She was wearing a simple yet elegant fitted black dress, carrying a designer bag and wearing sunglasses, despite the sun having set half an hour earlier. As she approached I realized I could not recall her real name.

"Mr. Stone," she said offering me both cheeks. Awkwardly I kissed as required.

"Lukasz," I said warmly.

"Patrice," she said slightly more coolly.

We sat side on to the bay in an uneasy silence.

"Have you always liked boats?" and "How are you today?" we asked over each other. More silence.

"Are you going to take your sunglasses off?" I asked.

She did – red eyes.

"Not much sleep," she explained.

"Ah," I said. "I have always loved boats. Thank you for asking. How are you?"

A petite blonde waitress in her early forties appeared alongside our table with two menus and a wine list.

"Madam," she said passing Patrice a menu. "Monsieur," I received the menu and wine list too which I passed back. "We won't need that, thank you."

"Very well, Monsieur. The dishes of the day are on the inside cover."

Patrice was gazing into the darkness of the bay. Looking at her I doubted she had much of an appetite.

"Drinks to start?"

I answered for us both. “Water, still. Thank you.”

If the waitress assumed that this was a first date she must have known it would not run to a second. She left us, returning quickly with a jug of water.

“So?” I asked gently.

“As I said on the phone, I cannot take any more of this,” Patrice said, turning back to face me. “How many more people have to die?”

I took my time considering my reply. Whatever I said would sound accusatory, but that could not be avoided.

“You’re closest to them. The assassins are on your team, not mine.”

“Not as close as you were on Thursday. Those cuts look painful.”

“Someone trying to make a point.”

“How did they make their point?”

“By ramming a three ton Chevy Blazer into my stationary car – with me in it.”

“Were they trying to kill you?”

I shifted uncomfortably in my seat. Should I answer that?

“No,” I lied. “I believe Thursday’s incident was designed to intimidate me.”

"And has it?"

Nice try Too-Bright.

"Perhaps what you are about to tell me tonight will be more influential?" I said.

"Do you think they will kill me?"

The question surprised me. Patrice had spent her entire life knowing the answers to questions before they were asked. Had she really been reduced to asking advice from a total stranger? From her sanguine look, weakened voice and those exhausted eyes, I was prepared to believe she had.

The waitress reappeared, taking our orders and bringing us our water. "Fish special twice," I said. "Well, Patrice, you know who they are. I do not," I said pouring water into two glasses.

"I do not know where to start," she said biting her lower lip. Her gaze returned to the bay. I thought she might cry. Justifiably. She was terrified.

"Let me start for you," I said. Our meeting tonight is confidential and without prejudice to my client, Lloyd's and your client's insurance claim for the Actual Total Loss of motor yacht 'AZUL' agreed?"

Legal language intended to put her at her ease.

"Agreed," she said almost smiling with relief.

This could be the turning point; crucial. Unless I fouled it up.

"Now, for those of us who were not blessed with attending law school that means that this meeting never happened. Agreed?"

"Agreed," she said through a broken smile and, finding the energy to raise her glass added, "To the meeting that never happened."

We chinked glasses of water.

"So, from the beginning. Please."

The faint smile vanished from her face.

"When I completed college in the United States, V.S., that's my senior partner, the lawyer you met, offered me a pupilage in his chambers. In his day Lukasz, he was awesome. Whenever he was in court I would try and work out a way around school so that I could go and hear him."

"How old were you?"

"Not very old, nine, perhaps, ten."

"And this started your ambition to become a lawyer?"

"More than that, I idolized him. Other girls wanted musicians or film stars. So far as I was concerned V.S. was the greatest man alive."

"Had you heard other lawyers perform at that young age?"

"Of course, the lawyers opposing him!" she said excitedly. "He never, ever, raised his voice; he never took cheap shots or tried ill-placed humour. He was poised, measured, and reasoned in his arguments. I would sit there listening to his arguments wondering how did he think of that?"

Our meals arrived.

"Go on," I urged.

"Well, eventually one of the Officers of the Court noticed my regular attendance whenever V.S. was before the judge. He mentioned it to V.S. and he called my parents. He asked them if they knew about my regular attendance at court, and if so whether they minded. My father was a prominent businessman in the British Virgin Islands, but even he was intimidated by receiving such a call from such a revered man. My father told V.S. he had no objection. V.S. then invited me to visit him in his Chambers with my parents."

"And you went?"

"Did I? No one could have stopped me! It was like an invitation to walk the red carpet. V.S. was so charming. He gave the little speech about his grandfather in London as he did to you but back then it was delivered with pride and passion, not the stale thinly veiled threat you received."

Patrice pushed her food around her plate and took some on her fork.

"V.S. has been practicing for a very long time," I said gently "Perhaps he should retire?"

"It's not his age Lukasz but I will get onto that."

"So what next?"

"V.S. said that provided it did not interfere with my school studies, I was welcome to visit his library and read his books anytime his legal secretary was in Chambers. With that he opened the top drawer of his desk and presented me with a primer on English Law. Inside the flyleaf he had written 'Patrice, Whatever we are required to do we must do it with honour and integrity. Without integrity we have no reputation. And without reputation we are nothing,' and then his signature."

"Quite something."

"Yes, but I didn't need telling, I had seen him in court at least fifty times by then."

"So you read your primer and went to the library as often as possible."

"Yes. I was there so often that when I was about fourteen they put me to work. It was photocopying to start with but then I moved onto trial exhibits. All of the time it was, 'Honour. Integrity. Reputation.'."

I ate some fish.

"What was his practice?" I asked.

"All sorts of things. Some criminal defence but only if he believed the accused was innocent. He did a lot of trust and offshore investment work as you would expect. The rest was higher end probate and land claims."

"Land claims?"

"If you can prove your family was resident in the British Virgin Islands at the time the Quakers abolished slavery, you are entitled to land."

"Is it worth anything?"

"It depends. Maybe a million dollars an acre."

"Worth claiming."

"He did a lot of pro bono work too. I helped out on that but by the time I went off to college in the States, trust work was the mainstay of the business. Boring really, but I think the appeal of the courtroom was waning on him."

"So you went off to the United States for three years? Four?"

"Four. I kept in contact with V.S. but during the vacations I did internships around the world."

I wasn't surprised. I was surprised, however, that she was so candid with me. I decided to press a little harder.

"Where exactly were the internships?"

"Washington, London then Tallahassee, Florida."

"So you never came home to the islands in those four years?"

"My parents came to see me."

"You have a Masters in Law?"

"Yes and I am licensed to practice law in several countries, including yours. I was going to settle in London but then my mother became seriously ill. V.S. heard about her condition and offered me a pupilage. These maybe small islands, but to be offered such an opportunity by someone

I still regarded as one of the greatest lawyers on earth and certainly the most honest was too good to resist. So I came home."

"When was this?"

"Early 2001. I started on a Monday morning. V.S. was at a meeting at a trust company head office. I hadn't been left anything to do so I started looking at the current case list and the client database."

I was losing her.

"And?"

"And? And I was shocked."

I returned to my fish.

"Why?" I asked casually.

"Why? Where had all the triple 'A' rated clients gone? Some of the names I didn't recognize. I had been off-island for four years remember, but some of the names I did recognize…"

"Crooks?"

"We must always allow for Damascus road experiences Lukasz, but so many? Just as I had finished reading the name of the last one, (a particularly shady trust company) V.S. returned to Chambers."

"And?"

"That was my second shock of the day."

"Go on."

"He looked like a skeleton. Gone were the laughing eyes, the quick movements, the wit. It was so distressing."

"What did you do?"

"What I wanted to do was resign on the spot, but then I had to be there because of my mother."

"Is she still alive?"

"In a way."

"I'm sorry." I eased off. "Patrice, why are we here?"

"In mid-2001 Chambers received a phone call from Florida. A gentleman wished to establish a BVI Company for the ownership of a luxury yacht."

"A less than rare occurrence?"

"Of course, I was sitting opposite V.S. when he told the caller that we could send him all of the forms via post or e-mail. All he had to do was sign and return them. The client appeared to be in a hurry and insisted that he meet with V.S., and any banker and accountant of V.S.'s choosing. A one-stop shop. Everything sorted in one meeting. V.S. agreed and the meeting was arranged.

On the day of the meeting I was due in court. The judge had been delayed down island on another case, so I was in my little room in Chambers when the American arrived. I couldn't see the man but his voice was familiar. I stood up quietly and using the mirror in my compact and a bit of contortion I got to see him."

"What could you see?"

I think both of us had given up eating at this point.

"Oh Lukasz, it was ridiculous. His outfit… He might have been in place in Hawaii, although I doubt it. More jungle flora in that shirt than I'd ever seen before and the shorts! If he believed he would blend in with the cruise line tourists he was wrong."

"Did you see his face?"

"Oh, yes."

"Did you recognize him?"

"Yes, straight away."

"Who was it Patrice?"

"The firm I was interned with in Tallahassee had various political interest groups as clients."

"Lobbyists."

"Yes."

"There are several favoured sites for lobbying, one of which is a sort of camp outside Tallahassee. During government sessions it is in use every night. The government officials set up a league of how many consecutive party nights they can survive."

"The record?"

"I've heard of several one hundred nighters."

"It was at one of these parties that I had met our appallingly dressed new client."

"Who was he Patrice?"

"Joseph Lamb Junior."

I think I stopped breathing at that point. Slowly I said, "You… You are the corporate lawyer for AZUL Yachts Incorporated, the sole owner of 'AZUL'. You are telling me that Joseph Lamb Junior was the beneficial owner of that yacht?"

"Yes," she said stoically.

"How can I use that information without identifying you? The BVI Registry is impenetrable."

Now sitting composedly, as if a great weight had been lifted from her shoulders and dropped onto mine, she reached inside her handbag and pulled out an envelope.

"What's this? A love letter from Joe?"

"A copy of the certificate of incorporation for AZUL Incorporated. signed by Joseph Lamb Jnr. And... And the registration documents for 'AZUL' – the real ones. Not the ones you've been given."

She closed her handbag and stood up.

"The killing has to stop Lukasz." I watched her leave. She hesitated at the top of the step, turned and walked back to me. "One last thing. Find out who Jack Mills is. I'm afraid you are on your own with that one."

I sat at our table for another half an hour. A tanned couple, French, I would say, strolled along the dock, two small blonde girls running ahead of them in tiny life jackets. They stopped beside a ten metre sailboat waiting for their parents to catch up. They all boarded still laughing. That is what boating should be – fun, I thought. Not death, injury and ruined lives.

I decided not to open the envelope until I was back at my hotel. I found our waitress behind the bar.

"Is your friend alright Monsieur? She seemed distressed?"

"I think she will be fine now. Thank you for asking," I said paying the bill in cash and leaving a generous tip.

....

In my hotel room I closed the curtains and opened the envelope Patrice had given to me. The documents inside were exactly as she had described. There in front of me was the signature of Joseph Lamb Jnr and above that a photograph of the man himself. What had Patrice meant about Jack Mills? The only Mills I knew had a boat six thousand miles from here.

I sent a text message to Rachel.

"Hi. Strange question for a Saturday night, but what's Mills' first name? Have a good evening. Lukasz."

After sending it I picked up the room phone and called Francesca.

"Good evening, it's Lukasz Stone."

"Good evening Lukasz," she said cautiously. At Casa Casaurina we had agreed that I would only contact her again if there was 'significant danger' to Drew's investments with Lamb. "Where are you?"

"It is probably best I do not say. Is this conversation being recorded?"

"No."

"Good. Your financial analysis and suspicions were correct. Joseph Lamb Jnr did own 'AZUL'."

"Sole owner?"

"Yes."

"I don't take any pleasure in being right."

"I can imagine. Since we last spoke my experts have been working on failure analysis."

"Their conclusion?"

"They have not issued their final reports but that is how I have them working. I have given a naval architect and a failure analyst the entire specification and build plans for the ship. I then instructed them to work out the most efficient way of sinking the ship as quickly as 'AZUL' sank. They have identified a particular bulkhead and frame joint as the weakest link. Are you with me so far?"

"Yes."

"My Salvage Masters have identified two pieces of the hull which show the hallmarks of an explosion. The edges of the steel are blown in shards and bent outwards."

"That means a bomb?"

"Not just a bomb, but a bomb from within the yacht. Now where do you suppose those pieces of steel came from?"

"The weakest bulkhead and what was it?"

"Frame."

"Bulkhead and frame joint."

"Exactly. So what we have here is literally an inside job. The bomb was placed inside the yacht by someone who knew the yacht and the exact point to cause instant destruction."

"The yacht was unique. You must have a very short list of suspects."

"Minute. I think we can safely rule out the shipyard workers. Why would anyone fly from Hamburg to San Juan just to blow up a ship they had taken great pride in building? Where's the motive in that? Then there's the naval architect and build manager. I have met him. He is devastated by the loss and truly believes the owner is going to sue him for negligence. We can rule him out. That leaves the Designated Person Ashore and the owner. Either way it leads back to Lamb."

"Was the boat overinsured?"

"No."

"So what's Lamb's motive?"

"That? That I don't know. Did anything important come to light in your analysis that you didn't tell me at Casa?"

"Nothing that would help you. I couldn't figure out how Lamb was making such great returns, but no one was complaining."

"Francesca, I promised to call you if I found out anything that could harm Drew's investment. I cannot prove it yet but I believe Lamb, or someone acting on his instructions, blew up that boat."

"That's desperate."

"And he kills anyone who gets in his way."

"What do you want me to do?"

"I want you to persuade Drew to take a vacation outside of the U.S. I know it'll be difficult because he's his own man, but get him to use prepaid credit cards – lots of them. Tell him to use cash to get as far from Florida as possible. Is he still the largest investor in Lamb's investment scheme?"

"So far as I know."

"Then he is in the greatest danger."

"Oh Lukasz, no!"

"Oh Francesca, yes. When he's far away from there, tell him to contact Lamb and demand a sizeable withdrawal."

"How much?"

"How large is the fund?"

"It's supposed to be in the neighbourhood of a billion dollars."

The same amount as the insurance on 'AZUL' I thought.

"And Drew's stake?"

"Twenty-five per cent; two hundred and fifty million dollars."

"I wish my parents had taught me binary codes."

"How much should he withdraw?" she asked ignoring me.

"He holds twenty-five per cent of the fund, but he has introduced his friends to Lamb so Drew is more significant than his stake alone. He lead them all in, he can lead them all out again. Tell Drew to go for a seventy-five million dollar withdrawal with payment into his nominated bank account within forty-eight hours."

"That's fast."

"I only have a few days before this case gets taken away from me. Once he has done the deed, get Drew to report to you what Lamb said. You call me. Agreed?"

"Agreed."

"One last thing. Does the name Jack Mills mean anything to you?"

"No. He's not one of the investors so far as I recall. Not

a name I've come across."

"Thanks. Goodnight."

Ping. Rachel – a text.

"Evening, Mills' first name – Mark."

I was disappointed. I prepared for bed. I locked Patrice's paperwork in the safe and climbed into bed.

Lights out.

Ping. Rachel.

"Sorry Lukasz. Spilled drink on the phone. Name's Mark, but everyone calls him Jack."

53

30 November 2008
London

I returned to London from St. Martin via Paris. I assumed that the suspension of surveillance Patrice arranged ended at Charles de Gaulle or London Heathrow at the latest. These guys were good, much more professional than Francesca's crew. Clearly they were trained in espionage. And murder?

On the plane from St. Martin I had, for the first time, analysed the manner in which Lamb's people killed his targets. Thirty-nine crew members killed efficiently with no chance of survival. Banksy killed by a single bullet to the back of the head on the relaunched Mills boat; that took a lot of effort, and no small amount of resources. Lomas undoubtedly seduced by girls, drink, drugs or, let's be kind, just tempted by a few days sailing in the Caribbean, delayed his return to a grey British winter and perhaps a grey British life. Then I remembered my first impression of Johnson – military. Correctly used, 'Captain,' can only ever be a naval man. In his Examination under Oath he testified that he had been in the navy before coming ashore. I had assumed merchant navy. What of captain Sharpe? He looked military too. Was he one of Lamb's men sacrificed for the scheme?

What about Natalia? From the description of the car wreck described by the ICU nurse, no one could have imagined she would survive. By the time they had realized she had Natalia was at the hospital with around–the-clock medical care. The opportunity for finishing the job, even for a trained killer must have been negligible. I wondered what happened to the assassin that failed in his mission. These were not the kind of people to forgive and forget.

From the little I had learned about Lamb he would not soil his hands with murderous work such as this. Yet these assassins could not work alone – they required a controller. A person loyal to Lamb, who could almost read the paymaster's mind, provides solutions, lethal solutions, while leaving no trace.

I jotted a few notes of timeline between the murders and attempted murder of Natalia. Timelines are often time consuming and require assumptions but are an illuminating tool in my business. The 'AZUL' timeline was very short; I worked the routings and logistics. It was impossible for one person to have attempted Natalia's murder on the west coast of Florida, dumped their damaged vehicle, then flown to San Juan, Puerto Rico, gained access to the yacht and planted the bomb. There weren't enough hours between all of the events. Likewise one person could not have flown from San Juan to London (I knew for certain there were no direct flights), then driven to the Hamble, and lured Banksy to his death, in such close proximity to the bombing of 'AZUL'. However I plotted and schemed (just as the killers must have done) it was impossible for one person to achieve. He would have to be omnipotent – an ever-present force of evil.

The bomb itself was, from what I could see, designed for purpose. It had blown the shell plating away from the bulkhead vertically, and then shredded the surrounding steel horizontally at the waterline. From what Hargreaves had said the aft third of the ship would have tried to overtake the forward two thirds such was the force of the explosion – that required expertise and planning. Sitting in my seat with a reading light above my head illuminating my sketched timelines, I realized, far later than everyone else judging by their warnings, that the people behind the killings must be an elite military (or former military) team.

I thought of the jet bridge operator and his mock shooting. How did he get security clearance to be there? How did he know my seat number? Was it possible that Lamb's connections had brought him protection in my own country too and my death to my shore?

....

Rachel had arranged for me to meet Henry Coles on the main concourse of Paddington Station. The atmosphere was gloomy. The Penzance night sleeper was just emptying, some of the passengers seemed hung-over – all of them looked bleary-eyed. I watched the oversized hands of the large station clock click round and wondered what Henry had to tell me. I was seated at a small coffee bar pondering this when Henry strode up to me.

"Good morning, Lukasz. Miserable morning."

I was pleased to hear the characteristic strength back in Henry's voice. I stood to shake his hand.

"Good to see you Henry."

His grip was back too and with it the old confident, relaxed smile. I wondered what elixir had revived him.

"I'm hungry, let's eat."

Before I could say anything Henry was striding towards the escalators that ascended to a bar on the mezzanine level. Henry's a tall and handsome man. With his height, looks, money and former position at Lloyd's he could have got up to all kinds of mischief, but so far as I know, he never did. His credo was not dissimilar to that of the V.S. of old, although he would use fewer words to say it. "There is a difference between reputation and notoriety Lukasz. I only want reputation," I remember him telling me more than once.

I tagged along behind the hungry Henry. A group of twenty or so Japanese schoolchildren were between him and the escalator. Without a word from him the group parted in front of him. Reputation may be great Henry, but an air of greatness doesn't hurt either, I remember thinking.

The bar was lit mainly by a row of lights behind the optics, as a result the saloon was gloomy. Henry ordered our breakfasts and selected a corner booth from where we could see anyone entering the bar. Apart from a middle-aged couple ignoring each other behind newspapers the bar was empty.

"What happened to your face?"

"An argument with a Chevy Blazer; an invitation to cooperate."

"Are you cooperating?"

"No."

"Good. So how far have you got?"

"I know who the beneficial owner is."

"Really? Can you prove it?"

"Yes."

"What else have you got?"

"I know that the 'AZUL' was blown up from her inside. The bomb had been placed in the cabin of a former crew member; she had been fired two months before the sinking. Her cabin was adjacent to the weakest bulkhead and frame joint in the ship. I can prove that too."

"Can you link the bomb to the owner?"

"Not yet."

"Lukasz, you've only got a few more days."

"Three days including today to be exact. I have traced the former crew member whose cabin it was."

"When was she fired?"

"The sixteenth of September."

"The sixteenth of September?"

"Yes. Why?"

"Probably nothing; that's the day Lehman Brothers collapsed."

Foolishly I thought that fact was immaterial.

"Someone tried to kill Natalia, the day before the sinking. They almost succeeded."

"Loose lipped? Identified the owner?"

"She doesn't think she ever met him. The Boss's identity was never talked about. She thinks only the captain knew who he was. She was recruited by captain Johnson in Fort Lauderdale."

"You are doing well Lukasz."

"Even if I link the owner with the bomb, I still haven't got motive."

"You may not need one."

"How come?"

Our breakfast arrived. We waited in silence as the young waiter clumsily arranged cutlery and condiments. His bronze coloured name badge (pinned to his shirt lopsidedly) informed us that his name was Claude and he was 'happy to serve'. Henry's patience broke down.

"Would you leave us now please?" Claude left. "As you know the burden of proof in a fraud case is much harder on us… you… than any other claim." Henry continued, whilst staring into his food, "I seem to recall there was at least one case where the judge said the insurers only had to prove the fraud, the reason behind the fraud was immaterial."

"I didn't know that. It's pleasing, but I can't rest until I've found out what could possibly justify so much pain, death and suffering. I've made promises to that effect."

"Virtuous but you might not be given the opportunity," Henry said pointing to my largest scar.

"What did you want to talk about, Henry?" I asked rather sharply.

"As you know apart from you, virtually no one in the

London insurance market will have anything to do with me. Chum has done a very good job in keeping me isolated."

"He is scum."

"He is what he is," Henry said sternly. "About ten days ago I received a call from Ed Stanton. Do you know Ed?"

"No, I don't think I do."

"There is no reason why you should, he is a reinsurance placing broker. He placed some of our high level reinsurances. He was on holiday when 'AZUL' sank. One of the programmes he placed for us was our Total Loss Only Cover."

"How does that work?" I asked prodding a dry rasher of bacon.

"If a yacht or ship is sunk, destroyed or written off we pay out and then recover from our reinsurers. Our programme was set so that any claim for Total Loss in excess of twenty million dollars would be paid by the reinsurers, not us."

"I thought you hadn't got any reinsurance for 'AZUL'? Chum told me the certificates you gave me had all been cancelled."

"That's the thing. Ed said we'd cancelled it and he had always wondered why."

"Did you cancel the reinsurance?"

"No. Ed said that not only was the Total Loss Only cover on 'AZUL' cancelled but around one hundred other covers in excess of twenty million dollars had been cancelled too."

Henry reached into his jacket pocket and handed me a typed list of the names of one hundred vessels. I recognized some. Some were incomplete.

"As I am a former employee of the Syndicate, Ed could not give me the names of the hundred so I have tried to remember as many as possible. You might want to get Joe to check them."

"There must have been some documentation issued?"

"Ed said that he had received a call from Christian. Christian said that he and I had reviewed our reinsurance arrangements and decided we did not need the Total Loss Only cover at current levels and wished to cancel them. Ed thought it was odd but assumed we'd placed the cover cheaper elsewhere."

"What happened next?"

"Ed produced cancellation endorsements and brought them to Christian at the Box. I wasn't there. Ed returned the next day and collected them – all signed."

"Signed by who?"

"It appeared to be my scratch."

"Forgeries?"

"Forgeries. The only person who stood to gain by this was Christian."

"How?"

"As soon as any one of the hundred vessels became a

Total Loss the syndicate would collapse. You wouldn't have known anything about it but Christian had been pushing for a merger with the Leadenhall Syndicate for some time. I was against it."

"Why?"

"The Leadenhall underwriting strategy is not as refined or successful as ours."

"Why was Chum so determined?"

"The Chairman of the Leadenhall board was at school with Christian. I'm sure whatever remuneration they are negotiating for Christian is in the millions, plus shares. Lloyd's will be helping the pairing along."

"So by cancelling the reinsurance, all Chum had to do was wait?"

"Yes. Statistically a Total Loss would occur within eighteen months. Not a long wait."

"There's nothing you can do about this Henry."

"I know. It's his word against mine. Lloyd's hasn't the appetite for more scandal, so they won't help."

"Let me see if there is anything I can do."

"Forget it Lukasz. I'm done with them," Henry said looking down at his plate. "Will you come and visit me in Oslo?"

"Oslo?"

Henry smiled. “Oslo. The Scandinavian market believes I had nothing to do with the Syndicate collapse. Negotiations between us are advancing nicely.”

“Congratulations.”

“Thank you. One last thing Colombo.”

“What’s that?”

“The small chap on the Lloyd’s panel.”

“What about him?”

“A major shareholder in Leadenhall. He is the man who was at school with Christian.”

....

Coverack, Cornwall

I parked my car beside the Paris Hotel and stood breathing in the mild air looking out towards Lowland Point. Behind the point lay the infamous ‘Manacle’ Rocks once inside the formation no captive ship would escape – she would have to wait her time to be smashed to pieces by the relentless sea. The similarity to my investigation seemed as clear as the sea below me.

My mother had read me stories of the shipwrecks from my bed in our family home of ‘Rose Cottage’. My bedroom was at the front overlooking the harbour. Even in winter I would leave the windows open so that I could hear the sea.

I turned and walked down the road past the slipway and old lifeboat house. My old schoolmaster was standing with an easel by a sail loft painting in watercolours the harbour scene below.

"Come and see me Lukasz," he said without moving his eye from his artwork, in much the same tone as he had when I was a pupil at the school up the hill above us.

"I can't this time Archie. I'm leaving in a few hours."

He turned to face me. "Shame. Looks like you could use some rest," he added nodding at my injured face.

"Car crash, common in America," I said.

"I see," correctly assuming that there was more to the story. "Your mother's at the café."

I walked a few farther metres to the Old Post Office Café. My mother had her back to the door, an oversized mug in her right hand and a newspaper lay out in front of her.

"I was wondering when you'd turn up," she said without moving. Over her shoulder I could see that she had been reading an article of 'AZUL' from the open newspaper. She stood and hugged me with her left arm without meeting my eye.

I said nothing and sat down opposite her.

"Julie," she called towards the deserted counter. "White coffee for Lukasz please."

Julie appeared at the top of the staircase behind the counter, smiled in my direction and busied herself making my drink.

"Where did you get those?" my mother asked, gently leaning forward to touch around the larger gash on my face.

"Florida," I replied.

"Hmm," she said leaning back in her chair. "I don't suppose this has anything to do with it?" she asked tapping the newspaper.

"Who knows?" I said turning to look out into the harbour.

Julie brought my drink to our table.

"Lukasz, they have boats in London. You didn't drive all this way to look at a few dories and sailboards with your mother. What's the matter?" she asked folding her newspaper across her chest.

I turned back and took my first sips of coffee. I told her everything, including the parts a son should never have to tell his mother – the assassinations. I told her I had promised to find who was responsible and bring them to 'justice'.

When I finished I sat and examined my mother's face – nothing. She took a large gulp from her mug and rested it perpendicularly to the edge of the table.

"Lukasz, why did you come?"

"To ask your advice."

"My advice?"

"Yes."

“How many people have you made promises to?”

“Many.”

“Then you are in too deep for advice. Get on and do what you have to do.”

54

1 December 2008
London

My tube journey to Liverpool Street gave me time to evaluate what Henry had said. It explained why Chum had been so quiet he was consumed with plotting his future with Leadenhall. As a man with no ambition beyond carrying out his job, I could not understand how anyone could justify to themselves what Chum had done. What right did he have to ruin someone as genuinely decent as Henry Coles? What right did he have to smash up the Syndicate, create insecurity and undoubtedly cause redundancies? The enlarged Leadenhall Syndicate would not need two compliance officers, two Syndicate managers and so on. It would not be Noah's Ark.

Where did this leave me and my investigation? If I could prove that the loss of 'AZUL' was fraud, no payment would be made that would mean no need for a forced merger. We could get Ed to replace the reinsurance programme (presumably at about the same cost, as we would be claims free) the Syndicate would no longer have any claims against them and they could cross its collective digits that nothing happened to the other ninety-nine vessels while the process was being completed.

If something seems to be too good to be true it always is. The reality, I knew, was that with Henry Coles out of the way Chum would force through the marriage with Leadenhall and the twelfth floor at Lloyd's would officiate. On the positive side, if the merger did proceed, hopefully the distance between Chum and me would increase.

I pulled out the list of vessels Henry had given me from my jacket pocket. Some were ships and so meant nothing to me. I recognized several megayachts and a frightening number of even larger gigayachts over one hundred metres in length. Without the reinsurance cover if any one of them was lost Lloyd's would have to intervene.

At the Syndicate office door I took a deep breath; Rachel – the wrath. As I walked in she got up from her desk looking at me sternly. I felt embarrassed. Worse was to come. She walked, no ran, over to me and threw her arms around me in the middle of the open-plan office.

"Don't you ever do that again," she said.

I thought about explaining that I hadn't done anything but even I understood that would have been very wrong. Colouring, I decided to say nothing. She pulled away and looked at the cuts.

"That the lot?" she asked.

"The rest are bruises."

"You want a coffee?" she asked, nodding determinedly towards the kitchen.

"In a moment, I'll see you in there. I've just got to see Joe." I walked to Joe's desk.

"Lukasz, my boy. The last time my wife greeted me like that was when I brought her home a new Vauxhall Chevette."

"True love Joe." I pulled out Henry's list. "Would you look into your reinsurance arrangements on these vessels please?"

"Lukasz, this is twice in less than three weeks you have sounded like you understand insurance. Are you OK? Is it the trauma? So many of us are living vicariously through you, your public does not want you coming in from the cold, you know. We want more boys' own stuff."

"Perhaps you can come with me on my next outing? You too can come back with souvenirs like these," I said good humouredly.

"No thanks, I'm happy being Q to your Bond. Go and see Moneypenny," he said taking the list. "I assume if Chum asks what I'm doing its sudoku?"

"Well done Q. If you have any of those exploding pens in stock…"

"…leave one in Chum's office?"

"Good man."

I walked back to the kitchen area. Usually at that time on a Monday morning it was busy with staff talking about their weekend activities, Rachel had done well to clear the place.

"So what have I missed? Where's Chum?"

"Chum, I should imagine is where he always is – at Leadenhall's office. He is doing an admirably competent job of keeping no one informed as to what is going on."

"Has he talked about 'AZUL'?"

"Not with me. I reckon he believes you won't finish

your investigation in time and so it will be taken over by Lloyd's." She pressed the button for white coffee on the needlessly noisy coffee machine. We both stood staring at it. "Is he right?"

I explained what I'd learnt since we last met – or most of it.

"Chum seems to have lost interest in 'AZUL'. He believes whether it's a design issue or a bomb, either way it will get paid. The case that he is most interested in is Mills."

"Mills?"

"Mills. It is causing him 'embarrassment' with the Lloyd's broker. I am to tell you that you are to 'confine your efforts' to concluding that matter urgently."

"That suits me."

"What?"

"That suits me."

"OK," she said doubtfully.

"Do you have the Mills underwriting file to hand?"

"It's on my desk."

We left the kitchen aware that resentful and probably suspicious eyes were upon us. As we walked back to Rachel's desk the kitchen filled up again.

"Here it is," she said passing me a green file – green for underwriting, red for claims.

I leafed through the file until I found Mills application for insurance. "Date of birth: 1958; occupation: Retired." That's early. He had avoided stating retired from what? Military? "Address: A manor house in Surrey".

"He's not from Surrey," Rachel said.

"How do you know?"

"Because I have spoken to him three times."

"And?"

"And, he is American."

Fortuitously, Chum had assisted me. Making Mills a priority was exactly what I needed. I sat by Rachel's desk rereading both the red and green files. She was filling out a spreadsheet, humming quietly to herself. The Syndicate had insured a fifty metre Italian built sailing yacht, built to top classification society rules by a well-regarded yard in Italy. The slightly shabby town of Viareggio had established itself as a respected producer of all kinds of superyachts. I read the pre-risk survey. Nicely equipped, nicely presented. No major problems. A hose clamp required here, recalibrate the compass there, bring electronic charts up to date, replace a through hull fitting because of the joining of two incompatible metals! The usual fare. Cruising was Mediterranean then UK. No Caribbean or Florida. No hurricane exposure. Owner Mark Mills as Rachel had said on Saturday. Nothing to suggest any American connection at all.

"Who do we know with connections in the U.S. military?"

"Super Mario has connections everywhere," she said

tapping her mouse decisively.

"After my experience in Florida last week he might not want a connection with me."

"I'll call him. What do you want to know?"

I pushed my chair back. "Rachel, I hurt here… here and here. My face is like a snakes and ladders board. Remember what happened to Banksy? I won't let any of this happen to you."

"You think Mills is important?"

"I think I have underestimated him. Please call Mario and ask him if he is free for a telecon today."

"OK."

"And one other thing. Mills alleged his boat was stolen from Dartmouth."

"So?"

"I think there's a Royal Naval college at Dartmouth. Would you check please?"

"Yes, boss."

Shoeless Joe walked over to us. He looked uncharacteristically serious.

"Got a minute?" he asked nodding towards his office.

"Sure."

We walked to Joe's office. He closed the door and sat heavily in the chair opposite the desk. "Every single name on that list you gave me, every one of them has had its reinsurance cover cancelled. What was Henry thinking?"

"Henry didn't know anything about it."

"Looks like his scratch."

"It looks like his scratch; those signatures are all forgeries."

"We are exposed for… for… to billions."

"Yes."

"What are we going to do?"

"Think very carefully. Shall we meet again later this afternoon?"

"Sure."

I could see Rachel mouthing 'phone' through Joe's office window.

"Would you excuse me Joe, got to get this call."

I went into Room 6 and picked up the phone. "It's Mario, Lukasz," Rachel said.

"Thanks. Good morning Mario. Thank you for taking my call."

"I had to Lukasz. You retained me as your lawyer," he said coolly.

"Otherwise?"

"Otherwise Lukasz you're too hot to handle right now."

"I understand."

"I don't think you do. We had a visit from the Florida Bar Association last week, completely unexpected and unwarranted. They want access to all the files we have worked with you over the last five years."

"Why?"

"They didn't say. They don't have to explain they can do whatever they want."

I recalled Mario telling me that Lamb was head of the Florida Bar Ethics Committee, a position he was clearly abusing.

"How many cases have we worked in that period?"

"Seventy-five."

"And how many of those claims did we decline or negotiate?"

"Sixty-seven, all dubious losses Lukasz, but you can see where they are going with it."

"Trying to prove that the Coles Syndicate has a policy of not paying claims."

"Which means that the next one your client declines will lead them straight into bad faith litigation that will cost tens of millions of dollars in punitive damages and legal fees."

"But the syndicate does not have a policy of avoiding claims."

"Save it for the judge, Lukasz. Sixty-seven out of seventy-five. As your lawyer I am telling you to be absolutely certain before you decline another one. How is the 'AZUL' going?"

"Are you taking notes?" I asked.

"No."

I detailed Hargreaves and Randall's findings, the pieces of the hull found by Spider T. I didn't mention the ownership documents.

As I came to the end Mario said, "Would you hold on for one minute please Lukasz?" I heard him ask, "What is it Maria?"

I could not make out what Maria was saying.

"Lukasz, did you hear that?"

"No."

"We have just received a call from the British Virgin Islands – a law firm. They want to know if we are authorized to accept service of suit in the 'AZUL' matter."

"I did. I still have two more days."

"Thank you Maria. Please close the door."

"Lukasz, I am telling you as your lawyer and as your

friend pay the 'AZUL' claim. Pay it. You are out of your depth. These are powerful people. They've given you many warnings. The fun's over. You ignored them. They tried to kill you. Their patience has run out; dead, finished, ceased to be. At best your career will be over once they're finished with you, or more likely you will end up dead. Bombs are covered by the policy. It was a bomb that sank the yacht. Pay the claim. People are dead – loads of them. Do not join them."

"I will think about it," I said knowing I would do no such thing.

"Rachel said you needed my assistance?"

"Do you have connections with the military?"

"Of course, a couple of my old college buddies are high up in D.C.. What do you need?"

"It's not much to go on, but can you ask them to check out a Mark Mills. Also goes by the name of Jack, born 1948, now resident in the UK. Was he ever one of theirs?"

"Depends when he left for the UK. Chances are he did national service or 'nam."

"Then the same for captain Johnson. I will ask Rachel to send you his details."

"Pay the claim Lukasz."

"Please Mario, I won't ask for anything else."

"You better not or I will send you your dollar back."

So Lamb was starting to apply more pressure. Even

my own counsel was bailing out on me. I picked up the red Mills file and started to remind myself of the facts. The boat had allegedly been on a swing mooring in Dartmouth when she disappeared in early October, 2008. The watchman supposedly went ashore for supplies and when he came back the boat had gone. I had taken the watchman's statement which Rachel had typed up. I remember her bringing the transcript to me and remarking. "Doesn't know much about boats does he? Doesn't even know port from starboard."

"Not very observant either. That's a large boat to sail out of Dartmouth in daylight without being noticed. I spoke with the harbour master and all of the water taxi guys. Everyone remembers the boat arriving but not when she left."

We had circulated details of the missing boat through our network of repair yards and yacht brokers without success. I had started to compile my report which would have recommended payment of the claim had I not been interrupted by the yachts reappearance, and Banksy's claim that the Hull Identification Number had been changed. In the rush to get to Heathrow I realized I had not checked the HIN for myself. I called Evo.

"Morning Evo, Lukasz Stone."

"Mr. Lukasz," he said with little warmth, "How are you?"

"I'm alright Evo. How are things at the yard?"

"Quiet. It's not the same without him. What do you want me to do with this yacht of yours?"

"Not sure it is ours. Don't worry we will meet your

costs."

"So what can I do for you today?"

"Did Banksy ever say if he'd found the hidden number?"

"Not to me."

"Have you ever met Mr. Mills?"

"No, only his assistant. The name's Alexander something."

"What's he like?"

"Ice. You know what I mean?"

"I think I do."

"He looks like he's sneering."

"What's he like to deal with?"

"He says it's not Mills' boat. Think we both know it is, but I've played along – safest."

"Have the police got anywhere finding Banksy's killer?"

"All they've said is that it was a professional job. Three different SOCO teams have been over the boat, and brought the dogs in too. I got talking to one of the forensics team last week he hadn't found any clues."

"Thanks for your help Evo. The Syndicate's new boss wants the Mills case sorted as a priority so I will let you know what to do with the yacht once the police release it."

Clearly calling the builders and asking the same questions as Banksy was not a bright move. Even I could see that.

Next on my list of jobs? Call Hargreaves. As I dialled the number I thought how pleasant it was to be in a Chumless office.

“Rob, I thought I would just call and let you know where we are with ‘AZUL’.”

”Lukasz, my final report will be with you by the week’s end.”

“I wasn’t chasing Rob. I thought you would like to know that the salvage guys found some steel plating, frames and bulkhead which came from the part of the yacht that you and Harry ‘identified’.”

“And?”

“And I am going to e-mail you the photographs in a few minutes. They show a large force applied from inside the yacht. If you are in agreement please include that in your report.”

“It is always a sublime delight to be proven right, although I imagine Randall will take the credit.”

“I don’t want to get into that,” I said remembering clearly that it was Harry at Ladaj who had spotted the weakness first. “I still need you two to work together. Would a payment on account of your fees help?”

“That’s kind Lukasz but no. Randall is fine, but if you

ever tell him I said that, I would have to kill you."

You'll have to join the queue I remember thinking.

"Keep an eye on your inbox Rob. The pictures will be with you shortly. They are large files so it will take around ten e-mails."

"Lukasz, let Rachel do it. We've got deadlines remember."

"Rob, before you go, you presumably have worked with experts with knowledge of explosives."

"Yes. Do you want me to liaise with them? Show them your artwork?"

"I think not on this occasion. I want to keep you and Randall buffered." What I really meant was I want to keep you and Randall alive.

"Buffered?"

"Yes buffered. It's strategic."

"You're the client."

"Thanks Rob. So could you send me some names?"

"I will send them to Rachel."

I signalled to Rachel to come into the room. I could have phoned her but it always ended in laughter, misinterpreted by the rest of the floor.

"Chum has been on the phone," she said.

"Is it me or is it much more productive here without him?"

"Much. He wants a 'sit-rep meeting' with you at three this afternoon. In his office I assume."

"The end of peace and the outbreak of hostilities. How did he sound?"

"Irritatingly jubilant."

"As well he might. Even Mario is saying pay 'AZUL'."

Rachel fell into the chair opposite me, "No!"

"Yes. Lamb is starting to put pressure on him. Joseph Lamb Junior is head of the Ethics Committee of the Florida Bar Association. They want to review every file Mario has handled for the Syndicate. Something is rotten in the State of Florida. He has agreed to provide biographies on Mills and Johnson. We haven't got a photograph of Mills have we?"

"No. I did an Internet search on him, under both his names but nothing came up that could relate to him."

"Odd. He lives in a manor house which normally carries some noblesse oblige, even if it's only an annual dog show."

"I searched the satellite images too. The place is well defended – even got a filled moat."

"Ask Smudger to go down and see if he can get a picture of Mills."

"I can't do that Lukasz."

"Why not?"

"Because everyone who gets near Mills winds up dead. See what Mario comes up with."

"Point taken. Would you send all the Spider pictures to Rob Hargreaves please?"

"That I will do," she said.

"He is going to send you the names of explosives experts. When they arrive please look them over. I cannot visit any in the United States, so any European experts would be best."

"Yes Boss."

I lifted the receiver once more and dialled David Archer's number. Perhaps he wouldn't be hung-over?

"Hello," he slurred.

"David, it's Lukasz Stone from London."

"Who?"

"Lukasz Stone. We met. 'AZUL'?"

"Oh aye, Lukasz. How are ye?"

"Still plugging away at it. I thought I should give you an update, perhaps put your mind at ease."

"Jack Daniels did that for me last night."

"Very kind of him but I think what I am about to tell you

may suit you better."

"Go on."

"'AZUL' was lost to a bomb. We have found no evidence of any errors in design or construction. She was a well found ship."

Notwithstanding his whiskey induced stupor there was no reaction.

"Did you hear what I said David?"

"Oh aye, I heard ya."

"You don't seem pleased."

"I'm not. I had a visit a couple of days ago from two brutes. They smashed my place up pretty badly; not that I had a lot. I was told that if I did not cooperate what happened to my condo was what was going to happen to me."

"Cooperate?"

"Cooperate. They said if questioned, I was to say that during the design and build I may have been distracted at times by 'personal issues'."

"But you weren't."

"I can't take the risk of saying that Lukasz. These guys didn't just mean business – they were the business. I really must remember to thank my friend Henderson in Italy for getting me into this."

"Is he still in Viareggio?"

"Oh aye, working on another new build. The third for the same owner."

"Do you know who the owner is?"

"Oh aye."

"Can you tell me who it is?"

"I can. No bit of paper covering that one. A chap called Mills. Jack Mills."

....

In 2008, there were barely five thousand yachts in excess of twenty-four metres in the world super yacht fleet. It was a relatively small community. It was usual for owners to know each other and recommend captains, yards, and project managers. Instinctively, I believed the relationship between Lamb and Mills was more than that. Lamb was The Honest Lawyer. But who was Mills?

"Rachel I'm just going out – need to think. Tell me, when you searched for Mills on the web, did you search for Lamb too?"

"No. I assumed you knew what he looked like."

"No. Can you search again but this time for Lamb? He's a socialite so there will be thousands of images. See if you can find any of him with Mills."

"You think the two are connected?"

"I know they are. Proving it is another matter."

....

I walked down Minories, purposefully avoiding Lloyd's. I wasn't concerned by the condition of my face or questions about the 'accident' I just did not have time to stop.

As I passed through the underpass to St. Katherine's Dock I realized for the first time how well my opponents had me surrounded. There was only one exit – pay the 'AZUL' claim.

It is impossible to walk quickly around St. Katherine's dock. Firstly, on the south side the cobbles are too uneven. Secondly, there are too many yachts and barges to look at. Could I really give up the job I loved? Was the case really worth it? If 'AZUL' was paid it would be by the Lloyd's Central Fund not the Coles syndicate. The fund is so vast it would hardly notice. I learned years ago that emotional involvement in any case reduced my effectiveness. This was different. Over forty people were dead – what level of inhumanity had I reached if that didn't matter? The level of Lamb and Mills.

The bridge across the lock was up. Three ten metre sailboats and two motorboats of the same size were entering the dock. I was looking at the slowly manoeuvring boats as I became aware I was being watched from the other side of the bridge. I looked up; three middle-aged women, two teenage girls, three Chinese tourists and my observer. He smiled at me. He then raised his arm, tapped his watch and mouthed, "It's your turn. Next." By the time the bridge had been lowered, he was gone.

....

When I returned to the office I found Rachel closely

examining images of Joseph Lamb Jnr.

"He is rather good looking," she said.

"Too old for you."

"I like older men," she said scrutinizing the images. "He seems to know a lot of famous people. Most of the people he is glad-handing are 'A' list celebrities."

"Any luck finding Mills?"

"Not so far, no."

"I think I have just met one of his team."

"What? Where?"

"A guy at St. Katherine's Dock; he was taking quite an interest in me."

"That makes sense," she said turning to face me. "Joanna said that Chum met with Mills' personal representative this morning."

"Who's Joanna?"

"Chum's new secretary."

"Did he get her from an agency, or did she descend directly from heaven?"

"I don't think she'll be staying long. Do you want me to keep looking for Mills?"

"Please. I want to find out what the link is between

Lamb and Mills."

"While you were looking at your boats and making new friends, Rob sent me the names of three explosive experts. They all look about the same in background and qualifications, so I called them all. One is leaving tomorrow for a three week trial in San Diego. Another is on holiday, trekking the Alps on an elephant and the third said that if you are anything like Rob Hargreaves he would sooner blow himself up than work with you."

"Did you tell him that I'm not like Hargreaves?"

"Of course, I told him you are far more infuriating than Hargreaves – he never listens to anyone, doctor."

"How long have we been married?"

"Don't worry," she said gently patting my hand, "He laughed. You are meeting with him tomorrow at noon. His place."

"Where is his place?"

"Pisa."

"What's his name?"

"Dr. Philip Corbett," she said passing me his details. "He sounds very pleasant. Please try not to upset him."

Or get him killed, I thought. I sat by Rachel's desk and read about Dr. Corbett's life. Scientist, lecturer, adviser to the British Military – my own Barnes-Wallace. I looked at my watch which confirmed the worst. Ten minutes until my meeting with Chum. I considered what the minimum information I could give him was. The phone rang.

"Lukasz, this is Joanna. Mr. Unstead-Matthews will see you now." So Chum had trained her to use his full title?

"I will be right there. Thank you."

Rachel said, "Good luck."

I walked slowly to Chum's office, still undecided on what to say.

"Lukasz, good to see you. Come in, come in," Chum said rather too loudly.

"Would you like a drink? Joanna can make you something."

"No thank you Christian. I have to be on a plane in a few hours so if we could get on with this meeting please?"

"Of course," he said. "Please close the door." As I closed the door I felt the temperature drop.

"Sorry for the theatricals. Don't need the troops to know of our differences."

"I didn't know we had any differences, Christian," I lied.

"The events of the last two weeks have been distressing for us all Lukasz. These have been testing times." Chum settled back in his chair, a picture of contentment.

"How are you getting on, leading the Syndicate out of these testing times, Christian?"

“Quite well actually, but you really are not helping me at all.”

I took some satisfaction from hearing that. “I am so sorry,” I said suppressing a smile. “What appears to be the problem?”

“Let’s start with Mr. Mills. He is the most urgent.”

“We only have two days left to decide about ‘AZUL’,” I reminded him.

“I will move onto ‘AZUL’ presently,” said Chum, “the most urgent is Mills. Where are you with it?”

“I believe the boat at Banksy’s yard is Mr. Mills’s boat.”

“Mr. Mills disagrees.”

“I know he does.”

“And frankly, Lukasz, if anyone should know their own boat, it really should be the owner, don’t you agree?”

“Usually.”

“But not in this case?”

“No. The Hull Identification Number has been changed.”

“So without the hidden number, we have no way of knowing who owns the boat, or at least who it was built for? So how do you find the mystery numbers?”

“Talk to the builder.”

"Have you done that?"

"No. Banksy was doing that around the time he was murdered."

A thundercloud moved across Chum's face. "You are a dangerous man to know Mr. Stone."

My contempt for Chum had never been as honed and complete as at that moment.

"Meaning?"

"How are your injuries healing?" he asked, his eyes narrowing.

"Are you threatening me?"

"I have no need to," he sneered. "We will get onto that presently as well. I met Mr. Mills' man this morning. Have you ever met Alexander…?"

"No." Close enough to the truth.

"He is a very charming man. Most charming considering his employer has been waiting sometime for a cheque for, let me think… forty million euros."

I said nothing, evidently to Chum's annoyance.

"Do you know anything of Mr. Mills' background?"

"Only that he is retired, I do not know from what. He has a mansion in Surrey."

"Mr. Mills was a highly decorated marine."

Thank you Chum! At last! A use for you, albeit by coincidence.

Now to link Mills with Johnson and thereby to Lamb, and I had a case.

"You appear distracted?"

"Sorry Christian. I did not know of his military service. Please go on."

"According to his assistant and the broker Mr. Mills' military service was exemplary. He was in Vietnam."

"Christian, does the American military pay substantially more than the British?"

"You know it does."

"So much more that a soldier, admittedly a senior soldier, can afford a forty million euro yacht, a mansion and who knows what else?"

"I didn't ask Lukasz that would have been rude," Chum said his voice a half octave higher than usual.

It would have been useful, I didn't say.

"When did he immigrate to Britain?"

"Several years ago. What has any of this got to do with his yacht?"

I stared at Chum in what I knew was patent disbelief.

"Christian, it's a fraud case," I said very slowly as if

explaining it to a drowsy child. "The more we know of the owner the better."

"Fraud!" Chum was on his feet. I sensed those in the outer office looking at us. "Fraud! Are you mad, Stone? You haven't a shred of evidence. The man says your boat isn't his boat. Get it?" Chum sat back down, adjusting his tie.

"What do you want me to do Christian?" I asked wearily.

"Go and see the builders. Where are they?"

"Viareggio."

"Where's that, Italy?"

"You know it is."

"How quickly can you get there?"

"Tomorrow probably," I lied.

"Good. This has to be sorted by close of business on Wednesday. Understood?"

"Understood."

"Now 'AZUL'. I hope you've made more progress on that."

"We're still missing some links."

"What have you got?"

"Are you going to report what I tell you back to Lloyd's?"

"Eventually."

"Can you wait until the deadline?"

"Lukasz, don't make me raise my voice again. I am your client. Tell me what you know."

"I know who the beneficial owner is."

"How on earth did you manage that?"

"Documentation was given to me..."

"Have you..."

"...and before you accuse me of showing appreciation for local culture with a bribe, it was given to me voluntarily by a reliable source."

"I don't want to know."

"That suits me just fine. I also know and can prove, that 'AZUL' was blown up from the inside by an explosive placed next to the most sensitive part of the ship."

"So we can sue the builders or designers?" Chum asked happily.

"No."

"No?"

"No. There was nothing wrong with the design or the build."

"But you just said..."

"It was the weakest part, not weak. It was a bomb, Christian, a bomb tailor-made for the task."

"Where was it placed?"

"In the cabin of a former crew member."

"How do you know they were 'former'? You haven't recovered the bodies."

"I know that she was a former crew member Christian, because there are copies of an exchange of e-mails between you and the broker about her wrongful dismissal."

"Are there?" Chum asked quietly. Exactly the response I was looking for.

"There are. Late at night – around midnight. You rightly said there would be no coverage."

More likely you realized the cancelled reinsurance would be discovered too soon for your scheme with Leadenhall, I thought.

"There's never any cover for that sort of thing," Chum said, his confidence returning. "What else have you got?"

"Bud and Spider located the critical steel plating. It clearly shows the bomb was on the inside of the hull. I expect Harry Randall's report to concur."

"So we have a covered loss," Chum said smiling.

"On the facts as I've described them, yes," I said smiling back through thick self-loathing.

"When will I receive your report? The committee has informed me that you and I are to appear before them at nine o'clock on Wednesday with our, I mean your, conclusion and recommendations."

"Great."

"Isn't it just? That means that I expect you to conclude both investigations by Wednesday. You have annoyed some very influential people Lukasz. Your antics in the United States have raised more than a few eyebrows in the Room."

"My 'antics' Christian is my job."

"However you describe your actions, is your own affair. Lloyd's will not allow you to damage the reputation of this Syndicate."

That's your job I thought.

"How is the merger progressing Christian?"

"I am glad you asked," he said smiling again. "It is progressing well. The Leadenhall people are very progressive. Lloyd's is being very helpful in facilitating us."

"When do you expect the merger to take place?"

"Could be as early as next week."

"So soon?"

"Yes."

"I look forward to it."

Leaning forward, Chum said, "You've got to get through this week first."

....

"I thought underwriters never used the 'f' word," Joe said.

"Chum isn't an underwriter Joe, he's an undertaker. He buries anyone that gets in his way."

"Quite a performance."

"Desperate. He says the merger may take place next week. He wants me to conclude both the Mills and 'AZUL' investigations by Wednesday."

"Can it be done?"

"Only with a huge chunk of luck."

"What should we do about the cancelled reinsurances?"

"If the merger is that imminent we may as well leave them. Leadenhall will carry out 'due diligence' at some point and buy replacement cover."

"How is Henry?"

"About to move to Oslo. He is very much himself again. Do you know Ed Stanton?"

"Not well, but I know him. Market functions, the Franchise Board."

"Franchise Board?"

"You know... actually you probably don't; Lloyd's has a Franchise Board. They ensure that the good name of Lloyd's remains well, good."

"They ensure ethical behaviour?"

"In a way. Why?"

"Do you think you can get Ed to give you a statement about the reinsurance cancellations?"

"I can try."

"I will ask Rachel to find out where Henry was when he was allegedly scratching one hundred cancellation endorsements. Feel at liberty to use that information with Ed. If he is on the... what is it?"

"Franchise Board."

"Then surely he is under an obligation to investigate forged scratches."

"Sure Lukasz... I don't know how to put this..."

"Anyway you want."

"This isn't going to get me shot is it?"

I smiled. "No Joe it won't. Now if you'll excuse me, I have to go and see a man about a bomb."

55

1 December 2008
London Heathrow Airport

My mobile phone rang. Mario. "Got some news for you about Lamb and Mills. First off I got my guys in D.C. to check the records of the army, navy and air force on Lamb. Nothing, nada, zip. It may be an age thing, or medical, or who knows what, but Lamb never served his country."

"What about Mills?"

"Mills is much more interesting. I even spoke with someone who was in the army with him, or at least until he was kicked out."

"I like the sound of that. Go on."

"From what I gather Mills was always enthusiastic when engaging with the enemy. Unfortunately his discretion didn't match his enthusiasm."

"Let me guess – he was a murderous thug?"

"Well put. He was hauled before court martials twice for killing civilians. According to my source the killings were entirely avoidable. On the third occasion, which included children, the army threw him out."

"What happened next?"

"D.C. is not entirely certain. It was rumoured that he had gone underground sorting out problems for the mob."

"A mercenary?"

"Mercenary, assassin, I don't know which is the appropriate name. Not my area of expertise."

"A hired killer whatever title you give the profession."

"Exactly. He attracted the attention of the FBI for a while but according to their database the investigation was halted. No case to answer. I spoke with the investigating officer. It appears likely that Mills was told about the investigation. Shortly afterwards he sold up and moved to your country. Could you get him checked out there?"

"I can, particularly as there is an ongoing police investigation involving his boat. He told us that he'd retired."

"People like that never retire Lukasz the thrill of the chase, the hunt and the kill is too great."

"And the money. Judging by his home and yacht there's no hint of recession in the assassination industry. It's disappointing that there is no link between Lamb and Mills."

"Not so fast. Firstly they both grew up in a small town on the west coast of Florida called Ruskin; population, say, three hundred. I find it hard to believe they didn't know each other and I would go so far as to bet your dollar that they grew up together."

"Excellent!"

"Slow down tiger. What is wrong with you? There's more."

"Go on."

"Even though it was decades ago the guy at the FBI is still sore about his investigation getting canned. He said that he had gathered up a whole bunch of credible evidence that showed Mills was into everything from drugs, racketeering, running prostitutes. You name it Mills, was in there."

"So what happened?"

"The guy's boss's boss got a phone call from an attorney representing Mills. Have a random guess at who the attorney was."

"Joseph Lamb Junior," I said slowly.

56

2 December 2008
Pisa, Italy

Rachel had booked a hotel a short distance from Pisa airport. It was on the edge of an industrial estate and beyond that, only fields. I had asked not to be billeted in the city as I did not want Mills realizing I was there to do more than just visit his yacht in Viareggio.

At breakfast I chose a table which allowed me to watch the entrance and the other diners. No one seemed to be taking any interest in me, but I was taking no chances. At last the questions regarding the surveillance had been answered. The careless spies were Francesca's; the deadly ones were Mills'. In between mouthfuls of stale bread and stewed fruit salad I read my e-mails. There was one from Francesca which simply read:

"Call me."

I had an uneasy feeling about that one. I had started to trust her but her 'naivety', her poor attention to detail and her wayward client made me nervous. I would call her later.

Transport had become dangerous for me. If I hired a car I got rammed. Catching a plane, I received air-side death threats. If I hired a cab there was a chance that Mills had arranged it and would have me killed? Rachel had arranged a driver for me for the day, someone with connections with the Lloyd's Agent in Genoa.

My car arrived promptly at 0745 and took me to Dr. Corbett's address. Corbett's office was also his home, buried deep in the heart of a very narrow back street just off the river. If I was being watched it could only have been from the windows of a neighbouring building. In the tiny street, two boys and a girl played a ball game I did not recognize. The remainder of the street was deserted. As my driver opened the car door for me I heard the children's high-pitched voices reverberate off the high ancient buildings, as the terracotta coloured paint peeled from the masonry. Try and stay as innocent as long as you can kids, I remember thinking – there are too many people you should never meet.

I noticed the video camera above the call buttons. It was small and incongruous in its modernity against the crumbling building. It reminded me of Johnson's home. Hopefully the camera would be the end of the similarities. I pressed the call button for Corbett's apartment. There was a click and a whirring noise. I pressed the door open – neither of us had said a word. In front of me was a bronzed grill covering an ancient elevator. Attached to it was a scribbled note. I read no Italian but elevators are the same the world over. 'An engineer has been called. Waiting for parts.'

I took the stairs and arrived at Corbett's apartment. So far this meeting had not gone well.

Corbett was as I had imagined. Just over six feet tall, straight backed, brusque. He led me through into his study. The walls were lined with books and there were no pictures, photographs or ornaments. Corbett must have noticed me taking stock.

"In my line of work we live for today. I have lost too many friends to think about yesterday."

“Thank you for seeing me at such short notice Doctor Corbett.”

“Not at all,” he said flicking some imaginary fleck from his lapel. “Your assistant was very charming. How can I be of assistance?”

“I understand that you specialize in explosives?”

“I really wish I didn’t it is quite a depressing business.”

“I admit this has not been my most uplifting case,” I said.

“What case is that?” he asked fixing me with a rejuvenated stare.

“May I assume that whatever I tell you is in total confidence?”

“Of course.”

I believed him.

“Do you have any interest in yachts, Dr. Corbett?”

“None at all. I was army. I understand they build a lot of yachts up the road.”

“Have you heard of the yacht ‘AZUL’?”

“Of course; sank off Puerto Rico a few weeks ago. Many deaths.”

“Indeed. Has anyone called you in relation to that incident?”

"No. Why should they? I told you I was army."

"We believe 'AZUL' was sunk by a strategically placed bomb."

Corbett stiffened. "I will be the judge of whether it was a bomb Mr. Stone and, if so, if it was strategically placed. You stay with the insurance."

It was my turn to straighten my back. I was Corbett's customer not a military subordinate. I had had enough of being pushed around, first Johnson, then Mills, now by my own expert. Enough!

I continued. "I know it was strategically placed Dr. Corbett because I have found the two pieces of steel that were adjacent to it. My failure analysis team has identified those pieces of steel as the weakest point of the ship."

"So what do you need me for?" he asked meekly. I realized that his ready availability to meet with me had less to do with Rachel's charm than his lack of clients.

"Our failure analysis shows that the explosive sent a force vertically initially detaching the side shell plating from the bulkhead. It then shredded the side shell plating horizontally, we assume in an attempt to stop us finding the shards. I need to know what explosives could have been used to create both the vertical and horizontal forces."

"Would you like a drink?" Corbett asked buying time before providing an answer.

"No, but thank you."

"You understand that my opinion is entirely based upon

what you have told me? I have seen no evidence."

"My failure team is finalizing its report today. My assistant Rachel, who you know, will send it to you later today – encrypted, naturally."

"Naturally."

"So, what do you think?"

"There are several possibilities based upon the explosion pattern you have described."

That was not what I wanted to hear.

"But really only one certainty."

Corbett rose awkwardly and reached for a large grey book, torn slightly at the top of its spine. Sitting again at his desk but resting the book on his knees so he could face me he said, "Possibility one – fertilizer. Unlikely as it sounds, but do you remember the bomb in Bishopsgate?"

"Yes. It was not far from my office."

"Do you remember the vehicle the IRA used?"

"Yes. It was a tipper truck – huge thing."

"Exactly!" he exclaimed. "Looked like any building truck coming into the City. Fertilizer was an ideal explosive because it was plentiful and in ready supply back then. Unless you are a farmer it is not so easy to obtain it in large enough quantities now."

I thought of Mills' mansion. Was it a farm too?

"But we can rule fertilizer out immediately," said Corbett.

"Why?"

"For the effect you have described you would need such a vast quantity that the yacht would lean over. What do you call a sideways lean on a ship?"

"A list."

"Yes, list. Everyone would see it and the crew would feel it. And besides how would you get that huge quantity on board with no one noticing?"

"I see your point," I said looking down at the book between us. The crew could correct the list with ballast, but they would be bound to investigate and discover the bomb.

"Possibility two – dynamite. It is not widely known, but the vast majority of terrorist devices still rely upon good old TNT."

"Really?"

"Yes. Of course the sale of TNT has been strictly controlled for years. It isn't like buying fireworks. You have to show a need."

"Quarries?"

"It arrives at the quarry, then disappears," he said nodding. "But we can discount TNT too."

"Why?"

"Because it is indiscriminate in the damage it causes. At a quarry you use it to create a large lump of slate, aggregate, whatever. You don't care about the shape. You aren't expecting a ready-made sculpture."

"Understood."

"Possibility three? The certainty? Semtex. Look at this." Corbett opened his book and quickly found the page he needed, as if locating a favourite Bible verse. "Is that what you've got?" he asked passing me the book.

I looked at a photograph of a ruined semi-detached house. The portside of the pair stood unscathed, the starboard a pile of rubble.

"Catholic one side, Protestant the other. The explosive split the house down the middle then blew the detonated side to dust."

I handed the book back.

"Of course the bombers weren't very bright. The half left standing had to be demolished but you get my point?"

"Yes. And that was caused by Semtex?"

"Oh yes. The only explosive that I know of that has that surgical precision."

Corbett turned the page.

"It's only an approximation but this is what we think the explosive looked like."

He passed the book back and I examined a diagram of

a length of vertical explosive with horizontal arms off of it.

"That, Mr. Stone, is the devil that sank your yacht."

I handed the book back to Doctor Corbett.

"How easy is Semtex to come by, Doctor Corbett?"

"Compared to fertilizer and TNT? Very difficult."

"What if someone had a connection with the military?"

For the first time during our meeting Corbett smiled, verging upon laughter.

"In that case? In that case, they could have a barn full," he said.

....

En route from Pisa to Viareggio I called Francesca. She answered on the second ring.

"Lukasz, thank you for calling," she said breathlessly.

"Good morning Francesca. How are you?"

"Worried."

Rightly so.

"What's up?"

"Where are you?"

"It doesn't matter. What's up?"

"It's Drew."

"Yes?" I asked warily.

"He has done what you said…"

"Good."

"…sort of."

"How 'sort of'?"

I heard a large intake of breath.

"He called Lamb and requested the seventy-five million withdrawal."

"How did that go?"

"Not well. I was sitting next to Drew when he did it. He played his part rather well. If Lamb was straight he would not have been concerned by it."

"Unless he had something to be concerned about?"

"Right."

"So Lamb agreed?"

"He was very hostile but, yes, he agreed."

"Then Drew disappeared? No cards, no forwarding address, neighbours looking after the cat, cell phones off?"

"Sort of."

"'Sort of' isn't good enough Francesca. I think it's great that you two make money but when it comes to the grubby stuff, that's my domain. My instructions could not have been clearer."

"Drew is his own man."

"Put that on his headstone."

"Lukasz!"

"Don't 'Lukasz' me Francesca. Have you not been counting the corpses?"

"I'm sorry."

"There's no time for that. Get him out of there. I don't care where he goes just get him away," I said and hung up.

....

For a town that produces so many beautiful craft, Viareggio is a scruffy place. The sea surrounds it, then invades through the centre. All around the town, yachts, yachts and more yachts. Even in winter such as this, the sun bounced off the gleaming white gelcoats.

At the start of the downturn, shortly after the 'AZUL' matter in 2009, there was much speculation about which of the Viareggio yards would survive. The yard I visited about Mills survived and so I will not identify it. The Mills case had nothing to do with them. Neither did Banksy's death.

Security at the yard was a typically Viareggio affair. I presented my passport at the security gate noticing that the barrier over the roadway and a through route via the yard canteen were both open, rendering the security check pointless. I watched a dozen people use both lanes unchallenged while my passport was examined in painful detail. I knew from experience that the yard would not bother logging my visit so there would be no record of my visit for Mills to find.

Eventually the security guard finished with me and I headed into the main yard. I had two yachts from unconnected cases in for repair in there, so I had valid reasons for being there. I located them and pretended to survey them. I scribbled a few notes and then walked to the main building.

“Thank you for agreeing to meet with me.”

Bill Henderson, the project manager nodded.

“Are you building Mr. Mills’ new boat?” I ventured.

“Maybe.”

“I have only one question.”

“OK.”

“What was the Hull Identification Number you issued when you built the Mills boat?”

Theatrically my host stood and walked to a filing cabinet. After much searching, in the third drawer, he withdrew a file.

“There,” he said, pointing to a sequence on the open page.

I wrote down the code; IT-BVP890734599.

Banksy was right – golf was a zero.

Mills was wrong.

And me? I was in danger.

And I did not care.

....

I returned to my hotel and thanked my driver. I locked the door to my room, retrieved my laptop from the safe and started to write my report – or my last will and testament.

....

57

3 December 2008
Outside Pisa, Italy

Ping – text.

"I know you Lukasz Stone. JM"

No you don't.

"Not as well as I know you."

Send.

....

E-mail:

"Rachel. Get Lloyd's to bring the report meeting forward to 1500 today. No arguments. And make sure there is a television in the meeting room. My report attached. Distribution embargoed unless I do not make the meeting. Thanks, Lukasz."

....

I saw Alexander at the boarding gate. I waved and greeted him a very good morning; that bought me ten sleepy witnesses.

He ignored me.

I am angry Mills. You, Lamb and Johnson are going to see justice.

I called Francesca.

"Is he away?"

"Yes."

"Don't tell me where. Lamb was running a Ponzi scheme, wasn't he? Last in pays the first out?"

"I thought so but I couldn't see how it could work if the market crashed."

"Which was when?"

"When Lehman Brothers crashed."
"Which was when?"

"Sixteenth of September."

"When did 'AZUL' sink?"

"Two months later. You think Lamb was trying to keep the scheme going?"

"OK financial analyst listen to me, marine insurance is an oddity."

"How?"

"They do this thing to invite fraud called 'agreed value'."

"No?"

"Yes. We all agree that the yacht is worth 'x' we insure

it for that and irrespective of the real value, that's paid for a total loss."

"That's insane."

"Exactly. So, Lamb takes the cash in, pockets some then buys himself some insurance in an asset he knows cannot deteriorate if the world market takes a nosedive."

"That would make him the only Ponzi who's ever protected himself."

"Yes."

"He bought himself reinsurance – unlike the Coles Syndicate."

"Exactly. He bought himself reinsurance against a fifty-year jail term."

"That would be life for him."

"What do you want me to do?"

"Are you certain Drew is safe?"

"For once, yes."

"This is what you are going to do."

58

3 December 2008
London Heathrow

I dithered. I was in business class; Alexander was in economy. I made sure he got off the plane before me. The cheery crew wished him a good afternoon – he ignored them. You might have me killed Mills but you have no idea what I have left you as my legacy.

I had checked an empty bag into the hold. I assumed Alexander would not fall for such a stunt and hang around an unclaimed bag at the reclaim belt, but I wanted him to know my contempt for him was complete even if he succeeded in killing me.

I had to get to Lloyd's.

Ping. Rachel.

"Received your report. I called the Committee Chair directly. You're on centre stage at 3pm."

Train, tube, car?

Where was Alexander?

Wherever Alexander was, he was waiting for me. I decided upon the tube – more stops, more witnesses, more places to get off.

Within two stops I saw him. He smiled.

"Good morning," I shouted.

He turned away.

By the tenth stop the tube had become crowded. Alexander had edged his way towards me. By the twelfth stop he was behind me. I felt the muzzle of a gun pressed into my back.

"Madam, unfortunately the man behind me has a gun to my back," I advised the petite middle-aged woman in front of me. "If he shoots, the bullet will go straight through me and into you. I recommend you move."

In an accepting way that only the British commuter has, she stepped to one side.

"He's only joking," Alexander said coolly.

Despite withdrawing his weapon from the small of my back, Alexander remained close.

"Mills can't win this one," I said.

"Wanna bet?"

"I don't gamble," I lied. "I deal in facts, not odds."

"And the fact is Mr. Stone, you are going to die."

"If that makes you happy, sir."

He was not expecting that.

"It does."

"What's one more? Go on – do it here."

"What?"

"Kill me. Here. Now. You have twenty seconds before the next stop. There's no CCTV on this train, but maybe that would put you off? You like CCTV don't you? So does your friend Johnson. Met him at naval college didn't you?"

Alexander's breath was hot on the back of my neck. I thought of the peeling skin of the now dead Sweaty Lomas.

"Strange Mills' boat disappeared from the end of the college garden with no one noticing."

Alexander said nothing.

I turned to face him.

"Let me make this very clear to you. Whatever you do to me today will vindicate the report I filed with my office last night. They know who you are, what you are and a considerable amount of what you have done." I was staring into the only dead eyes I had seen except of a corpse. "Do you…" I demanded, "understand?"

"Yes."

"Good. Then listen very carefully." I lowered my voice, "I know who Mills' closest friend is."

"Who?"

"Ruskin."

At last, a flicker of life in those ebony, vapid eyes.

"Now, if roles were reversed and Mr. Lamb was standing here and he knew he had a choice to save himself, or you, which do you suppose he would choose?"

No response.

"Let me explain. You are a murderer. That's what you do. You kill, you get paid for it and you've killed so many times and have been paid handsomely for it. However, I am interested in the paymaster. Your stunt with altering the numbers of Mills' boat was amateur at best. You did not need to murder Mister Banks."

"I didn't kill…"

"Yes, you did."

The train was starting to empty out. I should have been afraid but I was too angry.

"I know you killed Mr. Banks. I am certain that you only carry out the most important jobs. In a way I am flattered you and your gun are here."

It was a taunt too far. He stood as we approached the next station.

"I will kill you Stone. Not today, but I will. And I am looking forward to it."

……………………………

At Monument Station I called Rachel.

"Hey," I said as calmly as I could.

"Hey. Where are you?"

"Monument Station."

"Lovely. Walk on over and I'll get you a coffee. There's time before the Lloyd's meeting."

I paused.

"I can't."

"Why not? It's a two-minute walk," she said, then, "Are your injuries…"

"No, nothing like that. Did you manage to get the full Lloyd's committee?"

"Full house."

"Chum?"

"I think he has reserved the best seat. He is expecting you to say 'pay'."

I looked at my watch.

"Rachel, in fifteen minutes time I want you to send my encrypted report to every committee member."

"And Chum?"

"No. Are you alright to say you forgot to copy him in?"

"Of course."

"Thanks. Now the really embarrassing part."

"I've told you, I haven't got a dress. And you have to ask in person."

"Rachel."

"Yes?"

"Send a car for me."

"You are joking? You are closer to Lloyd's than our office. You aren't turning into Chum Junior are you?"

"Rachel. Please."

....

My black Mercedes pulled up under the canopy at Lloyd's. My driver opened his door ready to get out and open mine but I was gone before he reached the door handle.

Inside I recognized one of the 'Waiters', the Lloyd's security guards.

"Bill I have a meeting on twelve. Can you take me up?"

Usually there would be forms to complete, but Lloyd's enjoys a risk, particularly from one of their own.

On the twelfth floor my eyes readjusted to the bright lights reflected from the light paint and steelwork. I was shown into the Committee Room. This was serious, the best china. In the front row sitting alone, was Chum. I saw the large screen television Rachel had ordered with delight. Time to do your work now Francesca.

The Committee welcomed me with more warmth than

at our last meeting.

"Lukasz, thank you for calling this meeting and for getting here so quickly," said the Chair. "But tomorrow would have been fine."

"Thank you all for rearranging you diaries to be here," I said quietly.

"So what is all this about?" asked Chum confidently. "Even I have not been briefed."

"Have you not read Mr. Stone's report?" asked the Chair coldly.

"Well no. Is there one?"

Well done Rachel.

"Yes," said the man from Leadenhall.

"What does it say?" asked Chum.

"Mr. Stone?" The Chair passed the floor back to me.

"My report, Christian, says this. The 'AZUL' was the most expensive and largest yacht ever built." I picked up the remote for the television – Rachel had produced a wonderful presentation. "She had five decks," (a shell expansion plan appeared on the screen,) "several cinemas, pools, the usual. She also had a weak point."

"Her designer," sneered Chum.

"And her strengths, not least of who was David Archer, her designer. This yacht could have withstood any marine peril."

"Clearly she did not!" Chum laughed in Leadenhall's direction.

"Except an expertly placed bomb."

"Really?" Chum laughed.

"Really?" asked the Chair.

"Bombs are covered Lukasz," Chum recovered.

"Not when they are placed under the direction of the owner," I said.

The Committee nodded in unison.

"Direction? We do not know who the owner is," Chum said.

"We do," I said producing the ownership documents Patrice had given me. I passed them to the Chair and moved onto the next slide, of the same document.

"The beneficial owner of 'AZUL' was a man called Joseph Lamb Junior."

I flicked the button 'TV' on the remote. The screen was filled with flashing blue and red lights. An overweight Sheriff was pushing a slightly built man towards a police car. I had found a use for Francesca.

Every committee member read the ticker tape running along the bottom of the screen.

"Lamb arrested. Ponzi."

There was silence.

"Lloyd's has funded a Ponzi?" asked the Chair.

"Only if you pay the claim," I replied.

"Eh…" mumbled Chum.

"Christian, enough," said the man from Leadenhall.

"Tell us the rest Lukasz," requested the Chair.

"It was very straightforward – if deadly. The man you have just seen arrested was connected with people at the highest level in the State of Florida and in turn with the government in Washington D.C. Admittedly he wasn't the largest Ponzi schemer of all time, but he was the most cautious. He realized that he needed reinsurance in case the market turned and his investors started to withdraw funds – funds that he had already spent. What better way than an agreed payout if his large yacht sank? When he saw Lehman Brothers collapse in September of this year, he activated the emergency plan. He arranged for 'AZUL' to be scuttled and it could have worked."

"Except?" asked Goatee.

"Except a man named Mills who was to execute the plan tried to discredit me with fraud of his own."

"Mills!" screamed Chum.

"Yes, Christian. Mills."

"He has a claim for a forty million total loss that Mr. Stone has handled so poorly that it has made us a laughing stock," boomed Chum.

"Really?" asked the Chair.

"Says here Mr. Mills is believed to be withdrawing his claim," said Leadenhall. "You can read my copy of Lukasz's report if you like, seeing as you do not have your own."

Chum was silenced.

"It's true Christian. Once I explained the mix up of 'Golf' for 'zero' in the hull identification numbers he was delighted to have his yacht back," I said.

"Great," Chum replied.

"Isn't it? The Mills boat recovered, the 'AZUL' a fraud. The Syndicate pays nothing. I told you weeks ago that the yacht that James Banks and I had found was his. You wouldn't listen. You played straight into his hands."

"I think we should adjourn and pass this to Lloyd's Counsel," said the Chair.

"Don't be so ridiculous Stone," Chum glowered.

"Mills needed a distraction from 'AZUL', preferably discrediting me in the process. Thanks to you he almost got away with it. One more thing, if I may?" I asked the panel.

"Which is?" Chum asked rolling his eyes.

"What reinsurance arrangements did the Coles syndicate have?"

"None," jabbed Chum.

"Really?" I asked him.

"None," he repeated, uncertainly. He could not be certain of what I knew.

"Why do you ask?" the Chair asked. "Surely you know that, otherwise we wouldn't be so interested?"

"I only know about boats… and how to find a fraud."

I passed Henry's notes to the Chair.

"Christian," I said.

"Yes."

"Who cancelled the reinsurances?"

He said nothing.

I watched Leadenhall grab the report back from Chum.

"Who cancelled the reinsurances?" asked Leadenhall gravely.

"I can explain…"

"It is the recommendation of this committee that a disciplinary investigation commence regarding the cancellation of the vital reinsurance programmes. Due to the seriousness of the allegations that Mr. Stone has made, you, Christian, will be prohibited from conducting business at Lloyd's until the investigation is concluded."

At that moment all eyes of the twelfth floor were on Christian Unstead-Matthews. All bar two – mine. I have thought about it many times since but I will never know why that at the exact moment I should have been watching Chum's downfall my eyes were drawn to the television still showing the arrest of Lamb. Goatee followed my gaze to the screen with obvious curiosity. It was then that it happened – a blinding flash and the car carrying Lamb lifted into the air. The explosion shook the television camera and Goatee recoiled as if he might be struck by shrapnel.

I stood staring at the screen. There was, I realized, a wearying inevitability to what I had just witnessed. The two boys from Ruskin; the game was over. Mills had won. I was aware of silence around me. It was only later that it occurred to me that it could so easily have been me in that shredded car. So Mills had left no loose ends. I wondered if he had murdered his old friend on his own account or been paid by the governor – or a higher authority? For the first time since this filthy case had started I felt overawed. I was so completely surrounded by jet black and scarlet evil that I found it difficult to breathe. I had escaped; survived. I was no threat to Mills and I had just witnessed the assassination of my adversary.

"Was that…?" someone asked. I cannot recall who.

"Yes, it was," I said shuffling the report in my hands. "Your insured. Your insured is dead."

As the silenced congregation broke up I saw Chum try to speak with Leadenhall.

"Don't even think about it Christian," I heard Leadenhall say.

"What?"

"Forget mergers, Lloyd's will ban you for life for this," he said.

My job was done.

Epilogue

I am sorry to have to e-mail this to you. You understand the circumstances. It's best that you don't know where I am. It's a shame though. You were reluctant to start with, a little coy but showed real promise towards the end. As accomplices go, you were not a bad one. Don't listen to Alexander, he's too much the puritan.

So I guess this is goodbye. I apologize. So American. Back to my roots.

It was a shame about Jay.

Him or me.

Stone brought me back to life. Thank you Stone.

Must go.

Did you here that? That knock? That knock at your door?

I told you at the beginning… they will come for you. Not for me.

....

Lukasz Stone will return in ‘STONE’

For extracts and more:

www.nicksmith.com

Thanks and acknowledgements

'The Secret Pilgrim' by John Le Carre. Various editions published by Penguin Books.

Sincere thanks to Elizabeth Murray, Jamie Atkinson and Yvonne Smith.

12556493R00219

Printed in Great Britain
by Amazon.co.uk, Ltd.,
Marston Gate.